Death and Cupcakes

Musgrave Landing Mysteries, Volume 1

Yvonne Rediger

Published by Brown Wolf Publishing, 2024.

Also by Yvonne Rediger

Adam Norcross Mysteries
The Wrong Words
The Right Road

Musgrave Landing Mysteries
Death and Cupcakes
Fun With Funerals
Condo Crazy
Storm Stayed

VIC Shapeshifters
Into the Wood
The Shape of Us
Hell Cat
Trusting the Wolf

Standalone
The Common Touch
Diving In Heart First

Watch for more at blackyvy50.wix.com/yvonnerediger.

Yvonne's story is an excellent mystery - great characters (adored Arlie - a character with spirit). I was captivated, everything plausible with a creative twist for the who-done-it.

- Susan Davis

Published by Brown Wolf Publishing
Saskatchewan, Canada

Dedication

Thank you to my beta readers Leslie & Joan and my husband Keith, who listens to all my stories.
Thank you also, to RCMP Sgt. Colin Douglas and the other officers of the Duncan Detachment for their advice as well as answering all my weird questions.
Any mistakes are solely mine alone.

Chapter One

"JANE'S EATS AND TREATS café," Jane Westcott said the words aloud.

The phrase still didn't sound right, like fiction. The café used to belong to Aunt Ethel and always had, but now she was gone.

With a deep breath in, and out, Jane cleared the negative energy from her mind. Sad thoughts weren't helpful.

She squared her shoulders and once again went through her mantra. The work didn't scare her, waiting on customers didn't scare her, and filling orders didn't scare her either.

Failure, now that scared her. Well, and being homeless, penniless, and unemployed, that too.

"Stop being dramatic," she told herself. The café was her home now, and her job. And it was past time to work on the penniless thing.

Jane grasped the kitchen drawer's wooden handle and pulled the heavy drawer open. Back in the day, the drawer had been a flour bin, and the one above, a sugar bin. The stainless-steel liners remained inside, but this drawer now held over thirty unique and colourful aprons.

She reached in and drew out the one on top. The pinafores were remnants of Ethel Crawly, and touching the worn fabric made Jane smile. But it was time to get this show on the road.

Quickly, she flipped the dark blue strap over her head and pulled her braid out of the way. A snap of her wrists and the ties wrapped around her waist, and she fashioned the indigo material into a bow at the small of her back. After one last adjustment to the skirt material, she turned and crossed the wide board kitchen floor to the farm table.

Jane scooped up the basket of muffins. She took a steadying breath, and then briskly strode through the connecting door to slide the blueberry-oatmeal muffins into the main display case of Jane's Eats & Treats. The muffins were still warm, and their fragrance filled the air and mingled with the comforting aroma of six other kinds of oven-fresh treats.

She glanced at the clock, ten minutes to six in the morning. *How did I ever get here?*

The journey from her old life in Vancouver had been a bumpy one. No matter how many times she told herself coming back to Musgrave Landing was her only choice. Even though a sound decision, her return to the only real home she had ever known still felt awkward and ill fitting. Like a dress that was snug in the wrong places and ten years out of style, but she would adjust, she had to.

Jane took a firm grip on her uncertainty, grabbed the light blend coffee carafe, marched the container over to the self-serve counter on the north side of the coffee shop and placed it next to the medium and dark blend matching carafes.

At least the tasks were familiar. Well, mostly, Jane consoled herself. "Cups, lids, spoons, cream, milk, brown sugar, white sugar, raw sugar, and sweetener." Jane recited the memorized list. "What am I forgetting?"

A quick glance out the north window showed her a line of cars and trucks. Commuters already queued up for the six-twenty Musgrave Landing ferry. These people would be her first customers.

The anxiety which had nibbled at the edges of her confidence started taking hungry bites. The emotion made her swallow.

It will be fine once I get going. It's like riding a bike. So, what if it had been fifteen years since she'd waited on any customers in the café?

The early April sun shone a weak light through the east windows. The rays had yet to touch the west side of Salt Spring Island. As a result, the temperature hadn't risen above a frosty level.

An antique-blue sky promised fairer spring weather to come as sunlight crept up the granite face of Stoney Hill and across the waters of the strait. Jane hoped the good weather meant she would be busy.

She could make out a vessel currently powering its way across the Samsum Narrows to make berth at Musgrave Landing.

The sight of the ferry made Jane realize she had to hurry. She dug her right hand into today's cotton apron pocket for the list.

Of course, all the pockets were empty.

She dashed back into the kitchen to gather her belongings. Each apron was unique and the garments were essential for running the café. Not only did an apron keep clothing from taking on stains, each one sported several pockets to hold personal items. Like the building's keys, the coffee machine's operations sheet, her cell phone, and the café's daily opening to-do list. All of which, she deposited in various pockets then picked up the cheat sheet.

Jane scanned the list. "Crap, the honey." She nipped quickly behind the counter and extracted the bottle, shaped like a happy bear.

"Okay, now that's got to be everything." Jane checked the paper one more time, just to be sure, and then scanned the interior of the small café looking for issues or missing items.

On impulse, she made a last dash to the far-left side of the building into the ladies' washroom just to make sure the room was neat and tidy. Clean meant sales, grubby meant customers would question the café's hygiene, which could be a death sentence to her new business.

While she was at it, Jane popped into the men's washroom, did a fast check, and then washed her hands for good measure.

Everything was as ready as it could be. "It's only nerves. Settle down, Jane." She needed to curb this talking-to-herself thing. A bad habit left over from her job on the mainland, but not something she had time to worry about right now. Jane swallowed her nerves and smoothed her hands down her apron.

The time had come. She stepped over to the fire-engine-red door, paused with her hand on the deadbolt to get a grip, on it and her nerves. With her lips compressed into a determined, firm straight line, she turned the deadbolt and unlocked the door.

The April wind retained a cool bite to its touch and crept under the threshold. This was a good thing, in Jane's opinion. Hot drinks would sell well.

A small black cat, with one orange ear, was outside as usual. No more than a kitten, the wee female feline had taken to hanging around the café door over the past weeks. Now she sat hunched on the old weathered planter by the parking lot entrance. The kitten was a slick little minx, Jane lost count of the times she'd evicted the little creature from the café.

"If you don't have a cat, one will find you," Ann had laughed at Jane's battle with the cat. She'd sipped herbal tea and watched, amused, as her sister gave chase.

It wasn't that Jane didn't like cats, but there were rules with regard to allowing animals around when someone was running a food centric business.

Jane opened a small cupboard by the door and extracted the bag of dry cat food. She stepped outside, filled the metal dish, and checked the water bowl. It was chilly but not close to freezing, the water was fresh and clear. Both dishes sat beside the post used to tie up customers' dogs. Unless they were a service animal, pets were not allowed inside the cafe.

The wee black creature lithely jumped down from her perch and sauntered over to the dishes. There was a definite question mark shape in her tail as she peered up at Jane with luminous yellow eyes.

"I'll come see you later. I have to work right now," Jane promised, and gave the kitten a cheek scratch then went back inside.

She flipped on the 'Open' sign and returned to her station behind the counter for a quick hand wash and waited for customers.

The morning commuters must have been watching for the sign to light. No sooner had Jane made it behind the counter, when her first customers left their cars and crossed the few yards to the café door.

As the new owner-operator, Jane greeted each customer with a cheerful smile. She quickly doled out sandwiches, muffins, cupcakes, breakfast bars, and hot breakfast wraps. She sold coffee and bottles of water along with the food too. The more sales she made, the easier the task of waiting on customers became until all her nervousness was gone.

The feedback cheered Jane on too.

"So glad you've reopened," said her first customer.

"Nice to have the café back," came from the fifth.

"How is Ethel?" A tiny white-haired woman with a cane, and a very pronounced widow's hunch asked. Jane's eyebrows twitched in surprise at this question. Musgrave Landing was a small village and most people knew everything, about everyone.

Then a younger woman appeared at the senior's elbow. She gave Jane a commiserating smile and lifted her eyebrows.

Maybe not everyone got the news. "Mrs. Vernon, Ethel passed away."

"A month ago," Jane said and added a napkin to the paper bag, which contained a chocolate chip muffin and pat of butter for the elderly woman.

"I'm so sorry, I didn't realize," the senior said and patted Jane's hand. "Was it the cancer?"

"Yes, at least she's not in any pain now," Jane said and swallowed her emotions. She was glad she could now hold it together when well-meaning people asked about her aunt. Each day, dealing with her grief got a bit easier.

"It's nice you started up the café again, Ethel would have wanted this."

Jane's polite smile broadened. Her aunt made Jane promise to do exactly that. Aunt Ethel's words echoed in her memory, *I don't have a lot to leave you, except the café and whatever is in it, is yours. Make it work.*

The coffee shop was a mad house for about eighteen minutes and Jane could not have been happier with the chaos.

The only exception was one customer with a sour expression and pursed lips. His height required Jane to look up, to meet the disapproving gaze of a man in his late sixties.

"What can I get for you?" Jane ignored his sour expression as a thin boney hand placed a to-go cup on the counter in front of her.

"Nothing," he said stiffly. "Just, the coffee."

Jane's smile faded as she charged the man for the small beverage.

He gave her exact change. "You didn't wait long to take over, did you?"

"Excuse me?" Jane frowned as she dropped the change in the register drawer.

"Ethel's barely cold in her grave and you took over her café." He looked Jane up and down, as though he found her distasteful. "Tell me, did you and your sister fight much over the property? I'm surprised you didn't sell it all and take off back to Vancouver."

Jane looked directly into his hard eyes. Aunt Ethel's customer service philosophy was still deeply ingrained in Jane's memory. *It can take a long time to gain a customer, and seconds to lose them.* Her aunt always gave clear direction on how to handle customers such as this. She would have advised Jane not to say anything to the man, even though his words hurt her.

However, Jane was not Ethel. After the trouble back in her old life, Jane resolved to never 'just take it' from anyone.

Instead, she smiled widely and held out her right hand. "I'm sorry, I don't know you. I'm Jane Westcott, Ethel Crawly's niece. I lived in Musgrave Landing for most of my life, until I left for university, then work. And you are?"

The older man blinked in surprise at her but took her right hand and shook it. "Earl Moffatt," he said in a clipped tone.

"Did you know my aunt well?"

His eyes slid sideways, and his moustache twitched. "Not too well, no, but I liked her."

"I loved her," Jane said sincerely. "She was like a mother to me and my sister. We both miss her very much."

There was an awkward pause. "I'm sorry for your loss," the old guy muttered as he snatched his cup off the counter and made a fast exit out the door to the parking lot.

"Ignore him, Jane. Earl's a curmudgeon," said a woman with deep black skin, dark brown eyes, and scarlet fingernails which matched her suit. She placed a large coffee on the counter.

"He certainly is something." Jane watched through the side window as the old man disappeared from view behind a truck. Then she turned back to her new customer.

"I'm Celine Nickels. I've lived in the village for about three years, so I only knew Ethel slightly. She was a nice woman, and I'm sorry for your loss too."

"Thank you, lovely to meet you, Celine. You work on the main Island?"

"Yep, I'm an accountant for MPG in Duncan." She placed one fist on a curvy hip and smoothed her raven hair behind one ear. "I'm glad you've re-opened the café. I'm not big on making my own coffee in the morning, but God help the office if I don't have one first thing."

Jane laughed. "Can I get you anything else?"

"I'll take a trail mix muffin for breakfast, please." Celine's eyes danced with mischief. "And a chocolate cupcake for later, thanks."

Jane returned Celine's infectious smile and put the woman's order together.

The ferry arrived and neatly coasted into its berth at the end of the dock. Sometimes there was a vehicle or two on the first run of the day, but usually the deck was empty. There was not much reason to go to Musgrave Landing before the businesses opened. That is unless one lived in the village these days.

However, this morning was different. An RCMP police cruiser rolled off the ferry ramp and onto the concrete wharf. Everyone in the café paused to watch, including Jane.

"That's not a usual sight," commented a man Jane thought was named Sam. He was a tall, muscular man in coveralls and a denim jacket. He drove the tow truck currently parked in the café's tiny lot.

Crime rarely happened in Musgrave Landing. Here, early customers fell silent as the white car, with yellow, red, and blue stripes along the sides, drove past the line of cars and trucks waiting to leave. Some of Jane's customers stared out the window and speculated out loud about the reason the police had travelled to the village.

"I wonder what that's all about," said Victor, a tall thin, algebra teacher who taught in Mill Bay.

"Probably nothing good," Nancy said, a dental assistant who worked in Duncan.

When Jane spoke to her customers, she made the effort to discover something about each as she served them. She wanted to know who they were, their names, and what they did. She hoped some of these people would become more than an acquaintance and customer after a while, like Celine.

"I'm sure we will hear all about it before the day is over," Kelly said, a teacher who taught chemistry and Celine's carpooling partner.

As the taillights of the police vehicle disappeared up the hill as the ferry signalled its readiness to accept passengers.

In seconds, the building emptied.

With the customers gone, Jane leaned heavily against the back counter. *Wow is it going to be like this every morning?* She certainly hoped so and straightened. With a lighter step, she went about the room, neatening the five tables. She replaced chairs and put stools back under the bar along the west window. Her next round of customers would be arriving when the ferry returned in roughly an hour.

Jane grabbed a cleaning cloth and moved to the self-serve counter when her mobile phone rang.

"Hey, Ann," she greeted her sister as she tucked the phone between her shoulder and chin, not an easy maneuver to perform with a smartphone.

"Hi Jane, how's it going?"

"Busy, crazy busy," Jane said cheerfully as she gathered up the carafes for refilling.

"Glad to hear it. Do you think you'll have to hire someone to help out?" Ann asked.

"I don't know yet, so far I'm handling the workload okay."

"Do you need me to come and help you?"

"No, but thanks for the offer all the same."

"All right, I'll see you around lunchtime then." Ann hung up and as usual, didn't wait to see if Jane wanted to say more. But that was Ann.

Their aunt and Ann shared the exact same mannerism. Only one of the things they had in common. More than once, Jane had to call Ethel back to add some piece of information the hang- up had cut off.

Ethel had bequeathed her house, which included a studio, to Ann who was also an artist. As Jane loaded the used dishes into the dishwasher, she thought about the last conversation she'd shared with her aunt in the hospital on the main Island. Her aunt had said, *I love you and Ann like my own daughters, Jane. Please know when I say you haven't an artistic bone in your body, I don't mean it as an insult. It's merely a fact. That's why Ann will get the house and studio.* The older woman lay in her hospital bed, a thin, pale, half-image of her actual self as she explained her last wishes. *Jane, I'm leaving you the café. You're a hard worker and I know you'll get it back on its feet.*

Ethel, ever blunt, always told people what she thought. And their aunt never pulled her punches. Over her career as a café owner, Ethel Crawly did not amass a huge fortune from her years running the business. But the three of them had lived a comfortable life.

Occasionally, Ethel rented out the apartment above the café for extra income. Now, Jane made the small apartment hers after moving in days after the funeral. Ann had done the same with the house three blocks away.

Even though there were still many bills to worry about, no mortgage was a huge benefit to Jane's financial situation.

"It's all up to me," Jane said as she replaced the coffee containers on the self-serve counter and glanced at the clock. Ten minutes and the madness would start again. But the short break did give her time to combine her prepped ingredients for the soup she planned to serve at noon.

Four kinds of sandwiches, already made, sat in the refrigerated display case. Some had been sold already with the morning coffee and tea. There was only a small margin to be made on food, but every little bit helped.

Chapter Two

After the busy morning, Jane looked forward to a small break once the lunch crowd was served. A few ferry workers dropped in to check out the revamped business and bought something for their lunches. Jane's pot of homemade chicken noodle soup was a popular choice.

Ethel used to run the café from six in the morning until one-thirty in the afternoon, Monday-to-Friday. If there were a Farmer's Market running, Saturdays too. Jane saw no reason to change the hours for now. She would see what her revenue looked like after the first week.

"Hey, you," Ann called as she breezed in at a quarter to one o'clock. "Got any soup left?"

"I do, would you like an egg salad sandwich to go along with it?"

"Absolutely." Ann dropped her flowing emerald-green wrap and oversized bag on a chair. She plunked herself down next to it.

"How's did the morning go?"

"Good, busy." Jane shared the same shade of chestnut-brown hair as her sister, but Ann wore hers short in a pixie cut. Jane's long hair was usually bound in a braid and hung down the middle of her back. Both sisters possessed the same dark, chocolate brown eyes as their mother and aunt, but that was where the similarities ended.

"Good for you."

Jane glanced at her sister as she assembled their lunch. Two years older, Ann was also four inches taller than Jane's five foot three. Ann loved bright shades, and Ann's clothing and makeup reflected this as did her paintings. Today was no different.

With her shape being a bit on the stockier side, Jane preferred earth tones and a more natural look. And she was fine with that, she acknowledged as she ladled soup into bowls. "My products are selling well and that's all I can ask." She had lots of bills to pay.

At forty-one-years old, Ann and never had to worry about money. She was divorced and received alimony payments from Andrew Kingsley, her ex-husband. The support cushioned her from real life.

Probably, Jane theorized, Ann had never gotten over Jack Birch and that was the reason for her sister's failed marriage. Now that both of them were back on the island, Jane wondered if her sister would seek out Jack.

She compressed her lips with this thought as she laid items on the table for their lunch. It was best not to think about Jack. Then, her relationship with Aaron came to mind, and how she'd considered marrying him. Thankfully, Jane woke up to understand who Aaron really was before their relationship got that far.

Jane hand over the silverware, and Ann quickly arranged the place settings.

No, the idea of sharing her life with anyone was behind her now. She took her seat and slid the bowl of soup closer to her. Instead, she needed to work as much as she could. The situation did not change because she was back in Musgrave Landing. It would be wonderful if...no. Her old desire from her youth was unrealistic, especially when she looked at her beautiful sister.

Jack wouldn't know what hit him this time around.

Focusing on her sister, she served them both from a pot of tiger blend tea. "How goes your beautification project? Did the mayor look at your plans?"

"Sort of, I got a whole minute of Tim's time. He listened but he said none of my ideas will fit into this year's budget." She sipped a spoonful of soup. "Mm." Ann swallowed her first taste. "Lovely flavour, Jane."

"Thanks. But you're not giving up, are you?"

"No, I'll track down each village councillor if I have to. Everyone works, which means it will take me some time. Tim was easy, as the assistant postmaster, I cornered him Saturday and made him listen. I plan on speaking to all the council members before the meeting." Ann sighed as she unwrapped her sandwich. "We have to get off our collective butts and figure out ways to bring people to Musgrave Landing or this place will continue to die a slow death. I thought using donated artist time and talent would be a no brainer."

"It is. Who doesn't want nice things to look at? The murals in Chemainus are well known and draw tons people there every year." Jane sipped her tea and frowned. "I thought there was grant money awarded for business stimulation?"

"There is, but apparently Musgrave Landing has been turned down repeatedly, according to Anita. The small amount of funding the village did receive, the council plans to put elsewhere, but she wouldn't tell me where. She just said no, they can't handle it, not in this year's plan."

"Maybe you can get more details at the monthly council meeting."

"I hope so."

As they ate, Jane noticed Ann looking around at the white walls of the café. "What are you going to do with all this empty space?"

Jane wiped her mouth with her napkin. "I was thinking of commissioning a mural for the top half, above the windows. A wall painting will give the customers and me something to look at on the not so nice days in winter."

Windows graced three sides of the café. Those facing east, with a view of the tiny parking lot, looked uphill along High Street to the village. A bank of four windows faced north, with a view of the ferry wharf, the road, and the trees from the haunted house. Three more windows faced west and overlooked the patio. The view beyond showed the calm waters of Samsum Narrows and the forbidding granite face of Stoney Hill.

At the moment, the sun glittered brilliantly off the Narrows. The light turned the water to shimmering diamonds and shone warmly through the French door. The black cat was in a sunny patch on a broken concrete bench outside, eyes shut, enjoying the heat.

"Oh?" Ann looked expectantly at her sister. "Were you going to ask me?"

Playing for time, Jane refilled their cups from the brown-striped teapot, her favourite because it poured so nicely. She considered how to tell her sister what she wanted without hurting Ann's feelings. Her sister's art was bigger than life and would overpower the room's small space.

Finally, she looked up to explain and her gaze snagged on the bare patio, the undisciplined row of tulips poking up along the border. Their red, orange, and yellow heads nodded in the light breeze. With resignation, Jane realized she had one more thing on her to-do list. Clean up the flowerbeds.

Then inspiration struck.

"Come outside with me for a minute." Jane stood and tipped her head toward the door.

"Okay," Ann said giving her sister a nod, and grabbed her wrap to follow.

The fresh air retained the spring chill even though it was past noon and the sun shone down on the paving stones.

"Look at this." Jane gestured to the side of the building facing the water. "The café is the first thing people see when they arrive on the ferry."

She watched as Ann studied the peeling white clapboard with pursed lips. On the north side, the bracket, which should be holding the café sign, was still empty. Jane had ordered a new sign, but the delivery was late. She hoped to see it by the end of the week.

"It's dull and uninteresting." Ann nodded and turned to Jane with an excited glint in her eyes. "What are you thinking?"

Jane could see her sister was already bubbling with ideas.

"You are great with colour. Do you think you can, or would want to, tackle the exterior? I'd love a mural of flowers, tulips, daffodils, and maybe pansies?"

As Jane looked at her sister, Ann's eyes narrowed as she looked at the offered canvas again. With brisk steps, her artist sister marched around to the north side. "What about here?" She cut her gaze to Jane.

"Here too, and the west side as well," Jane said as she folded her arms around herself. The chill penetrated her sweater and blouse, but she smiled through it as inspiration grabbed her sister with both hands.

"And the south side, what are your plans there?" Ann asked briskly.

"That side of the building still has the exposed red brick. I'd like to keep it."

"Good idea." Ann nodded.

"Will you do it?" Jane asked.

"This will be fun." With a dazzling smile, Ann abruptly turned and faced Jane. "I'll work up some sketches this afternoon and bring them by for you to look at as soon as they're ready. You can pick out what you like."

"Sounds good." Jane nodded. Her sister's re-born enthusiasm made Jane happy. "We can start the Ethel Crawly Beautification Project, right here, at the café."

"It's very fitting." Ann scrutinized the wall one more time.

Jane glanced at the strait. The ferry was not too off in the distance. "Come on, we have to finish lunch, my next shift of customers are on the way." She gestured at the white and blue vessel as it made determined progress across the churning water.

Chapter Three

When Jane locked the café doors at two o'clock, she did so with deep satisfaction. Her first day went better than she'd ever imagined. True, she'd experienced a couple of hiccups. The ancient coffee machine hadn't ground the beans fine enough in Jane's opinion, and several customers requested espresso which she couldn't supply. Things Jane needed to resolve.

One, she would read the manual again for grinding the coffee beans, and two, she would follow up on the delivery of her espresso machine from her supplier in Victoria.

Even so, those issues could not dampen her mood. She'd greeted a few old acquaintances and met tons of lovely new people. She'd also given her sister a new challenge. Best of all, she had actual money to deposit into her bank account and could pay some bills.

Jane hiked her purse strap higher onto her shoulder as she turned and came face-to-face with her neighbour, Arlington Birch.

"You quitin' already?" the elderly man asked his words sounded like an accusation. His wrinkled, seamed face scowled at her. Jane edged back from the tall, spare man.

Several days' growth of grey and white whiskers coated the lower half of his face and neck. Above his watery blue eyes, bushy eyebrows drew together in a frown. His navy coat and trousers hung slack on his lean frame. He looked like a good wind might knock him down, except there was steel in the old man's spine.

There were hints of Jack in his father's face. His son was taller though, and Jack's hazel eyes came from his mother. Jane wondered where the younger man she'd crushed on as a teenager was right now. Over the past weeks, she'd half-hoped to see him around the village.

"Yes, sorry Mr. Birch. I close around one-thirty, after the ferry leaves. There's no point in staying open. The next trip on the schedule is at four-thirty, with the commuters travelling home." Hardly anyone stopped at the café at that time of the day when Aunt Ethel ran it. People just wanted to go home after work.

"Keeping Ethel's hours?" His eyes examined Jane as though looking for flaws.

"Yes, that's the idea." She considered letting him inside and offer to serve him when he gave her a sharp nod.

"Makes sense." He looked down at his feet for a moment. Was he disappointed?

"Long day otherwise," Mr. Birch said in a clipped tone as he glanced back up at Jane, his frown eased slightly. Then he turned his attention toward the tulips, grass, and weeds in the flower boxes and planter.

"That's true." Jane waited for him to say something about the tangle of plants on the street side of the building. She really needed to get going on the landscaping.

"I'll stop by tomorrow, earlier." He spun on his heel and strode briskly back up the hill.

"See you then," Jane called after him.

The Birch house was directly across the road from the café. Mr. Birch maintained the property meticulously. His cedar hedge was laser level with no protruding off shoots. The plants wouldn't dare. Each of the shrubs and flowerbeds were clipped, sculpted, and weed free, with the black soil exposed. No wood chips as a short cut, using them would be cheating. Mr. Birch practiced what Aunt Ethel called aggressive gardening.

Jane crossed the road and strolled by his house. Mr. Birch was no longer in sight. She paused to study his property. It took a second, but she spotted what she was looking for. The garden gnomes Mrs. Birch placed about the yard decades ago when Jane was a child. The little concrete men wore faded red caps and assorted shades of jackets and pants. They peaked out from behind Sitka spruce trees, around hydrangeas, and other various places in the yard. Jane, along with Ann, and a few other village kids had raced against each other in a game that Jack had led to find and tag the gnomes. Simpler times.

Mrs. Birch had allowed the kids to play in the yard as long as they did not get too rambunctious. There would be juice and cookies around three-thirty, then she would shoo everyone home. Sometimes, Dirk Ipkiss got booted out of the yard early if he broke something or made the girls scream by tossing earthworms at them. Good times.

Across the street, kitty-corner from the café sat a huge Victorian-era stone house. The structure stood farther back from the shore, surrounded by ancient walnut and chestnut trees. When Jane and Ann were kids, they told each other the three-story monstrosity was haunted. Once, Jane thought she saw a man standing at the window, on the second floor. No one else ever saw the man. Jane knew she'd seen something and after that, believed the old house was truly inhabited by unsettled spirits. She still remembered the flutter she had experienced in her belly when walking by the house.

Jane smiled at how odd she'd been as a child. The tree growth over the last couple of decades obscured the house completely now. Sad how no one had ever taken it over. When Jane had asked Aunt Ethel why no one lived there, she'd said the property remained tied up in some family legal battle after the owner passed away. It took Jane a moment to remember the family name but it came to her, Highmere, that was it. Someone in their family had disappeared too, if she remembered correctly.

Jane hiked her purse strap over her shoulder again and walked on by. No premonition triggered any creepy feelings and she found this somewhat disappointing. She still had a lot to do today, time to get going.

The village no longer housed any industry other than the ferry and a small marina down the rocky shore from Jane's café. Musgrave Landing had become a bedroom community. The village survived on urban workers wanting to live in the country. The ferry terminal was the largest employer, what with some of the crew living in the village.

Empty storefronts lined the High Street and many houses were for sale, most for over a year or two. The once well-maintained street was now heavily pockmarked with potholes.

Get a move on Jane. She shook herself from her thoughts as she continued up the hill. *The errands won't do themselves.*

Her first stop was the village office. A woman sauntered down the concrete steps, coming toward her.

"I'm not sure you want to go in there." The woman swung her designer handbag strap over her shoulder, making the gold bangles on her wrist clatter. Her platinum-blonde hair, pulled back from her round face, cascaded down her back in corkscrew waves. She tucked strands behind one ear, exposing large lobes and dangling gold drop earrings.

"Why not?" Jane stopped short of the concrete steps.

"The administrator is fighting with a councillor." She rolled her eyes with their shocking blue lids in commentary as she strolled past Jane down the steps in a cloud of floral perfume.

Jane shifted aside as the woman moved on, hips swaying in her tight, black knit dress and matching jacket.

She walked up the steps and frowned at the office door. Jane didn't want to get caught up in some argument, but she needed to complete her business.

Raised voices penetrated the wooden door. The combatants weren't loud enough for Jane to hear everything, but words like 'money,' 'stupid,' and 'regret' were among those she could make out. Certainly not very professional to fight in a public building where they could be heard, but not her problem.

She reached for the door handle and the door abruptly swung open.

"Sorry," Jane said automatically and stepped back to allow the man to exit.

"Jane? Jane Westcott?"

She looked up into sky-blue eyes. His curly golden-blond hair was the same as when they were kids. "Dirk Ipkiss? Wow, you look great." Jane greeted her old friend with a wide smile. His fit, swimmer's trim body was new. He must have dropped at least seventy pounds since the last time she'd seen him.

He grasped Jane's wrist and led her away from the door. "Thanks, I feel great, if older." He flashed brilliant even teeth at her, those were fixed too, Jane noted as she allowed herself to be led.

"We've all gotten older," Jane said ruefully.

"You're as beautiful as ever though."

"Sweet of you to say so," Jane said, even though she had never thought of herself that way. Ann was the beauty.

Jane looked at Dirk and thought how surprising people turned out sometimes. He'd been overweight, buck toothed, with a face full of acne. Now his skin was smooth, almost flawless. "It's been what, fifteen years?"

"That's right, I saw you once at Christmas," Dirk said with a nod. "I heard you moved back and reopened the old café."

First Ann, and then Jane had left the village to go to university in Vancouver. Later, both took jobs there and shared an apartment, until Ann's marriage to Andrew Kingley. Neither sister spent much time back in Musgrave Landing, apart from the occasional holiday. Most times

Aunt Ethel travelled to Vancouver to visit them. When Ethel's cancer became terminal, all their lives had changed.

"Yes, today was the first day I was open for business."

"Not bad for only being back on Salt Spring Island for what, a month? I'll have to drop by for a coffee," he leaned slightly forward, "and a treat." His tone turned a touch suggestive.

Jane arched an eyebrow, and said, "Sure, we open at six and close at one-thirty, weekdays."

"Would you consider selling the property to me? I'd give you a good price."

Jane stared at Dirk, surprised at his offer. Before thinking it through, she asked, "What would you pay me for it?"

"Fifty thousand," Dirk responded promptly.

Jane burst out laughing. "I don't think so, but thanks all the same."

"Let me know if you change your mind," Dirk said without missing a beat. "What are you doing on the weekend?" He leaned one hip against the handrail.

"I have tons to do. I've only completed the work on the inside of the café, so far." She pulled her sweater tighter as a gust of wind made the loose strands of her hair flutter in the chilly breeze.

"Can I help in any way?"

"Oh, lovely of you to offer, but Ann and I have it under control. Now, I really must get going." She quickly stepped around the man. "Please stop by though," she tossed over her shoulder, and then escaped into the village office.

"Hello!" Jane called out over the odd quiet of the place. Silence.

After a moment, a round, vertically challenged woman bustled into view from a back office and advanced on Jane. Her face was flushed, all the way up to the tips of her ears, and she was blinking rapidly, possibly to stem tears.

Jane felt empathy for the woman. She knew it was hard sometimes to control your emotions at work. Especially, if your boyfriend gave you trouble.

"Good afternoon, how can I help you?" Her name tag read Anita.

Jane approached the counter. "I've come to pay for my business license." She extracted the notice out of her worn brown-leather messenger bag. "It's still valid." She added the extra form. "This is the request to have the business name changed from Ethel's Place to Jane's Eats & Treats." Jane gave the older woman a quick smile.

"Why are you changing the business name?" Anita frowned at the paperwork.

"For tax and legal purposes," Jane answered.

Anita lifted her eyes to study Jane. Tightly permed curls framed the woman's oval face, hair colour leaning closer to orange than blonde. "Fine," she wheezed and added a long-suffering sigh for good measure. The woman began reading the papers again and her lips moved slightly as her eyes passed over the words. Then she glanced at Jane, assessing her. "Your sister's the artist."

"Ann Westcott, yes, she is." Jane nodded in confirmation.

Anita sniffed disdainfully. "Newcomers, always wanting to change things," she mumbled, and then continued louder, "that'll be a hundred dollars even."

Jane laughed; she couldn't help it. Anita must be referring to Ann's beautification project.

"What's so funny?" Anita frowned up at her, and Jane felt positively tall.

"There have been Crawlys in Musgrave Landing since it was founded over two hundred years ago. We aren't new." Jane allowed a smile to settle on her lips. "Where are you from, Anita?" She arched an eyebrow at the shorter woman.

Anita blinked as if in surprise. "I'm originally from Saint John, New Brunswick. I've lived in Musgrave Landing for the past ten years, me and Tim," she said firmly and proudly. "But you're a Westcott?"

"Our mother was a Crawly, Ethel's sister. Ann and I came to live here with our aunt as children." Anita didn't need all the details of her and Ann's early life.

"You liked it so much you and your sister came back and bought up your aunt's property?"

"Something like that," Jane agreed. She held up her credit card. "I'll use this to pay."

Anita typed some numbers into her computer and reached out her hand for the card.

"It's fine, I've got it." Jane's smile turned a little tight as she picked up the key pad to insert her card. These days, no one touched her bank cards or her credit cards. She trusted no one, other than Ann. Well, and Andrew too, he was her lawyer.

Neither woman spoke as the transaction processed, this left an uneasy silence between them. Anita's sullen expression and bitter mood could be attributed to the earlier loud conversation with Dirk, but Jane got the feeling this was Anita's natural disposition.

As a consequence, Jane kept her expression neutral but decided not to let the other woman's comment go unchallenged. "For what it's worth, Ann is trying to make the Musgrave Landing like it was when we were kids, an interesting place to visit, with flowers and artwork scattered around the village. Her project could bring in a few tourist dollars."

Anita clicked her tongue in clear distaste and sniffed. "Change will bring new construction, noise, and disruption. We like things how they are now, nice and quiet."

It didn't look like Jane could say anything that would be taken in a positive light by the town administrator. She merely took her paperwork and tucked it away in her bag. "Thanks."

"Have a good day." Anita never broke a smile.

After leaving the village office, Jane stood on the sidewalk across from the post office, eyeing the building. She hoped the next person she talked to would be more pleasant. The day had started out so good, and right now, she struggled to swallow the bad taste in her mouth.

Resolutely, Jane used the crosswalk and climbed the post office steps. A wheelchair access ramp was built beside the steps. She had not noticed it before on her visit last week. "It looks like some things around here can change after all." Jane opened her purse and dug for her keys as she swung the door open.

It was a relief to enter the dim interior of the lock box area in the post office and be out of the brisk wind.

Jane found her business-sized postal box along the bottom row on the south-side and inserted the key. No doubt there would be a large stack of brown envelopes loaded with forms to fill out documents from several government agencies. When one ran their own business, not everything could be done on-line.

She opened the little door and peered in, one item. Frowning, she grabbed it and then relocked the box.

The white cardboard notice told her to see the postal assistant. Jane made her way through the glass and wood double-doors to the customer service counter. No one else was around. "Hello?" she called out to get someone's attention.

"Hello." A painfully slender woman with brilliant red hair popped up at the wicket. "How can I help?"

"I don't seem to have any mail, except this note." Jane passed the card over.

"Oh my, strange, I know you have mail. I sorted some of it myself. I'm Mina, by the way. Welcome to Musgrave Landing."

Jane thought about explaining again, as she'd done in the town office but merely said, "Thank you. It's lovely to be here."

"Let me check this number." Mina stepped over to a metal rack of shelves that held numbered parcels and cardboard boxes, also with numbers. "Ah ha." Mina grabbed a shoe box sized container off the next to the top shelf.

From where Jane stood on the other side of the wicket, she could see a note attached to the cardboard box.

Mina read the note and turned back to the counter to extract a heavy hardcover ledger. She ponderously opened the book and ran her index finger down the row of box numbers and names beside them.

Even upside-down Jane could see her name beside 'Box 550' and it was crossed out. The new name, ATS Enterprises, was printed underneath. In the comments was Tim Stanhope's signature.

"Uh," Mina said, hesitantly. She looked at Jane with wide eyes. "It looks like box five-fifty has been assigned to someone else."

"What? How can this be?" Jane asked. "I signed the papers and the postmaster personally issued me the keys last week."

"Be that as it may, it belongs to a different business. I'm supposed to ask for the keys, please." She held out one, long fingered hand to accept them.

"I think there's been a mistake, I'd like to speak to Bea. I have all my correspondence set up to go to that number and I've paid the yearly rent for it."

"I'll just be a moment." Mina scurried away and disappeared around the corner.

A moment later, Bea Merryweather strode over to the counter. "Hi Jane, what's going on? Is there a problem with your mail?"

Mina trailed the older woman only as far as the parcel shelf.

"There's a problem with the box number, it's been issued to someone else," she said and tried not to sound annoyed.

"I am so sorry for the mix-up, Jane." Bea gave her a gentle smile then turned to Mina. "We need to fix this problem. Assign one of the mid-size postal boxes to," she paused to read the name in tiny script above Jane's struck out name. "'ATS Enterprises', I've never heard of this business."

"Me neither," said Mina.

"Explain it to them when they come in." Bea pushed the ledger over toward Mina. The postmaster strode over to the shelf and took down the cardboard box and returned to the counter. She slid the pile of mail over to Jane. "Again, I'm sorry for the mix-up."

"Thanks, Bea. It's no problem."

"How was your first day?" The older woman leaned her elbows on the counter.

"It went well, thanks." Jane decided not to add—up until the last hour or so anyway.

"Glad to hear it." The older woman gave her a gentle smile. "I'm sorry I didn't make it down there today, but I certainly will tomorrow after my run. We all have to support each other." Bea gave Jane a firm nod.

"That would be great. See you tomorrow then, and thanks." Jane beat a hasty retreat.

As she exited the building she thought, how weird was the bank going to be?

Chapter Four

Thankfully, the bank was not weird at all. Tony-Joy, the teller who assisted Jane with her first business deposit, was easy to speak with and friendly. She advised Jane how much and what type of money to keep on hand for the cash register float. Toni-Joy also gave Jane a deposit bag for transporting her funds and then ordered cheques for her. The rest, Jane could do on-line as needed. All in all, reviewing the day as she walked down the hill toward home, it had gone fairly well.

Once back at the café, she set about readying things for Tuesday morning. She removed all the current day's baking from the display case and wrapped each item in cellophane for placement on a tray labelled 'Yesterday's Delights'.

She was out of sandwiches and breakfast bars. Only one breakfast wrap and two chocolate-on-chocolate cupcakes remained. It pleased her to think the customers liked her baking and other items.

She planned to clean the display case and public areas, and then to replenish her products. She would eat dinner in between those tasks, somewhere, and got busy with the chores.

Half an hour later, she wrung the floor mop out for the last time. As she set the mop aside, someone knocked firmly on the café door.

Curious, Jane stepped around the counter and peered out through a window. A pleased smile curved her lips as she hurried forward and opened the door.

"Hi stranger." She grinned up at the broad-shouldered man. Jack Birch grinned right back at her. Jane felt her heart light.

His wavy auburn hair, tamed into a short style, exposed a firm jaw and strong cheek bones. Hazel eyes sparkled with humour as his grin exposed even white teeth.

Jane's breath caught. He looked so good in his faded jeans and forest-green golf shirt. Jack had remained fit after all these years. Seeing him now caused the turbulent emotions from her past to surface.

"Hello Jane, it's so good to see you again." His sincere words touched her and she welcomed them like water in the desert.

Jack leaned down and caught her in a one-armed hug.

Surprised by his action, Jane still welcomed it and returned the gesture as she grasped his muscular shoulders. The brief contact made her eyes close, and she seized the opportunity to breathe in his spicy aftershave.

Then, he released her. "Happy opening day," he said while offering her a flower arrangement of pink roses, purple lilies, and violets with his other hand.

"Oh, Jack, these are lovely. Thank you so much." Jane accepted the flowers in the white vase, the ceramic cool against her fingers. She looked at Jack. "Come in, please."

"Sure, just for a minute."

Jane crossed to the counter and placed the flowers beside the cash register, giving them a slight turn to display the arrangement from a better angle in the best location. In this location, she could enjoy the flowers all day long.

"I'm sorry I didn't get the flowers to you for your opening this morning," Jack said as he closed the door. "I was obligated to go to Victoria today."

"You didn't have to do anything. The flowers really were sweet of you though. Especially considering you went to the trouble of coming all the way over to the village."

"It was no trouble. I'm moving back, as of today too. I used to come over Mondays to check on Dad, but with my old territory closer to Comox, it was hard to get out here. So, I asked for a change and it came through a couple weeks ago. I've sold my condo in Duncan and moved back to the village."

Jane blinked. They would be neighbours again, across the street, and possibly see each other every day. Her heart sped up a notch. "To help your dad?" she asked.

"Yeah, and because I missed Musgrave Landing." He studied her, and added, "Among other things."

To cover her confused fluster, Jane nodded. "I saw your dad today, he looks well. He stopped by for a moment, but I'd just closed up. He said he'd be back tomorrow. I haven't seen either of you since Aunt Ethel's funeral, how have you been?"

"I'm good. I don't think Dad's eating enough though." Jack's expression sobered.

"He did seem to be on the lean side," Jane said with a nod.

"I doubt he bothers to eat half the time. Now that I'm living here again, I know he will, at least once a day."

"No doubt it's a good thing you've moved back then."

"It was rough for him after my mom passed on last year. I think he's gotten a touch more eccentric too." It was obvious Jack worried about his father. "But how have you been? Busy I would guess getting ready to reopen." Jack turned his attention to the café and looked around.

"It has been crazy, but it's going okay. It was a good first day."

"Glad to hear it. Musgrave Landing could use a shot in the arm right now. It needs a wider tax base and new businesses to bring in new blood. The population at Whisky Corner helps and hopefully the planned new road will too. "

"A new road, going where?"

"From here, it will link up to Whisky Corner, and continue on to the Fulsome Harbour road."

"This new road will give us access to the majority of Salt Spring Island, and ferries to Vancouver," Jane said with excitement.

"It's a good time to be starting a service-based business." Jack grinned.

"Yes, and timely. Ann wants to get the ECBP up and running. The project will hopefully promote the village and bring in more people. The new road will certainly help encourage traffic to the village, too."

"ECBP?"

"Ethel Crawly Beautification Project, something we came up with as a memorial for Aunt Ethel. It's also Ann's new passion."

"I see," Jack said carefully. "How is Ann?"

Jane felt her expression slip into neutral at his question. "She's great. Ann has a new challenge, beside ECBP, painting the outside of this building." There was history between Ann and Jack, she reminded herself, and she should be happy with a friendship with Jack, nothing more.

From Jack's careful expression, Jane realized he must still have some feelings for Ann. Maybe now with both of them back in the same town, the two of them could reconnect. If they did, she would be happy for them. Jane forced a bright smile.

"Will you let her paint the place purple, green, and puke yellow?" Jack gave her a smirk.

Jane could not help but laugh. "No, she's over that particular 'colour shock' phase."

"Good." Jack gave a shiver. "It took me two days to repaint the plant shed for Mom."

"Sorry."

"Not your fault. It was a long time ago and we were kids." Jack waved her concerns away. "Are you taking donations for ECBP?"

"We probably will, but right now Ann's busy chasing town councillors to get grant funding for the project. She has a proposal to offer at the next council meeting, including a three-year vision."

"Interesting, I hope it goes well for you both. It's a nice way to remember Ethel. Let me know when you start collecting donations, I'd like to contribute."

"Thank you, that is very generous of you, Jack."

"No problem, I can help fundraise too, if you like." They looked at each other for an awkward moment. "Well, I guess I better get going. Vimy will be getting antsy and I have some unpacking to do."

"Vimy?" It was Jane's turn to ask for clarification.

"My dog, he's in the truck." He tipped his head toward the parking lot. "Dad will have dinner ready too."

"Wait for a second." Jane dashed behind the counter and into the kitchen beyond. She snagged the leftover cupcakes and put them into a carryout box, then returned to the café. "I'm sorry I don't have anything for Vimy, but here you go, something for dessert."

"Thank you, Dad loves sweets." Jack peaked under the lid. "Chocolate is my favourite."

Jane smiled softly. She knew what Jack's favourites were.

"What does your dad like?" Jane folded her arms and leaned on the counter.

"Maple, caramel, stuff like that."

"As coincidence would have it, the featured treat tomorrow is double maple cupcakes."

"I'll make sure to tell him." Jack gazed down at her for a moment.

Did he have something more to say?

"Have a good evening," he said finally.

"You too, and thanks again for the flowers."

Jack gave her a nod and then left.

Jane straightened and shifted away from the counter to lock the door.

She paused to stroke one pale pink lily petal before returning to her cleaning tasks. Jane savoured the warm feeling Jack's thoughtfulness triggered. Then she spotted a small white envelope hidden amongst the flowers. She plucked the note out of the holder and extracted the card from its envelope.

Jane,

Welcome back to the village. Congratulations on opening your café.

Good luck!

Love Jack

The note, handwritten in Jack's terrible scrawl, meant more to Jane than the flowers. He'd gone to the effort himself instead of ordering the arrangement through a florist. He did not dictate the card, or pay for delivery, but did it all himself. The extra effort meant Jack was a true friend.

Jane ran her fingertip over the endearment and his signature, and then sighed.

What if...no.

Jack never showed any interest in her beyond friendship, and the way he had just spoken of Ann reminded her of it.

The shortage of teenagers in the village had drawn all the kids close in age into the same group, Ann, Dirk, Jack, Jane, Chester, Hanna and a few others. They used to hang out as a group, rather than paired off. Jack was five years older than Jane, but now the gap in ages didn't seem so great. At thirteen and eighteen, it had been huge. Especially once Jack left for university, a lifetime ago.

Even so, Jane slid the card into the top apron pocket, a small one in the bib of the garment, over her heart.

JACK STOOD IN THE DYING light beside his truck with his hand on the door handle. He paused to watch Jane read his card and then tuck it away in her apron pocket. She didn't put the card back with the flowers or toss the note away. He took this as a positive sign.

There were many things in Jack's daily job that put him in harm's way, but none of them scared him as much as blowing this chance with Jane. He needed to go slow. This had to be done right.

When Jane picked up the wash bucket and went back into the kitchen, he opened the truck door.

She had a lot on her shoulders. From what he heard, Jane experienced a bit of trouble back in Vancouver. He didn't have any specific information, but he knew Ethel had been worried about her niece. She and his dad had been friends and they talked.

Jack doubted Jane's circumstances had changed much since her aunt died. She had to be grateful to inherit the business. Even though, it appeared Ann got the more valuable inheritance, the house, studio, and surrounding land would be worth more than the old café property.

Still, there was some value to the location. Waterfront property went for astronomical prices on the mainland and

Vancouver Island. Salt Spring Island, though, was a bit more remote. The smaller island didn't see quite as much of an increase in the value of real estate as quickly as the mainland did, but it had climbed. Especially since Vancouver had become warier of foreign buyers. He wondered if Jane knew what she had.

A bark sounded inside the truck cab.

Jack climbed in and glanced fondly at the dog. Vimy sat on the floor below the passenger seat on his special piece of carpet, far safer for him to travel in the truck lying on the floor than on the seat. The German shepherd stared at him, tongue lulling as he showed an enticing canine smile.

He tucked the bakery box beside him and then leaned over to scratch the soft fur around Vimy's ears. "You want to get going, don't you, boy." Jack closed the door and turned the ignition key. "Past your supper time, isn't it?" He smiled and rubbed the German shepherd's ears one last time, and then put the truck in reverse and backed out of the tiny lot.

It would be a late night, a lot of stuff to unload, personal items, some tools, and his clothes. Most of the furniture went with the sale of his old place, but he managed to bring his widescreen television, high time to upgrade his dad.

Jack didn't regret leaving Duncan behind. Other than work, and a few friends, he had no reason to live in the small city.

Sure, he would still commute daily. Jack put on a lot of miles in a week, but what difference did it make if he added a few more so he could live back in Musgrave Landing?

The benefits were certainly here. His dad would welcome his company and he would be out of that multi-tenant building he'd lived in for the last few years. Jack hated apartments, but it was what he could afford at the time.

Coming home provided a yard for Vimy too. He pulled up into his usual spot in the doublewide driveway. His father had left the exterior lights on for him.

The best thing though, was Jane back in Musgrave Landing. Nothing would be the same.

Chapter Five

Come on, you aren't going to empty yourself. Jane picked up the floor-washing bucket and hauled it into the utility room / laundry room to dump out the dirty water. She called that job her last chore. It was time for something to eat.

Jane stowed the bucket and mop as her cell phone rang her sister's theme song.

"Hey, you," Jane said, and then thought about sharing Jack's visit to the café. She wondered why Ann and Jack had never been a couple. Jack certainly ticked all Jane's boxes. But Ann's question distracted her from this train of thought.

"Jane, did you receive an unusual letter today?" A hesitant note was threaded through her sister's voice.

"I picked the mail up but haven't gone through it yet. I've been prepping for tomorrow. Why?"

"Put the kettle on, I'm coming over." Ann hung up. Jane tapped the end icon and pocketed her phone, shaking her head. *Now what?*

By the time Ann arrived at the kitchen door, it was full dark, and Jane was starving.

"If you want tea, fill the kettle, I'm heating up some leftovers. Are you hungry?" Jane asked as her sister entered and closed the outer kitchen door.

"I could eat." Ann dropped her wrap and purse onto a kitchen chair. "But scratch the tea, I brought something better to celebrate your first day."

Jane turned from making up plates of leftover baked ham, with scalloped potatoes and a side of broccoli, so she could see what Ann was talking about. "Lovely, I could use some wine, glasses are to the left of the sink."

"I'll set the table." Ann placed the bottle of Chardonnay on the wide-board farm table. "I love this kitchen more than mine," Ann commented. She moved around the exposed red brick walls and stainless-steel appliances as she collected dishes and utensils. "No wonder Aunt Ethel practically lived here."

"I love the three-minute dishwasher cycle." Jane put one plate into the industrial microwave and hit the button. "I can see why Ethel bought it instead of an espresso machine."

"The racks are a bother though." Ann put down woven sage-green place mats on the table before adding the place settings and wineglasses.

"I figured out if I stick them over the rinse sink, they aren't in the way."

"Ah, good idea," Ann said as she poured the wine.

"So, what's this about a letter?" Jane grabbed the warmed plates out of the microwave and carried them to the table.

"Sent from Aunt Ethel," Ann said and gave Jane a steady look as her sister took her seat. "But first things first, let's toast to your success." She waited until Jane picked up her glass. "Happy opening day." They grinned at each other as their glasses clinked and they sipped.

"Okay, no more stalling, give." Jane picked up her fork.

Ann cleared her throat and put down her glass. "I received a letter from Aunt Ethel in today's mail. She must have directed her lawyer to hold it until now."

"And, to be sent out after her funeral?" Jane popped a broccoli floret into her mouth.

"Yes, I think so."

"Can I read it?"

Ann dug into her massive bag and extracted a cream envelope.

"I can tell just by looking, it's Aunt Ethel's stationary. That, and the cursive handwriting." Jane accepted the envelope. "I always wished my handwriting was as good as hers. Cursive writing is becoming a lost art, not to mention using a fountain pen." Jane scanned the letter. "This says the same thing as her will. You own the house and all of its contents."

"Yes, but look how she stresses 'content.' It's like she means something by it."

Dearest Ann,

My kindred spirit. I charge you with utilizing my studio, now yours, to its fullest extent. Realize your full potential, for you are amazing.

The house, studio, and the land are yours, always and forever to do with as you will. Find what makes you content, for contentment is important in life. Find your key, to your contentment, and you will never have to worry about anything again.

Until you do, do not sell the property. You do not want any regrets.

Your loving aunt,

Ethel

Jane glanced up at her sister and handed back the letter. "It's lovely and weird at the same time, to say the least." She used her napkin to blot a stray tear, her aunt's words stirred up emotions all over again.

"Did you receive a letter?" Ann was working on her broccoli. She always left the vegetables for last.

"Oh, let me look." Jane wiped her fingers on the napkin and pushed out the chair next to her where she'd deposited her box of mail when she'd gotten home. Excitement built inside her at the thought of receiving a letter from her aunt. The deposit bag was on top and she placed it beside her. "I have to put this in the strongbox later."

"You're killing me, Jane." Ann sighed impatiently.

"Don't get your panties in a bunch." Jane leafed through the brown envelopes and flyers, and then paused. "No." She went through the envelopes again. "There's nothing here from the lawyer. All this stuff is for the business." She gestured at the pile of mail, nothing personal for her.

"Maybe your letter will come tomorrow," Ann said with a shrug, unconcerned. She grabbed her wineglass to take a drink as she re-read her letter. "This has to mean something."

"Of course, it does, she loved us, and she didn't want us to make any rash decisions. I can understand it, especially when I think of the house. It's been in the family forever."

"And this building, even longer," Ann shook her head. "No, this feels like there is more. She's trying to tell us something."

"What, like speaking from the grave? Then why didn't she just come out and tell us before?" Jane got up and collected their empty plates to load into the dishwasher. The task helped get her mind off her disappointment.

She left the dishwasher door down as a hint for Ann to load the rest of the dishes while she crossed to the stainless-steel oven a few feet away to set the preheat temperature.

"I don't know. Sometimes our auntie could be wily." Ann refilled their glasses, ignoring the dishwasher's maw.

"She liked a good joke too," Jane said skeptically, as she retrieved the cupcake batter out of the fridge and popped the lid off the container. Instantly, the fragrance of maple was released into the room. During the lull between ferries, she'd mixed together the ingredients for tomorrow's feature treat.

"Is there dessert?"

"No cupcakes, I gave the last two to Jack." She plucked a wooden spoon out of the red vase she used as a utensil holder and gave the batter a brisk stir. "But there are muffins on the YD tray." Jane set the container down on the counter next to the lined-up baking tins and donned plastic gloves to add cupcake liner papers to the pans.

"Jack Birch?" Ann stood and strolled out of the kitchen into the café. She came back with the whole tray of Yesterday's Delights.

Jane merely raised an eyebrow at her sister. Her sister was fussing.

"How is Jack?" Ann feigned a casual interest.

Her tone made Jane glance over her shoulder at her sister again. She closed her teeth over her first response and said nothing.

Ann opened a cupboard and took out a rectangular basket, then lined it with red and white deli paper from the box on the counter.

Instead, Jane said, "Jack is fine, he's moving back to the village. He stopped in to congratulate me on opening day. He asked how you were too." The cupcakes went into the first oven and she set the timer. Jane walked back to the cooler and slid open the door to extract the six muffin batter containers; blueberry, oatmeal raisin, trail mix, chocolate chip, fruit explosion, and cinnamon-brown sugar, Jane's own recipe.

"Oh?" Again, with feigned casual interest. "Did he give you the flowers?" Ann asked as she arranged the items to her satisfaction in the basket. She kept a blueberry-oatmeal for herself and a chocolate chip muffin she placed by Jane's wineglass.

"Yes, and it was very sweet of him to think of it." Jane filled the muffin tins with batter. Her sister's faked lack of interest would be hilarious, if she didn't feel a slight pang of envy.

Ann took the newly loaded basket out to the display case as Jane continued to fill baking tins with batter. When she returned, Ann placed the used tray in the dishwasher. She took the hint and loaded the rest of their dinner dishes into the machine, sans their wineglasses.

Jane knew they would have to discuss Jack, at some point. Especially now, that she was staying in Musgrave Landing for the foreseeable future. It confused her as to why Ann had not made a move on Jack. Plainly she had feelings for him. However, her divorce might explain it. Maybe her sister was scared of being hurt again or maybe she was waiting for Jack to make the first move?

It could be Jane needed to have a discussion with Jack about Ann. The thought made her heart twist, for all of them.

"Now back to this letter." Ann dropped back into her chair. "What do you think?"

"We should go on a treasure hunt?" The muffin pans went into the second oven. Jane closed the door and set the timer, then rejoined her sister at the table.

"A treasure hunt would be fine if we knew what we were looking for." Ann braced her chin on her fist as she toyed with the cellophane wrapped muffin, idly spinning it in a circle with her other hand.

"It's fairly obvious what we should be looking for." Jane checked the level of wine in the bottle then the level of her sister's glass. Her own was half-full. "Did you walk here?"

"Yes, I did. What's obvious?"

Jane picked up her glass for a sip, and then remove the cellophane from her muffin as she thought it through.

"Jane, you're doing it again." Ann gave her sister a stern look. "What is obvious to you?"

"You have a key to find. Once you have your key, we will know what the 'contentment' is. All will be explained, I would guess."

"Maybe it's a million dollars."

"Sure, it is," Jane said dryly. "Anyway, you're not hurting for money."

"I have a huge house in need of renovations. I could use money." Ann twisted her lips.

"So could I. The bank hasn't refunded me a dime of my savings from the hacked accounts."

"It will take time, but Andrew is good at his job. You will get your money back." Although the divorced couple didn't speak much, Andrew did not hesitate to take up his former sister-in-law's case. "Have you...heard from Andrew lately?"

Jane swallowed her bite of muffin and shook her head. "I should call him for an update." She rubbed the bridge of her nose and breathed out a long sigh to dismiss her past misfortunes.

"We need to find a key, huh?" Ann changed the subject as she broke her muffin in two. "Piece of cake."

"I'm still confused. Why didn't Ethel give you, us, the key? Assuming I have a letter coming too. Why didn't she tell us straight out what this is about?" Jane popped the last bit of moist cake and chocolate chips into her mouth.

"You know how she was." Ann ran one gentle hand over her letter, evidence she enjoyed the texture of the heavy cream paper or maybe because their aunt had handled it. Jane didn't know.

"She must have told us a hundred times..." Jane looked expectantly at her sister.

"Anything worth having, takes hard work," they both said at the same time and then grinned at each other.

Jane looked down at her hands as she folded her crumbs into the cellophane. "Did you ever want our mother to be more like Aunt Ethel?"

"No. In my heart, Ethel was our mother. Much more than her sister ever could or would have been. I'm glad Mom dumped us here. I can't imagine what it would have been like traipsing after her from one third-world country after another. No thanks."

"All water under the bridge." Jane nodded and ignored the black feelings that bubbled up. The last image she recalled of her mother was the exuberant smile on her face as she waved good-bye. Jane and Ann had stood beside their aunt, watching the ferry depart. Sometime later, they'd received news their mother was dead.

"An ocean full," Ann added with forced brightness in her tone. "Come on, I'll help you get the rest of the food ready for tomorrow. I don't feel like going home yet, and I'm feeling generous with my time."

"Thanks, I'd appreciate it." Jane stood, and they cleared the rest of the table. "Did you track down all your councillors today?"

"Only two, Weldon Ingram and Dirk Ipkiss," Ann said as she washed off the tabletop. "I did speak my piece, and they both seemed receptive to the ECBP. Especially Dirk, he's tasked with applying for provincial and federal grant funding."

"At least some progress then," Jane said and handed Ann the box of gloves.

"There's something else, the monthly council meeting has been moved up to tomorrow evening." Ann snapped on a pair of gloves.

"Why?" Jane dumped sandwich fixings on the table while Ann laid out two kinds of fresh bread, multigrain and white, in neat rows.

"Who knows, but it means I'll be tied up tomorrow evening."

"I appreciate all your help, but you just get the votes you need to move the project forward. I think I will have to look for someone to help me out part time. Running this place is a lot for one person. I'm not sure how Aunt Ethel managed it."

"If I get three votes out of the five council members, I'll have it." Ann looked over at the cream envelope, next to Jane's pile of mail. "If I don't, maybe Aunt Ethel will provide funding for her namesake's project."

Chapter Six

At a little before six on Tuesday morning, Jane couldn't help but glance out the window and down the street. She hoped Jack would stop by before taking the ferry back to Duncan.

"I only want his opinion on my cupcakes," she said aloud as she flipped the switch on the open sign and it lit up. Then, "Jane, you are pathetic. And you talk to yourself way too much." At the very least, she could be honest with herself inside her own head, about how she felt about Jack. It started with friendship, then a crush, and evolved over time, to something more. Unfortunately, Jack loved Ann and there was no denying it. Why else had he never married?

This morning, Jane took extra pains with her look, just in case. She pulled her thick brown hair up into a bun with a clip to allow a flirty rooster tail to bounce enticingly at the back of her head. Curling tendrils framed her face to soften the look. She liked how her natural golden highlights grabbed the early morning light and hoped someone else would too.

Usually, not one for makeup, today Jane broke that rule and added a touch of eyeliner and natural lipstick. Jack probably wouldn't notice anyway, but the extra effort made her feel better. Besides, what could it hurt to look good?

Her first customers strolled in, and she didn't have time to think about Jack or anything else for the next ten minutes. Breakfast wraps needed heating, lunch items needed bagging, and tea and coffee needed dispensing, to say nothing of ringing up the sales.

True to his word, Dirk Ipkiss strolled in with the first rush. "Good morning, Jane, you look lovely."

"Thank you, Dirk, what can I get for you?" Jane took in his brown tweed blazer, blue dress shirt and tan slacks.

Dirk made a show of flashing his gold watch. "I'll take a fruit muffin and a large drip coffee to go. I have a meeting shortly with some vendors."

Was he trying to impress her? She suppressed a smile and efficiently put the muffin into a brown bag as she added, "To-go coffee cups and lids are at the self-serve counter. That will be three-fifty, please."

He stared at her for at least thirty seconds. "Oh, yes, of course." Then dug for his wallet and handed her a five-dollar bill. Jane had his change ready. "Have you thought about my offer?" he asked and grabbed the change.

"What offer?" She frowned.

"My offered from yesterday, to buy the café." He gave her a chiding look.

"Oh, I thought you were joking. Fifty grand is far too low."

"I can see I'll have to rethink my offer."

"If you like." Jane shook her head, he could do what he liked, but she wasn't interested in selling.

"Have a good day, Jane."

"You too," she said. Jane watched as he put one quarter into the ECBP Donation cup and pocketed the rest. Then Dirk wandered over to talk to someone else.

The chipped, lime-green ceramic mug had sat beside the cash register since forever. The change went to various charities when Ethel ran the place. It seemed fitting to continue the tradition.

The ferry coasted into its berth at the end of the dock. For the second time in two days, an RCMP police cruiser rolled off the ferry ramp and onto the concrete wharf. And again, everyone in the café paused to watch, including Jane.

"I bet it's about Tim," said Nancy, the middle school teacher. A few heads nodded in agreement.

Jane frowned, it was apparent she was out of the loop.

Dirk pushed past Victor to get to the door and abruptly exited.

Victor slid his large black-framed glasses up his nose as he took a sip from his dark roast coffee. He scowled at Dirk's rudeness. "What's his problem?"

As the morning progressed, Jane forgot about the arrival of the police until the officer pulled into the café parking lot. The sun had risen higher, but the air remained cool. The officer advanced to the entrance. The constable wore a light grey uniform shirt, dark navy uniform pants with side cargo pockets, and a reflective yellow stripe up the side Over the shirt, she wore a body armour vest, with 'police' written on the back. She also both wore a utility belt, with her side-arm service revolver, cuffs, flashlight, Taser, and radio attached.

There were a couple other compartments on the black belt, and Jane wondered briefly what they contained.

The café was empty, except for Jane. Jane smiled as the lanky brunette entered the building. The cop, in her mid-thirties was trim in an athletic sort of way.

The next ferry, a good fifteen minutes out, would be transporting the commercial vehicles with business deliveries for the village and the hamlet of Whisky Corner.

"Good morning, Constable Havelange." Jane read the last name from her name tag.

The officer's dark eyebrows went up in surprise. "Well done. Most people mangle my last name," she said, walking up to the display case.

"I assumed your name was a French pronunciation." Jane shrugged. "What are you in the mood for today?"

"Close, my name is Belgian." The constable smiled and looked over the sandwiches and baked items. "I'll have a large dark roast coffee and a fruit explosion muffin, please."

"To-go, or would you like the muffin warmed up? The coffee is behind you." Jane took a square of wax paper from the shelf and used it to extract the largest muffin from the tray.

"Warmed up please, I think I have time before the next ferry gets here."

"You do," Jane confirmed as she heated the muffin and readied a plate with a knife and pat of butter.

The food was exchanged for money, and the officer sat down at the closest table to enjoy it.

Jane busied herself tidying the area behind the counter. The new espresso machine was supposed to arrive today and the location where the machine would sit behind the half-wall needed to be cleared. Jane wanted to wash the spot down too.

"How long have you run this coffee shop?" Constable Havelange asked as she buttered her muffin.

"I reopened yesterday." Jane wrung the cleaning cloth out in the hand washing sink. "Before that, my aunt, Ethel Crawly used to run it."

"Then you pretty much know everyone in Musgrave Landing?"

"I did, I'm relearning. I lived away for quite a while, until my aunt got sick."

"She isn't still ill?"

"No, my aunt passed on last month."

"I'm sorry for your loss."

"Thank you." Jane went back to scrubbing the counter and backsplash.

"Do you know Tim and Anita Stanhope?"

"I've spoken to her." Jane paused and looked over the short wall at the cop.

"Do you know anything about their relationship?" Dark eyes gave Jane a penetrating gaze.

She compressed her lips as she thought about what to say. "Not really, no. But by reputation Tim can be disagreeable, and so can Anita, but then so can we all." She hesitated to say judgmental statements about people. But this was the police asking questions, her responses weren't gossiping. "Tim is the mayor and his wife Anita is the town administrator."

The constable nodded and wiped her mouth with a napkin. "I know. What I'm interested in is do you know if Tim Stanhope ever walked out on his wife before?"

"No, I've only ever seen him once in the post office, where he works."

The cop pulled her occurrence book out of her jacket side pocket and flipped it open. She extracted a pen and made a note. "You were working yesterday? Did you see him take any ferries off the island?"

"Yes, I was, but he didn't come in here and I didn't notice him leave on any of the trips."

"Thanks." She flipped the notepad closed. The officer was quiet as she ate and sipped her coffee.

Jane realized a radio should be playing or something. The silence felt awkward.

The chair scraped against the floor as the cop got to her feet and walked to the display case again. "What flavour are those cupcakes?" She put her plate and knife in the grey bin for used dishes as she spoke.

"Double maple, would you like one?"

"Can I have six? If they are half as good as that muffin, I'll need that many. I have a couple of office clerks I owe a treat to, and those would fit the bill."

"Certainly." Jane plucked a flattened bakery cardboard box from the shelf, and deftly put it together before loading the box with cupcakes.

The door opened as Jane gave the constable her change. A brisk wind from the north had picked up and it wanted to suck all the heat out of the room.

Jack Birch and Mr. Birch senior stepped into the café. Fighting against the brisk north wind, Jack hung on to the door and quickly closed it.

"Good morning, Jack, Mr. Birch."

Jack's eyes found her, and she loved the way they creased at the corners when he smiled.

"Good morning," Mr. Birch returned her greeting, narrowed his eyes at her, and then shook his head in what Jane felt was dismissal.

"How are you this morning?" Jack asked as he walked up to the counter. Mr. Birch hung back.

Jane opened her mouth to answer.

"Well, hello Jack," the constable interrupted as she put away her change.

"Hi Lea. Wait, why are you here?" Jack's gaze came level with the cop.

"Nice to see you too," she said raising her eyebrows, like she expected more. Then she turned to his father. "Good morning, sir."

Jack made quick introductions between his father and Constable Havelange.

Jane bit her lip and then frowned. Jack appeared all eyes for the female RCMP officer.

Mr. Birch nodded to the cop and turned away. He selected the table farthest from the counter, but close to the electric fireplace. The fake displayed pushed out a decent amount of heat, a good reason to sit in front of it on this chilly morning.

"Your call out—it's nothing serious I hope." Jack's eyes studied the constable's face.

"Nothing that involves the Conservation Office," she began, then paused and frowned. "Correction, have you received any reports about bears hanging around Musgrave Landing? Specifically, Eldon Trail?" The constable picked up her box of cupcakes and stepped toward Jack.

"Not that I know of offhand," he said and shook his head. "I'll check the logs when I get to work."

"I'd appreciate it. Tim Stanhope is missing." All eyes moved to the constable. "He went for a walk around Eldon Road, as is his usual practice around six-thirty Sunday night. He hasn't returned. I couldn't see anything obvious when I drove the road. Which made me wonder if a bear might have got him."

"Or it might have been a cougar attack," Jack suggested.

"There are cougars on the island too?"

"Oh, yes," Jane said. "One walked down Kings Street when I was a kid. The village was much busier then and the animal wasn't much worried about people."

The constable studied Jane for a moment. She removed a business card from her jacket pocket and offered it to Jane. "Call me if you hear of anything about an attack or if anyone spots Tim Stanhope around town."

Jane took the RCMP officer's card and glanced at it before she tucked it into her apron pocket beside her key ring. "I will."

"I stopped in at the post office and spoke to Bea Merryweather, she hasn't seen him either. He also didn't report for work yesterday or this morning and he didn't call in. Pass the word along for anyone who's seen him to call the

Detachment and ask for me." The cop moved to the door. "You too, Jack. You have my number."

"What about Search and Rescue? How long do you want to wait to scramble a team?"

"It's policy to wait forty-eight hours for an adult, especially for someone who is familiar with the area." The officer looked steadily back at Jack. "If you want to go out there and have a look, I've got no objections."

"I might do that," Jack said with a nod.

"Thanks," she said to Jane, lifting the box.

"Thank you for stopping by." As the door closed behind the officer, Jane turned to look up into Jack's hazel eyes. "What can I get you, Jack?"

He returned her gaze, and briefly, they were caught up in the moment. Then Jack blinked, and the moment was gone.

"Extra-large coffee to go please." He cleared his throat and tipped his head toward his father. "Dad will have the breakfast wrap." He took out his wallet and offered Jane a twenty-dollar bill. "You having coffee and juice Dad?" he tossed over his shoulder.

"Just coffee thanks." Mr. Birch sat with his hands flat on the wooden tabletop, looking around the café.

"Make it two coffees, please."

Jane turned and opened the fridge. The appliance sat behind the counter in the back corner, and she selected the plumpest breakfast wrap and placed it on a white ceramic plate.

She took the time her back was turned to compose her expression. "You can grab your own coffee if you like, everything's on the self-serve counter," she said over her shoulder, happy her voice stayed steady.

Everything she'd ever felt for Jack was still there, not imagined. Like coming home, when he'd hugged her last night.

She swallowed and pulled on disposable gloves. Opened the bacon and egg tortilla to sprinkled shredded cheese on the inside, rewrapped the deli paper around it, and popped the plate into the stainless-steel microwave mounted over the sink.

Now, she was prepared to look back at Jack. "Do you want a wrap too, or a breakfast bar?"

"I'd love a muffin, please. You pick for me." His back was toward her as he mixed the two coffees across the room.

Jane selected a trail mix muffin. Again, she made sure it was the largest one in the basket. "Heated up?"

"No thanks."

By the time she popped the muffin into a brown paper bag, with butter, plastic knife and a napkin, he'd walked back with the coffee.

He didn't look at her.

Jane compressed her lips in resignation. *So, this is the way it's going to be.* Deal with it, Jane, put it away. At least she hadn't said any of it out loud.

She placed Jack's muffin beside the cups and briskly took his twenty off the counter. Jane wanted to give them their breakfast on the house, but money was too tight at the moment.

"That's weird about Tim going missing," Jane said, grasping for something to say as she counted out Jack's change.

"Yeah, and the more I think about it, the more I'm sure something may have happened to him. I'm going to take a drive down Eldon Road and have a look on the trail with Vimy. Lea might have missed something." He stuffed the muffin into his jacket pocket. "Thanks, Jane." He took the coffee cups to his dad's table.

The microwave toned. Jane served the wrap to Mr. Birch and moved away giving the men some space, but Jack wasn't staying.

Jack paused at the counter and offered Jane his card. "You can call me too if you hear anything."

She took his card, careful not to touch his hand. After the handing him his change earlier and brushing his fingers, she knew it was best not to touch him.

Jane met Jack's eyes, this time with a slight frown. "The constable asked me if Tim Stanhope took the last ferry back to the main island last night," Jane said on impulse. "Is she stationed at the Duncan Detachment?"

"Yeah, we have crossover responsibilities, if we catch a poacher or they get an animal sighting in a residential area."

"It's good to keep the lines of communication open," Jane said with a neutral tone. *Think about something else.* What was it to her if Jack was interested in the cop?

The parking lot door flung open, and Ann stumbled in. She juggled her giant purse and attempted to keep the door from slamming against the wall. "Ack! Help!"

Jack hastily put down his coffee and rushed to grab the door from Ann.

"I've got it." He deftly slid an arm around Ann's waist to haul her into the café and close the door.

"Thanks, Jack." Ann pushed her flyaway hair out of her eyes and smiled warmly at him as he removed his arm.

"Sure, no problem. I'll see you all later. Bye Dad."

Mr. Birch gave his son a wave as he munched on his breakfast wrap.

Jane watched him drive away to the sound of the ferry's arrival. It berthed, and trucks began rolling off. Jack had forgotten his coffee on the counter. She looked at her sister and noticed her flushed cheeks.

"You're up early," Jane commented as her sister dropped her belongings into a chair and helped herself to coffee.

"My head is too full of ideas. I needed to get the sketches over to you, so you can have a look. I'll have to make a run into Duncan for paint and supplies." Ann set her cup down and dug a portfolio out of her bag.

"Can't we buy what you need from Hillman's Hardware?" Jane dumped the water from her scrubbing and rinsed the sink. She was ready for the new espresso machine.

"I suppose," Ann said doubtfully as she opened the folder.

The phone rang, and Jane picked it up to look at the number and sighed.

"Jane's Eats & Treats."

"Hello, my name is Paul, and I'm calling about the computer."

Jane grimaced, and hung up, dropping the phone into its cradle on the counter. "Scammer," she muttered. She picked up a plate of ginger snaps and snagged Jack's coffee off the counter as she went by. It would be a shame to waste it. If he came in tomorrow, she'd give him a free coffee.

"Those guys don't give up easily," Ann said and made room for her sister at the table. "I've had five calls in two days."

Jane waved the interruption away. "Anyway, the point of the ECBP is to support local businesses and the village, right?" Jane looked at Ann's drawings. She noticed out of the corner of her eye that Mr. Birch paid close attention to them.

"True, I guess I can get the supplies locally," Ann said and slid the folder closer to her sister. "What do you think?"

Jane looked down at the rough sketches of her café building. Ann drew realistic flowers on the outside walls, red poppies, orange and yellow tulips, and deep blue pansies. Except they looked huge, the flower heads were the size of manhole covers. The flowers intermixed with deep-green leaves and grass on a white background.

"I love these, Ann. They're perfect." Jane grinned at her sister, and Ann flushed with pleasure.

"Shouldn't the rest of the building be blue, like the sky," Mr. Birch asked over Jane's shoulder.

Jane jumped. "Mr. Birch, you gave me a fright." She hadn't heard him come up behind her.

"Humph," Mr. Birch muttered and moved back to his table. "The sky should be blue," he muttered.

"Thanks, but I want people to notice the café. I don't want it to blend in," Jane answered, a touch sharper than she meant.

"Like people wouldn't notice flowers three feet wide," he muttered to himself as he picked up his coffee cup.

"White will make the flowers stand out more and create interest," Ann agreed, ignoring Mr. Birch's comments. "Now, on to the interior," she said. Ann shuffled papers and pulled out a new sketch. "Tell me if you like these, if not, I can come up with something else."

The next drawings showed the café's interior walls from a three-dimensional perspective. The drawing displayed a view of the Samsum Narrows with a pod of orcas and dolphins. Some, coming out of the water, while seals watched from a rocky island on a clear summer day. "These are good too." Jane nodded as she examined the sketch. "Is that Burial Island?"

"If it's done right. And yes, I thought the island would work. We can make it look as though the whales are diving in and out of the windows." Ann pointed to the three casements she included in the sketch. "I know an artist who could tackle this easily. Ben is very talented."

"What do you think, Mr. Birch?" Jane handed the sketches to the old man.

He looked surprised when she consulted him, but willingly took the drawings. He studied them for a moment. "These are good," he agreed with a nod and held them up to the windows as if he was imagining the mural. "This design fits."

Ann flushed darker this time and smiled at Mr. Birch's comments.

"Can I get an estimate for both commissions?" Jane asked as she accepted the drawings back from Mr. Birch.

"Of course, I'll price the supplies, and then go talk to Ben Sinclair. I'll give you separate estimates from each of us and the supplies."

Jane stood and helped her sister packed up her drawings.

"Did you hear Tim Stanhope is missing?"

"No." Ann looked at her in surprise as she sipped her coffee. "What happened?"

Mr. Birch grunted and picked up his coffee mug again. "He's stepping out on his wife. Probably, Anita finally decided to do something about it. I told Jack the same thing."

Jane raised her eyebrows at the old man. "He's missing, that's all we know for now."

A large truck pulled into the parking lot and distracted her from the gossip.

"I hope this is my espresso machine arriving." She got up and went to the door to meet the driver and receive the invoice.

"Nice job with the doors." Mr. Birch nodded at Ann as he sipped his coffee.

"Thanks, they did turn out well."

"I'd have helped you remove the plywood, and such, if I'd known what you were up to."

"It wasn't too bad of a job. Jane and I tackled it together." Ann pushed up the long sleeves of her grape and emerald silk blouse.

"Too bad about the original doors, whoever broke in messed them up pretty bad while Ethel was in the hospital. I couldn't leave the openings exposed. The weather would have gotten inside."

"There was a break-in? Here?" Ann asked.

At these words Jane looked back at them with a worried frown.

"Yeah, a while ago, two in a week," the older man said as he leaned across to Ann's table and took a cookie from the plate. "I told Ethel about it when she called me to check on things." He dunked the ginger snap into his coffee, and then aimed the soggy mess at his mouth. The cookie disappeared in short order.

"Ethel never mentioned anything to me." Ann looked at Jane as she closed the door on the wind. The driver returned to the truck to extract her shipment. "Did you know Mr. Birch was keeping an eye on the café while Aunt Ethel was in the hospital?"

"Yes, she mentioned it to me."

"Did she tell you about the break-ins?"

"No." Jane looked at Mr. Birch. "You put the plywood over the doors?"

"Yeah, that was me. I checked the house too, but nothing happened over there." He shrugged. "It's a good thing I was looking after things though."

"Why is that?" Ann asked.

"Cops didn't want to come over to check it out because I couldn't tell if anything was stolen." He shrugged his boney shoulders. "You should have a report from the insurance company coming to you through the mail. I called them for Ethel."

Jane slid her eyes toward the kitchen and the neglected pile of envelopes on the kitchen table. She would have to find time to go through them, soon.

"So, where did you put my plywood?" He picked out another cookie.

Chapter Seven

Jack drove past the post office, village office, bank, and B&H Country Grocers, a cluster of houses, and then took a left to travel down Eldon Road. He glanced at his dog, Vimy, laying on the carpet with his black head on his tan paws, eyes closed. The dog was used to travelling with Jack everywhere work took him.

He frowned as he left the village behind. Tim Stanhope walked the trails around the village frequently. Had Tim's wife made that plain to Lea? Jack doubted Musgrave Landing's mayor had gotten lost. Lea's assumption about a bear attack was possible, but unlikely too.

However, Tim was in his early sixties and carried some extra weight. More likely, the man experienced some kind of medical issue and couldn't get himself back to the village.

Jack knew exactly where Tim and Anita lived, the last house before the turn to Eldon Road. Their house offered easy access to several walking trails, which originated in the village and ran all through the woods. The locals used the paths to walk their dogs or for biking as well as hiking.

One trail was a particular favourite of Tim's. This path led past the back of their house, joined up with Eldon Trail, and then on to Mount Bruce, a higher degree of difficulty and quite a distance from town. This made the trail a less popular route for the locals to take for their daily strolls.

Tim liked to be by himself in the woods. Jack found this out when he came across the mayor several times when walking Vimy on this same trail. Tim ignored the dog and Jack. He stalked right by them going the other away, taking the blue path which led to the mountain's west exposure. "Make sure you clean up after that dog," were the only words shot over the older man's shoulder as he strode away.

As a responsible dog owner, of course Jack carried the required bags to pick up after Vimy. But Tim's attitude didn't encourage Jack to strike up a casual conversation.

Even though Jack thought it unlikely, there was a real possibility the mayor had encountered a bear or a cougar. People had to be careful when walking the trails, best to take a walking stick and bear spray. Jack knew people got complacent with increased familiarity of an area. They thought they were safe, the same as when they were in their backyards. Unfortunately, Jack knew from experience in SAR, search and rescue, the second people didn't respect nature and the dangers, bad things could happen.

He drove past Lara Finkle's pink and white house and then pulled into the small hiker's lot, just large enough to hold six vehicles at the main trailhead. Jack's truck was the only one parked there.

Vimy's head lifted immediately. His ears pointed forward, alert with the change in routine.

"It's time to go to work," Jack told him, and Vimy stood. "Want to help me find somebody, boy?" Jack turned off the engine. "Let's see if you remember your training." He opened the glove compartment and extracted an extra-long nylon leash. The type Vimy understood meant he was tasked with a challenge.

The German shepherd leaned toward Jack, and he clipped the leash onto the dog's wide collar. Vimy tensed with excitement, ready.

Jack didn't have to urge Vimy to leave the truck. He barked once as soon as Jack opened the door and hit the ground right behind him.

"Give me a second, buddy. Here," Jack said the command, and Vimy returned to stand beside him. Still, the dog looked out into the woods, already searching.

Jack put on his coat and reached behind his seat to pull out a holstered canister of bear spray. He clipped the defensive mechanism onto the right side of his leather belt. Grabbed his phone out of the holder and went to tuck it into his jacket pocket, but the device slipped out of his hand and hit the gravel.

"Ah, damn," Jack muttered, as he leaned down to pick up his phone. He wiped the dirt off. The face appeared scratched, but the smartphone looked okay. The battery read a quarter charged, he hoped it would be enough as he tucked it into his coat pocket. He should have plugged it into the charger when he got in the truck, but he'd been distracted. Partially, the distraction was caused by his concern for Tim Stanhope, and partially, by Jane and her deep brown eyes. The way she'd looked up at him. His reaction had been immediate and needed to be curbed, at least for now. He'd think about it all later, he had to focus on the task at hand.

His jacket sported the logo and crest of the Conservation Office, provincial flag, flower, and crown, along with the words Integrity, Service, and Protection, as did the cap he put on. He took his job seriously. The motto was more than mere words to him.

Over his coat, he added a reflective orange and yellow vest. Last week, bear, cougar, and wolf hunting seasons had opened. Jack doubted many members of the population of Musgrave Landing would have purchased a tag for any of the allowable game, but it didn't hurt to be cautious.

He closed the truck door and pocketed the keys. If he couldn't find Tim Stanhope, he would scramble the local Search and Rescue team to comb this trail, end-to-end, and if nothing were found then the teams would fan out to check the other trails. He wasn't going to wait forty-eight hours.

"Ready, Vimy?"

The dog glanced up at him and gave one bark. Tension made the German shepherd's posture rigid, with only the very tip of his tail moving in a wag.

"Let's go. Hunt. Hunt boy. Find him." Vimy dropped his nose to the ground and did a complete circle around his owner.

Jack had to move the leash in a circle as well, to allow Vimy freedom of movement. The dog, in search mode, moved forward to the entrance of the trail and Jack jogged to keep up. As soon as they made it to the trail junction, where it split in four directions, the dog's tail dropped. He surged forward into a run, nose down in the leaves and pine cones.

Jack was forced to run to keep up with the former K-9 officer.

Chapter Eight

By noon, the day had warmed, and the wind dropped. The new espresso machine arrived, as did some other supplies, but still no sign appeared for the outside of the coffee shop.

Jane opened the back room and directed the driver to place her shipment on the floor. She hurriedly cleared a spot and the driver eased the pallet into the open space. At one time, the storeroom served as her aunt's office, but over the years it'd become the catch all for supplies, extra stock, as well as odds and ends of furniture.

She and Ann attempted to clear out the space and reduce the clutter, but more remained to be done. The room was piled high with junk accumulated over several generations and would require more time to be cleaned out than Jane currently had to spare.

The basement had been just as bad. It cost her a couple hundred bucks to get all the paint cans, trash, and a wealth of other near trash items removed. All that was left down there were the wrought iron patio tables, most in poor shape.

Even though it was practically empty, she still found the basement creepy. The damp smell and shadowy corners were perfect for trapdoor spiders. The huge, yet, innocuous creatures made Jane shutter. She'd come across two in her lifetime, and that was far too many in her opinion.

Jane pushed those last thoughts firmly away. She planned to sort the newly delivered items and unpack the espresso machine as soon as she got a free moment. She looked around the old office as the driver offloaded his dolly.

Perched on the old desk was a vintage black radio covered in dust. Jane picked it up and unwound the cord. If the radio worked, she'd put it in the café.

As the driver returned to his truck for another load, Jane plugged in the ancient wireless, and it lit up. She tuned in the station from Duncan and light rock played out of the speaker.

"Good, you're coming with me." She shut off the device and coiled up the cord.

The café didn't have a safe but instead, held a strongbox bolted to the wall in the back corner. Jane had cleared a path to it a week ago. She stared at the metal box for a moment, thinking. She would have to look through the metal box again to see if she could find the key mentioned in her aunt's letter.

Jane recalled recipes and assorted yellowed documents inside, as well as an old cigar box which contained her grandfather's medals. His old pistol was recently donated to the village museum.

Still, Ethel used to keep the makeshift safe locked since it was where she put the daily cash and the till float money. She kept the key to the strongbox on the ring which lived in her left apron pocket.

Jane saw no reason not to keep these same habits. If she kept to what was familiar, she always knew where to find the café keys. It comforted her to keep some things the way her aunt had, making the transition feel less strange.

Presently, there was no time to indulge in any investigation. The last of the items was offloaded and Jane signed for her order. Several of the commercial drivers had stopped back at the café for lunch while they waited for the return ferry. A couple stood in front of the counter.

Serving the drivers would bring in real money, and she needed to concentrate on tangible things instead of some fantasy key. Hopefully, there would be a similar letter for her in today's mail. It felt odd to be left out.

Stop being pathetic Jane.

She frowned at her sensitivity. Of course, there would be a letter for her. She'd tucked Ann's letter into her pocket to return to her absentminded sister the next time she saw her. Jane had meant to do that this morning, but Ann left while Jane was with the delivery driver.

After thanking the trucker, she closed the storage room door and headed back behind the counter. Ten minutes later she was finished with the last of the commercial drivers.

"Thanks." Jane handed the man who drove the oil tanker his change. He nodded, then gathered up his sandwiches and coffee and made for the door. Some of the drivers had returned and clustered together in groups outside. They stood around their queued trucks. Some of them smoked and drank coffee as they chatted together. Others climbed into their rigs and took an early lunch.

Inside the café, a couple of locals sat on the stools in front of the narrow counter, staring at their smartphones.

Cindy and Hanna, a couple from the village, were at the table close to the patio door. The soup of the day sat in large bowls in front of them. They also nibbled egg and cheddar cheese quiches and drank mugs of extra-dark roast.

Cindy told Jane earlier they planned to walk onto the ferry as foot passengers and take the connecting bus to Victoria. The couple talked in low, cautious voices with each other, and the odd word surfaced, such as baby, adoption, and natural childbirth.

Jane tried not to listen in. To cover the conversation, she nudged the radio's volume nob. The music helped create the illusion of privacy for her customers. She'd wiped the radio down, and Mr. Birch offered to place it on the high shelf above the coffee mug cupboard for her.

The next table was occupied by Bea Merryweather, the postmaster or was that mistress? Jane was just happy to see the locals supporting her business. If this kept up, she would definitely need more serving help.

As she thought about getting an additional pair of hands to deal with the work load, Jane glanced to her right, at the self-serve counter. Mr. Birch was there tidying up. He turned and brought the medium-roast carafe over to the counter. "This one's empty."

Jane gave the older man a steady look. He was clean-shaven today. His hair neatly combed, and he wore a navy long-sleeved shirt tucked under the belt of his khaki trousers. She raised one eyebrow at him.

His expression was innocent, as they looked wordlessly at one another for a moment. Then Jane exchanged the carafe for a full one.

"Would you please put this one out for me, Mr. Birch?"

His watery blue eyes met hers. "Certainly," he said with a slight smile.

Mrs. Elderberry entered from the parking lot and tottered on high heels to the counter. Her pure white hair sported one streak of purple on the right side. She was dressed in black yoga gear with a book tucked under her arm.

"Hello, Jane." The older woman's apple cheeks bunched up as she smiled.

"Good afternoon, Mrs. Elderberry, what can I get for you?" She had the sweetest disposition of anyone Jane knew. Her fluffy white hair always reminded Jane of the whipped meringue Aunt Ethel used to top her lemon pies, although the purple streak was new.

"Raspberry tea in the brown stripped teapot please, it pours so nicely."

"Certainly, can I get you anything else?" Jane asked.

"A ham and Swiss cheese sandwich as well. I have a few minutes before the ferry gets here." She laid her Linwood Barkley mystery on the counter as she dug into her black purse, shaped like a tiny backpack.

The ferry signaled fifteen minutes later. The drivers and passengers got up from the counter along the wall, taking their to-go cups outside and climbing back into their rigs.

Mrs. Elderberry, Bea, and the other locals finished their meals also and filed out to get into their cars or walk onto the boat for the trip off island.

"That was wonderful soup, Jane." Hanna waved as she escorted Cindy out the door.

"Thank you," Jane called after them.

Without comment, Mr. Birch helped Jane clear the empty tables. She loaded the used dishes and cutlery into the dishwasher as he washed the tables quickly and efficiently with the disinfectant spray and one of the cloths Jane handed him.

"It's lunch time for me now. Would you care to join me, Mr. Birch?" Jane asked as she wiped her hands on a towel.

"I would, thank you." He finished straightening the chairs.

"Is vegetable soup and a turkey sandwich, okay? I like to eat the slow sellers."

"Sounds good to me," Mr. Birch said with a smile. He helped transport their lunch to the closest table by the counter.

Once seated, she handed him a napkin and spread one on her lap as she regarded the father of her old friend. It should have felt awkward, but it didn't.

"Mr. Birch, can I ask you something?"

"Certainly," he said as he added pepper to his soup.

"Would you be interested in a job?"

"Depends. Do you think you can call me Arlie instead of Mr. Birch?" He raised his salt and pepper eyebrows at her.

"I can, if you can take orders from your kid's childhood friend."

"Deal." Arlie held out his right hand.

"Deal." Jane shook his hand, smiled, and then picked up her spoon. "How mechanically inclined are you? We have to figure out how to assemble an espresso machine after lunch."

A grin spread over his wrinkled face. "I'm a mechanical engineer, Jane. I think we can handle it."

Later, as Jane cleared their dishes, Arlie organized the parts and manual for the new machine into a neat row on a flattened cardboard box on the backroom floor.

The largest piece of the machine was already in place behind the half wall. Arlie had run home for his toolbox to connect a water hose to the machine. Now, he knelt behind the counter with heavy black framed glasses balanced on the end of his nose. He peered through the lenses and adjusted the connections to his satisfaction.

The café was empty of customers when the door swung open, and Jack stalked in.

Jane turned to ask if he wanted lunch. She could clearly see by his body language he was in an agitated state. At the last second, he caught the door before it banged against the wall, due to the force of his entry and not by the wind.

From the corner of her eye, Jane noticed the small black cat stealthily glide in behind Jack and scoot under the armchair by the windows on the west side of the café.

She ignored the cat. Jack's agitated state drew her attention instead.

"Can I use your phone, Jane? My cell is dead, and my charger in the truck won't activate it."

"Of course, is something wrong?"

"I must have damaged the phone when I dropped it."

Arlie gave Jack a nod and returned to his work.

"Here you go," she said and offered him the portable handset.

"Thanks," he said and spied his father behind the counter. "What are you still doing here, Dad?" he asked as he punched in some numbers.

"Working. What are you still doing on the Island?"

"Finding dead bodies," Jack said tersely and lifted the phone to his ear.

"What?" Jane stared at Jack. The clean cutlery she had been putting way, forgotten in her hand.

Jack held up one hand to forestall any further questions. "Hi Lea? This is Jack Birch. I'm still on Salt Spring. I've found Tim Stanhope." His eyes met Jane's and there was an odd coolness in his gaze as he studied her. "No, not a bear attack, but he's dead. He's been murdered." Jack paused to listen and turned away from Jane, pacing back and forth along the west windows.

At these words, Arlie stopped the assembly of the coffee machine and stood, staring at his son. "I thought he was kidding," Arlie said blinking as he removed his glasses.

Jane dumped the last of the silverware into the basket. She would wrap them with napkins later. She watched Jack too, and she and Arlie openly listened to Jack's side of the conversation with the police.

"No, I'm not overreacting." He paused. "Because he took three slugs to the chest, that's why."

"Holy crap," Arlie said and leaned back on the counter folding his arms.

Jane merely shook her head in disbelief and covered her mouth to trap any exclamations behind her teeth.

"It's a close grouping, not made by a rifle. I'd say a handgun."

"Oh, my God," Jane whispered, she was unable to stop the words from escaping.

"No, I didn't touch anything. I'm at Jane's café. I'll wait here for you and the coroner. The body isn't easy to find, you'd need a tracking dog if I don't show you." He looked over at Jane. "What's the phone number here?" She rattled it off and Jack repeated it to the constable, and then hung up.

"Do you want something to drink?" Jane grabbed a mug off the shelf.

"Do you have any whisky?" Jack wiped his face with one hand, half-joking.

"No, sorry."

"We do at the house." Arlie walked over to Jack and grasped his son's arm.

"No, Dad." Jack put his own hand on his dad's arm in return. "I shouldn't, not before talking to the police. But thanks."

"All right," Arlie said and squeezed his son's arm in what looked to Jane as a comforting gesture. "Not a pleasant find, I'm sure."

"No, it wasn't. I doubt I would have found him if it weren't for Vimy. By the look of the body, I'd say it's been laying there since he disappeared Sunday night, but I'm no forensic expert." Jack paced again.

Jane poured him a strong cup of coffee from a fresh pot. She thought he could use a hug or something when she touched his hand as she passed him the mug. Their eyes met briefly, and then Jane pointed to the self-serve counter. "Put some sugar in your coffee, it helps with the shock."

He followed her advice then left his mug on the table. "I have to wash up," he said and then detoured to the washroom.

"What happened?" Jane asked after he returned.

"Vimy is trained to track people. The plan was to walk the trail, but Vimy found Tim's scent right away, and we hauled ass over half a kilometer. We found him down a side trail. Vimy must have smelt the blood, or something, possibly the cordite residue. Tim was covered with ferns and tree limbs." Jack shrugged then folded his large frame into one of the wooden chairs.

"The killer wanted to hide the body," Arlie said.

"That's my guess." Jack took a deep swallow from his mug. "Ah, damn." He placed the cup down on the table.

"What?" Arlie asked.

"I should have had Vimy track for the gun. It might still be there if the killer ditched it. I never thought about it at the time." Jack picked up his mug again and sucked back another healthy swallow.

Jane grabbed a large ceramic bowl and filled it with the last of the vegetable soup. She placed the gently steaming bowl in front of Jack with utensils.

"Where's Vimy now?" his father asked.

"Is he in your truck? Did you want to bring him in?" Jane asked.

"No, I took him home."

The phone rang. Arlie grunted and returned to the counter to answer it. He looked at the display. "Not the cops," he told Jack then hit the button. "Hello. Jane's Eats and Treats."

Jane thought about why Jack didn't call the police from his house, but she didn't mention it. It was clear by his disjointed explanation he was disturbed about finding the body. As if reading her thoughts Jack looked at her, and she could understand his actions as well as the troubled look in his eyes. "Thanks," he said and picked up the spoon.

"Who's this? Josh? What's the scam of the day, Josh?" Arlie leaned against the counter.

"Vimy needed to be fed and watered after our trek into the woods. I'll have to go back for him. Take him out there again to see if he can find the weapon when the police get here." Jack spooned some soup into his mouth and closed his eyes in appreciation as he swallowed. "This is good, just what I needed." His eyes found Jane's again.

"No problem," she said as she slipped into a chair across from him.

"My credit is at risk? Really, well, that's terrible." Arlie continued his conversation with the scammer. Jane glanced over her shoulder at Arlie. He opened his eyes innocently wide at her. She shook her head at the older man's antics and got up to go back to the display case.

She opened the sliding door and grabbed a couple items.

"I think you need more than the soup," Jane said to Jack as she set a roast beef sandwich and cupcake beside his mug.

"Does your mother know you're a criminal? Have you explained to your family how you make money by victimizing old people? You should be ashamed of yourself."

Arlie ended the call and returned to the espresso machine, picking up a screwdriver.

Jane blinked at Arlie's words.

"It's his hobby. He likes to mess with the scammer's head," Jack explained between bites.

"Arlie, you didn't have a double maple cupcake. I made them especially for you."

"Arlie?" Jack asked and raised his eyebrows in surprise at her.

The grey head snapped up, visible over the half wall. "Time for a tea break," he said and clambered to his feet again.

Jane dodged Jack's questioning look because she'd used his father's nickname. Instead, she returned to the display case and picked out another two cupcakes. She added loose tea and hot water to the brown striped teapot. The Earl Grey blend was for her new employee.

"Tell me what's going on here," Jack said to his father.

Jane figured he wanted to get his mind off from finding the body.

"Jane needs some help around here, so she hired me." Arlie took the teapot and cups from his boss. Their eyes met, and Arlie gave Jane a worried, puckered frown.

Her lips twitched, but she gave him a small nod. She would not give Arlie away. He'd been obvious by the way he hung around all morning that he wanted a job. If he needed employment for social or monetary reasons, well, not her story to tell.

"I have so much to do, and business is picking up every day. I need an extra pair of hands, for sure." Jane joined the two men at the table, and Arlie poured his boss and himself a cup of tea.

"Generous of you, Jane." Jack gave his father a long steady look as he reached for his dessert. He'd inhaled the sandwich and soup, leaving nothing but crumbs.

"Not at all, I need help. It'll be good to have someone wait on the customers while I'm making the soup or warming up orders. I have food prepared ahead, but it goes fast. And at some point, I'll have to do some of the cooking during the day instead of in the evening."

"Not the most enjoyable way to spend your evenings," Jack commented. He finished off his dessert and folded the paper liner to drop onto the sandwich plate.

"It's not like I have a social life, so it doesn't matter. I need the café to be a success. That's the most important thing," Jane said. She pulled her eyes away from watching Jack's tanned fingers encircle his coffee mug, and she extracted her cupcake from its paper.

"Some restaurants buy mixes and prefab food," Arlie said as he broke his cupcake in two moist chunks, making it a sandwich with the frosting in the middle. He paused to inhale the maple aroma, clearly enjoying the moment.

"I don't ever want to do pre-fab food. I'd reduce the menu first."

"We have menus?" Arlie swallowed his first bite of cake.

"One," Jane said and pointed to the wall behind the cash register. The blackboard paint converted the wall to a menu. "Ann drew that up for me." The multi-coloured chalk listed all the café's offerings. She picked up her cup to sip the dark brewed tea. "How's your hand writing? You can put up the feature treat of the day every morning."

"Will do," he agreed. "This cupcake is delicious just the right amount of maple," Arlie told her. "Thank you."

"It's very good," Jack agreed as he narrowed his eyes at his father.

Jane could see he wasn't completely sold on the idea of his dad working for her. She hid a smile. Was Arlie acting out of character? "Thanks, I'd like to start make my own bread too."

"Own your supply chain, good idea." Arlie nodded, licking icing off his fingers. "What about buying from vendors that meet your standards? Gladys Wyatt bakes good bread. She sells it at the community centre once a week. I get mine from her. Maybe you could order some to see if you'd be happy with her bread?" Arlie suggested.

"There's an idea," Jane agreed then looked across at Jack. He'd gone quiet.

Arlie glanced between them then got to his feet. "That machine won't install itself. I imagine you'd like to try it out today too?"

"Yes, please," Jane agreed with a hopeful tone.

He nodded with a grunt and took his tea with him behind the half wall.

"What are you thinking Jack?" Jane reached across the table and touched his hand. Again, she broke her no touching rule. She'd just have to ignore temptation.

He lifted his head and green hued eyes studied her seriously for a moment. "Did you have anything to do with

Tim Stanhope? Were you seeing him?" Jack asked in a low, harsh voice.

"Are you crazy?" Jane pulled her hand back as if she got scalded. "No, of course not."

"Then why would Tim have a letter addressed to you in his coat?"

"What are you talking about?" She frowned and pushed the last half of her uneaten cupcake away.

"I noticed an envelope sticking out of Tim's inside jacket pocket. I could see your name on it. It looked like a personal letter."

"Well, that's creepy. I don't know why Tim Stanhope would have a letter for me in his pocket, but I do know he tried to give away my post office box to ATS Enterprises. I got it straightened out yesterday with Bea."

"I see," he said, his tone sounding doubtful of her response. Jack looked at her steadily.

"You think he was sending me something?" Jane asked, her tone coming across sharper than necessary. His doubts had affected her.

"Could be. It wasn't just a regular envelope, it was cream coloured stationary."

The tiny hairs on the back of Jane's neck rose. What were the odds?

Today's apron was green and white pinstripes. Staring back at Jack, she slowly slid her hand into her bottom apron pocket and extracted Aunt Ethel's letter to Ann.

"Did it look like this?" Jane laid the letter on the tabletop beside the cupcake.

"Exactly like that. Same writing too, I'm fairly sure," Jack said. His eyes shifted from the letter to study her face.

"This letter is from my aunt. She had it sent to Ann after she died."

Chapter Nine

"There's no sign of anything from the road," Jack said. "No evidence Tim Stanhope entered the trail from Eldon Road. It's more likely he started on the trail from his house."

"No vehicle either?" Constable Havelange asked as she set her fists on her hips, pushing the sides of her yellow rain jacket apart. "I didn't see one earlier this morning."

"And you're right, there's no car or truck parked anywhere around," Jack agreed and looked at Inspector Zeffler, Lea's boss. "Vimy led me right to the body on a branch trail. It's roughly half a klick in, and three hundred feet off the main trail. The bush is thick," Jack explained his first trip into the woods this morning to the RCMP officers and the man from the coroner's office. There were no other vehicles on the one-thirty ferry. The coroner's vehicle, the police SUVs, and a van took up the available space.

The new arrivals stood around Jack in a loose circle. He felt vaguely uncomfortable being the centre of attention.

Jane and Arlie watched the question-and-answer session from behind the counter. The authorities declined any offering of coffee, and Jack was happy his father did not see fit to offer his colourful opinions about Tim Stanhope and his marital situation, again.

Present were Constable Havelange, Inspector Zeffler, and another male constable in a navy-blue Sikh turban, Jack did not know his name yet. They also brought the coroner, a short balding man in his late fifties. The other people accompanying this group waited outside.

The cops and coroner took in everything Jack said with serious expressions and the new constable jotted notes.

"Where did you enter the trail?" Zeffler, a man of medium height, but broad, like he lifted weights in his spare time, wore a white shirt, grey tie, dark grey suit jacket, and dark trousers. The shade of grey made his jet-black hair and heavy eyebrows look darker.

"After the pavement ends, there's a dirt road that continues on. Kids go there to hang out. North of Lara Finkle's house, past a stand of big-leaf maples, there's a small dirt lot for hikers. I parked there and entered from the road."

"Anita Stanhope, the victim's wife, said her husband walked the trails every evening after supper. She never mentioned he would have started off from a trail by their house," the constable put in. "That would put the body at least four or five kilometers from home, including the connecting trail." The cop acted annoyed with herself, probably for not looking farther down the trail, Jack assumed.

"As I said, you'd never have found Tim without a tracking dog," Jack shrugged. "No one would have, at least for a while." They didn't disagree with the obvious fact finding a body would be impossible in the dense foliage. Not without a K-9 like Vimy.

"All right," said the Inspector. "Let's get out there."

"Would you like me to pick up my dog? We could check the area for a weapon."

Zeffler tipped his head and the shorter man looked up at Jack for a moment. None of his thoughts showed. "That would be helpful, thank you," he said after a moment. "It would take us a day to get a K-9 from Nanamio or Victoria. Your dog will speed things up."

"I'll stop by my house first and pick up Vimy then." Jack gave his dad a nod and allowed his eyes to drift over to Jane briefly before leading the authorities out.

A fine misty rain began falling as he drove to his father's house. He left the truck running as he approached the gate and whistled for Vimy. The black and tan dog charged good-naturedly around the side of the house and abruptly lurched to a stop at the gate.

Jack smiled slightly at Vimy's enthusiasm. Training kept the shepherd inside the fence. The dog was more than capable of clearing the four feet of wood.

"Let's go to work, boy." Jack opened the gate and clipped on the leash. He led the way to the truck and the dog willingly jumped in the passenger-side door to sit on the carpeted floor.

After he climbed into his side of the truck, Vimy stretched his neck to lay his chin on Jack's knee. This action was a request for attention, a calming technique for both of them.

"Good boy." Jack slowly relaxed as he scratched the dog's ears. With a resigned sigh, he backed out of the driveway. Unfortunately, as a member of Search and Rescue, Jack had found more than one body in the woods. However, this was the first time he'd found one which was obviously a murder victim.

He hated days like this.

Jack turned back down Shore Road and met up with the authorities. He led the parade of vehicles through town, among the cop vehicles following him was an ambulance with the BC Coroner's Service logo. A white paneled van followed the coroner's vehicle. Jack suspected the van had something to do with collection of evidence at the scene.

People on the street paused under umbrellas to watch the unusual procession pass by. Jack knew gossip was flying fast and thick through the village by now. Someone would no doubt talk to Anita, but he hoped not. It would be better to get the facts from the police than assumptions from the locals.

Once out of the village, Jack sped up on the deserted road. Within minutes, they parked their vehicles in the small hiker's lot.

He wasted no time putting his gear back on. He and Vimy stood at the head of the hiking trail and waited for the police and coroner to join them. The rain was a small annoyance, but the moisture could make tracking the gun more difficult. Absently he ran the leash through his hands as they waited.

A woman and man from the coroner's office carried a backboard and walked over to wait patiently beside him.

The man appeared bored, but the woman looked around her with interest after she exchanged names with him.

"This is the first time I've been out here. It's a nice spot." Her name was Edna.

Jack frowned at her remark, but quickly realized she referred to the hiking trail and not a good location for a murder. Finally, the police and their retinue had organized and he and Vimy led the way.

"Let's go, boy." They struck out at a brisk pace, making the others jog to keep up.

In a handful of minutes, the dog led the group straight to the body.

Jack knew from experience how this type of thing went, so he and Vimy held back some ten feet from Tim Stanhope's prone form. Not a pleasant sight, Tim's face and body were covered by broken off ferns and spruce boughs as though the killer tried to hide the body and then gave up. The plants did nothing to disguise the smell.

"Shelberg," Zeffler waved a younger man forward. He was the photographer in their party and had first crack at the scene. Shelberg took at least a hundred shots of the whole area, by Jack's reckoning. Finally, the young man appeared satisfied and stepped back.

"Tell us what you touched, Jack," Constable Havelange requested. The three cops and coroner service people were now kitted up in white disposable coveralls, bootees, and gloves.

"I lifted the plants to see if Tim was alive. I felt for a pulse in his neck after I saw the entry wounds."

"Anything else?"

"No, that's it." Jack shook his head. That was also when he saw the envelope protruding from inside Tim's coat, but he hadn't touched it. His sleeve must have nudged the coat open and the letter slid out.

After the coroner carefully moved the plant matter aside, more pictures were taken and the envelope with Jane's name on it was also uncovered. The cream paper almost glowed in the dim light, hard to miss.

The letter lay half-fallen out of Tim's inside pocket, exactly where Jack had found it. When he saw Jane's name on the envelope, he had been shocked, disconcerted, and maybe, yeah, a bit angry.

Even now, after Jane's logical explanation, he still harboured some doubts. Why would Tim have a piece of Jane's mail in his possession? It seemed more likely Tim was sending Jane a note. But then, why would Tim do that when he could walk down to the café to speak to her, or call her? Whatever the reason, he didn't like it.

Jack liked even less, the fact he doubted Jane. Was he using this situation as a reason to stall? He was not a risk taker by nature. To tell her how he felt was a risk, bigger and more life altering than he cared to admit. Yesterday he thought he was ready, but now...

The letter was the first thing the corner extracted. The coroner's people were all gloved up, as was Lea and Zeffler. The letter was carefully passed to Lea, and she read the address. She turned and looked at Jack, lifting one eyebrow in query.

For his part, Jack looked steadily back at her.

There were dark stains on the letter.

Lea turned it over, and he could see the envelope was unsealed. The other constable stood close by and opened a plastic bag for her to place the article into, but first she drew out a single sheet of paper. She read it and showed the other constable, then dropped each into a separate, clear zip-top bag. Like the items removed from the jacket and trousers, the letter was handed to the inspector for examination.

Jack hadn't read the letter Jane showed him earlier, but it was a no-brainer to see the two envelopes matched, as did the paper of the letters. He hoped Jane was not somehow involved in any of this, but it was hard to ignore the letter. The uncertainty made him fidgety–he couldn't stand around watching this.

Six feet from the still form–now covered and positioned on the backboard–lay a narrower side trail which was barely more than an animal run. "I'm going to get Vimy to search for the weapon. Is that okay with you?" Jack looked to the inspector.

"Yes, that's fine." Zeffler gestured to the other constable. "Pannu, go with him."

"Yes, sir."

Jack looked down at his dog, and Vimy looked expectantly back at him. "Find the gun. Find it," he told the canine. "Track."

The dog dropped his nose to the ground and began a sweep.

They started in the area around the prone shape of Tim Stanhope. Vimy was in deep search mode again and moved back and forth in a grid pattern.

Nothing.

"Let's try down there, this way, boy. Here." Jack led him back up the wider track, which would take them back to the road. "Track it, where's the gun?" Vimy complied and took the lead with Jack in the middle and Officer Pannu bringing up the rear.

"How far down here are we going? Right back to the road?" Pannu asked after a couple of minutes of jogging behind Jack.

"It shouldn't be too far, people are generally lazy. Or so my buddy Soto told me. He was Vimy's original owner."

"Your friend is a cop?" He jogged easily behind Jack.

"Yep, from Victoria K-9 service. Soto had Vimy for five years." Vimy kept up a ground eating pace on every walk, Jack was used to it.

"That's an average dog's service term."

"It is," Jack agreed. "When Soto was assigned to take on a new K-9 partner, he couldn't keep both, so he gave Vimy to me. I volunteer with Search and Rescue, so he's a good fit." Vimy was more than that to Jack, they were buddies.

The shepherd paused and then turned left, leaving the trail. Jack jogged behind, "Good boy," he praised as he pushed slough out of the way. The clingy plant grasped at his jean-covered legs. Gamely, Pannu kept up.

The dog stopped and sat down and looked up at Jack.

"Is it here, boy?"

He received one bark in answer.

"Point to it."

Vimy dropped his nose down to the ground in front of his chest, with his paws outstretched.

"Good boy. Come on. Here." At the command, Vimy came back and glued himself to Jack's side.

Pannu approached the location Vimy alerted on and began carefully moving brush aside. Then he leaned farther in. "I see it."

Jack dug for the yellow tennis ball he kept in his jacket pocket. "Good boy," he told the dog and tossed the reward to the shepherd. Vimy deftly caught the ball and bit down, tail wagging.

The cop snapped on black latex gloves and reached among the branches of slough and ferns to extract the gun. "An old pistol," he commented as he held it away. Pannu ejected the clip then pulled back the slide to remove the round in the pipe.

"Is that a Browning-Inglis?"

"Yes, a 9mm." Pannu extracted an evidence bag from his coat and inserted the clip and the loose round. "Would you hold this please?" Pannu offered Jack the bag.

He took it gingerly.

"Do you know much about these?" Pannu asked casually as he fed a black plastic zap-strap through the open breach, looped it, and close the seal.

"No, only about the one I've seen on display in the Musgrave Landing Museum." Jack handed the evidence back and Pannu slipped the pistol, now made safe, into the bag. "One of the villagers loaned it from their grandfather's belongings. The pistol is included in an exhibit about locals who fought in World War II."

"Ah," Pannu said with a nod. He lifted heavy black eyebrows which practically reached his navy-blue turban as he looked at Jack. "We now have another suspect to add to our list."

Jack did not ask about who was first, he suspected he knew.

Chapter Ten

Jack tried to remember who owned the pistol displayed in the museum as he drove behind the constables back into the village. The museum had unveiled the display on Remembrance Day over five months ago. He knew the exhibit included an officer's army uniform, medals, and photographs, but he couldn't recall who had donated the uniform or the weapon.

The team split up after the inspector thanked Jack and Vimy for their efforts, and Jack was asked to return to the village with Constables Pannu and Havelange.

The inspector suggested he accompany them to speak with Anita Stanhope, the widow. Jack didn't understand why. Possibly, because Tim's widow knew who he was, and they wanted someone familiar there for when they told Anita about Tim.

A stop at the Stanhope residence had proved unsuccessful, Anita wasn't home.

"Do you find it odd Anita reported her husband missing and she still went to work?" Jack shook his head as they walked back to their vehicles.

"The longer I'm in this job, the weirder I find people are and the harder it is to know what normal should be," Lea said with a shrug.

Jack arrived at the village office first. Instead of going inside, he strode across the street to the post office.

He held the door for a mother and her two kids, all decked out in rain coats and rubber boots. The children ignored their mother's warning and charged down the steps to jump straight into a puddle in the broken sidewalk as Jack entered the building.

"Mina, is Bea around?" Jack held the lobby door open as he addressed the postal clerk.

"Bea! Jack wants to talk to you!" Mina didn't even turn around as she sorted parcel notification cards.

The postmaster poked her head around the corner. "Hi Jack, what's up?"

Jack waved at her in a 'come here' motion. And the woman trotted over carrying a fist full of envelopes in her right hand. He realized the time, after one o'clock–the postal truck had been and gone. The two women were sorting mail, but it couldn't be helped. Bea needed to know what had happened.

"You need to come with me to Anita's office. It's about Tim, grab your coat."

"Oh!" Bea trotted back into her office and returned with her coat on. She swiftly opened the gate and closed it behind her. "Mina, first class is done. You'll have to handle the rest until I get back."

"Righto." Mina nodded as she walked away from the counter to deliver the parcel cards to their post office boxes.

Jack escorted Bea across the street in the drizzle. Lea and Pannu stood by the building's main door, obviously waiting for him to return before they went inside.

"Where's Tim?" Bea asked as she took in the police vehicles and the cops.

"The officers will explain it." Jack gestured toward Lea and Pannu.

At the sound of an approaching vehicle, he turned. The coroner's van trundled down the main street. Bea's head snapped right to watch it proceed past them, down the hill, and toward the ferry dock.

"Oh no," she said sadly, covering her mouth with pale fingers. "Was it a heart attack?"

One tire of the van hit a pothole full of water and sent up a splash. To give the driver credit, it was practically impossible to drive the High Street without hitting some break in the paving, the place needed an injection of funds to fix the infrastructure.

The inspector's car pulled in and parked behind Jack's truck. The group waited for him to join them on the sidewalk.

"Mr. Birch, who is this lady?" Zeffler asked as he studied the older woman.

But it was Officer Havelange who spoke up. "Inspector Zeffler, this is Bea Merryweather, the postmaster. She was Tim Stanhope's supervisor."

"She's also a friend of Anita's." At least, Jack was fairly sure Bea and Anita were friends. From the way Bea flattened her lips and closed her eyes briefly then took a deep breath, maybe he was wrong about their relationship.

The cops glanced at each other, but said nothing.

Inspector Zeffler nodded and Constable Pannu swung the door open. They proceeded into the village office to give Anita Stanhope the bad news.

As the group crowded into the foyer, Anita lifted her orange, curly head. Her eyes narrowed as the five people filed into the small office. "Can I help you?"

Jack hung back, preferring to take up wall space. He noted her red-rimmed eyes and pale complexion, and wished he were anywhere else. But, if the cops wanted him there, he would stay, and he was glad he'd brought Bea with him though.

"Anita Stanhope, this is Inspector Zeffler," Lea introduced the senior member of their team.

"Is there somewhere private we can speak to you?" Zeffler asked.

Anita's mouth turned down and her glare hardened. "Here is fine."

"Please, have a seat," Lea instructed Anita.

By the set of her jaw, Jack thought the administrator might refuse. Finally, she dropped down into the office chair Pannu held out for her.

"Your husband has been found," Zeffler got right to it.

With the inspector's words, it was as though all the air inside of Anita Stanhope left her body. She had to know from his tone, it wasn't good. The older woman lifted her chin and stared at the inspector. "He's dead, isn't he?" Her tone suggested the ultimate finality.

The inspector didn't answer right away.

There was no easy way to deliver this type of news. Better to get it over with, Jack figured. He could not imagine how hard it would be to receive this type of information about a loved one. Let alone deliver it. This had to be worse than finding out your mother was dying. At least there had been time for long talks, and for him to say good-bye.

Bea stepped forward and placed a hand on the other woman's stiff back, rubbing it in a slow circular motion. "I'm so sorry, Anita," Bea whispered, and Anita dropped her chin to her chest as she took in an unsteady breath.

"Was it a heart attack?" Anita murmured the question. She stared glassy-eyed at her twisting fingers.

Jack looked closely at Anita. Was it possible she was the killer? She sounded sincere to his ear, but then he didn't know Anita well.

Lea ignored the question. "When was the last time you saw him?"

"I told you." Anita raised her head and glared at the cop. "Sunday night, after supper. He went for his usual walk. He said he'd be back in a couple hours. I waited all night." She took another long shuttering breath. "I left a message Monday morning at the Detachment about Tim missing. Then you showed up and were perfectly useless." Anita flung a hand at Lea.

"Why did you wait until the morning to call the police if you thought something had happened to your husband?" Zeffler asked.

"He...he sometimes stays away late." Anita's hands came together again, and she twisted them nervously in her lap. She made the skin turn red around her gold wedding band.

"Sometimes, if we have words, he'll stay away overnight. It's only happened a couple of times. Tim always comes home in the morning," she said the last words in a wheezy rush as tears slowly slid down her round cheeks.

"Did you have an argument on Sunday?" the inspector asked.

Anita nodded mutely.

Bea made a concerned noise and handed her friend a couple of tissues from the box on the desk.

"What was the argument about?" the senior officer pressed.

Anita shook her head and mopped at her face with the tissues. "Just stupid stuff, nothing important."

Lea and Zeffler exchanged a look as the constable extracted her note pad.

Pannu drifted farther behind Anita and Bea and wandered around the office. Jack watched the officer as he looked at the papers on the desk. Then he moved to the back of the building and walked in and out of the meeting rooms and the mayor's office as the conversation continued.

"When he stays away overnight, where does he go?" the inspector asked.

"He's got a friend he visits...sometimes." She clutched her hands together so tight her knuckles turned white and the tissues tore.

"What is this friend's name?" Lea held her pen to the notepad.

Bea looked away and bit her lip.

"I don't know," Anita said defiantly and dropped her head again.

Jack thought about the woman his father mentioned this morning, back at the café. The possibility Tim was cheating on his wife with another local woman. It would account for all the obvious awkwardness in the room.

A man was dead. This was no time for embarrassment.

"Lara Finkle lives on Eldon Road. It's the only house along there. Maybe she heard or saw something," Jack said in a low tone, and Lea wrote the information down.

"The pink and white house we passed?" Zeffler turned to Jack.

"That's the one," he said. He felt eyes on him and instinctively glanced at Tim Stanhope's widow. She glared at him coldly.

"Mrs. Stanhope, is Lara Finkle your husband's friend?" the inspector asked to confirm the information.

She continued to glare at Jack with her jaw locked.

"Mrs. Stanhope, please answer the question," Lea instructed.

Slowly Anita turned to look at the inspector and the constable. "Yes," she hissed in a low whisper. Her response did not sound so much sad, as angry.

"Where were you Sunday evening until this morning?" Lea continued with her questions.

"I told you, I was at home."

"Were you alone, did you call anyone?"

"I was alone, no, I didn't call anyone. I went to bed early, and lay there all night, waiting for Tim," she said with a frown. "What's happened to him?"

There was a long pause, and then Zeffler cleared his throat. "I regret to inform you that your husband is dead."

The phrase came out smoothly, if flat. Jack assumed the inspector must have conveyed these sentiments more than a few times in his career.

He, like the constables, had to remain impartial and at arm's length from the victim's wife. Soto told Jack the police usually looked at family members first as suspects. Then excluded them, one-by-one from their inquiries as it was proven each was not involved.

"I figured that out already, what happened to him?" Anita snapped at the inspector.

Jack waited for Zeffler to say Tim Stanhope was murdered. The tension in the room was thick with expectation as all three cops carefully watched Anita Stanhope.

"Your husband was shot in the chest."

Bea gasped in surprise and covered her mouth with her hand. Her eyes went to Anita.

The widow silently opened and closed her mouth, like a fish trying to breathe air and failing. She choked and dissolved into a torrent of tears.

"Can I take her home?" Bea wrapped an arm around Anita in a protective hug. She looked to Zeffler for permission, and he nodded. "Come on Anita, we should get you home." Bea helped the wailing woman to her feet.

Jack plucked a raincoat off the coat tree in the corner and draped the garment over Anita's ample shoulders.

The widow ran her hands roughly down her face, trying to get a grip on herself. "I have to lock up. Get out!" she ordered. "All of you." Anita snatched a ring of keys off her desk and glared at the officers and Jack.

Bea caught the inspector's eye and tipped her head toward the door, silently urging the group to exit.

"We will stop around to your home in about an hour or so, Mrs. Stanhope," Inspector Zeffler said.

"Why, what for?" Anita demanded impatiently.

"There are still a few details we need to ask you about for our inquiries," Lea said.

Chapter Eleven

After the police and Jack left, Jane felt more than ready to lock up and call it a day. She had to make up a bank deposit, and she wanted to talk to Ann.

Why did Tim Stanhope have her letter? Why was Jack upset about it? Did Jack think she was responsible for killing Tim? No, probably not, not by the way he explained the whole thing to the police while she was standing right there.

"What a strange second day." Jane flicked the switch off and the sign darkened.

"Why are you closing up?" Arlie was dumping coffee beans into the espresso machine to test his installation.

"It's time, well past two o'clock." Jane took the broom from the storage room and began sweeping the floor.

"You know those cops will be back. They'll need hot drinks if they're standing around in the rain all afternoon. Not to mention something to eat before taking the last ferry."

Jane paused with one hand on the deadbolt, while the other held the broom. "You think so?"

"Yep," he said over the hissing and squirting of the espresso machine as it went through its cycle. "Come and try this."

She left the lock open and turned the sign back on, then walked back to the counter. Arlie handed her a tiny blue ceramic cup. Jane dutifully sipped as Arlie watched.

"Mm, this is good." Jane took another sip of the potent coffee.

"Heh, want a latté?"

"I suppose we should test the steamed milk process."

Arlie nodded and glanced at the manual beside him. He picked up the stainless-steel pitcher, about the size of a creamer and meticulously followed the directions. In minutes, he had an indigo-blue mug brimming with a vanilla latté. He added a dusting of cinnamon then held out the brew to Jane.

"You're using me as your guinea pig." She narrowed her eyes at him but smiled as she took the saucer and cup.

"Yep, I am." He made a 'go ahead' gesture at her.

Again, Jane sipped one of Arlie's creations. "Oh my, this is so good." She took another drink.

Arlie flushed with pride as he fiddled with the machine and wiped down the surface.

"Do you think you could handle the place, while I run to the bank and get the mail?" Jane asked as she took the fourth sip.

"Of course, my girl, that's what I'm here for." Arlie's blue eyes sparkled.

"Great." Jane handed him back her cup and continued to sweep the floor, she planned to finish at least one task before heading uptown. As she got close to the armchair in the corner, one black paw shot out from under the chair and snagged the broom bristles.

Jane gave a chuckle and reached under the chair for the little animal. She extracted the purring fuzz ball and Ruby playfully batted at her fingers, and then looked at Jane with wide green eyes.

A glance out the window at the blustery spring afternoon, rapidly darkening, decided it for Jane. She carried the little female cat past the counter and into the adjoining kitchen. "Arlie, do you have any warm milk left?"

"I do. I'll pour some in a saucer."

Arlie found Jane on her knees on the multi-coloured rag rug in front of the kitchen sink. He handed her the saucer of milk.

"Thanks," she said. "This cat doesn't belong to anyone, does she?" Jane placed the milk in front of the kitten. Ruby immediately stuck her nose in it and sneezed, then went to work lapping up the milk.

"She's barely more than a kitten. I doubt she's ever had a home, not since she was born anyway. I think she was part of a litter found in a shed at the marina. Cats hang around there because Laurie feeds them in the winter."

"Laurie?" Jane asked.

"Laurie McDonald, the marina owner. She owns the restaurant over there too. Old Rufus left it to her last year, the whole kit and caboodle."

"I thought Dirk owned the marina." Jane ran a light finger over Ruby's silky fur while the cat purred like a chainsaw and lapped up the milk.

"Dirk Ipkiss? Hell no, he works for Laurie. Although, I think he likes to give the impression it's the other way around."

"I could see Dirk doing that." Jane also concluded his offer to purchase the café must be along the same vein, make-believe. "I wonder why Ruby's hanging around here if Laurie feeds the strays."

"Did you name that cat, Ruby?"

"Yes, I couldn't keep calling her 'that cat,'" Jane said as she rubbed the one orange ear, and Ruby purred even more. "She's been here on and off, for the past few days."

"I dare say Ruby is your cat now," Arlie chuckled. "If you don't have a cat, one will find you."

"I've heard that before." Jane glanced up at Arlie with a rueful smile.

"Sara used to say it, every time she took in a stray." Arlie blinked at the mention of his late wife.

Jane's brow puckered seeing Arlie's pain so close to the surface.

"I'll go clean up the espresso area." He turned on his heel. She watched Arlie stride away and was again glad she offered him a job. The man needed something to occupy him. Life must be lonely in that huge house by himself. No wonder Jack moved back to the village.

Finished with her milk, Ruby climbed onto Jane's lap, still purring. Jane continued to pet the sleek black fur. "We're going to have some ground rules around here though, Ruby. Seriously," Jane told the cat.

Ruby ignored her words as she settled in.

Chapter Twelve

Jack parked his truck next to the police vehicle. He was cold to the bone and felt completely drained. At least Vimy was snug at home sleeping on his pillow. A part of him wished he'd made the choice to go to work instead of driving out to Eldon Road.

No, that wasn't true, he supposed as he climbed out of his truck. He couldn't have gone to Duncan without looking for Tim Stanhope. If Vimy had failed to find Tim's body, he would have gone to Lara Finkle's house next, and to hell with everyone's feelings.

Once Tim was officially declared missing, the Search and Rescue team would have been called in. It made more sense for Jack to check out the surrounding trails first on the off chance he could resolve the situation and avoid putting anyone else at risk. Even though all the members were willing volunteers, each still had a job and family.

Officer Pannu had returned to the café parking lot a few minutes earlier, he glanced at Jack an ended his cell phone call.

His dad looked up from behind the counter as the two men entered.

"Coffee?"

"Yes, please," Jack gave his dad a grateful half-smile.

"One shot?" Arlie asked.

"Of what?" the constable asked.

"Espresso of course."

Pannu lifted one shoulder. "Sure, make it a double shot for me; I need to drive off this chill." He opened his wet jacket.

Arlie's chuckle had an edge as he placed two large mugs on the counter.

"I got this," Pannu dropped a ten on the counter and grabbed his mug. "It's the least we can do for you, Mr. Birch. You've saved us a lot of time."

"It's been no trouble, but thanks." Jack picked up his mug and took a shallow sip. Heat and caffeine shot through him.

"Ah," Pannu said and closed his eyes in pleasure after his first sip.

"When did you learn to make espresso, Dad?" Jack asked, over the rim of his cup, studying his father.

Arlie gave his son a level look before he returned to packing down the next round of coffee into something that looked like an ice cream scoop. "I wasn't always your father, you know. I had a life before you came along. I worked my way through university as a counter clerk at a coffee shop. That was before they called the position a barista."

Officer Pannu chuckled as he sipped from his mug.

The back door in the kitchen opened and closed, and Jane paused in the doorway. Her cheeks flushed and her bangs, wind tossed. She must have just returned from uptown. Jack stared at her as he cradled his warm mug between his cold hands. Their eyes met and held for a second.

A few strands of hair brushed against her rosy skin. The wind must have pulled them from her hair clip. When she hung up her coat on the back of the connecting door, he could see there were several types of food stains on her apron, but Jack thought she looked amazing.

"Jane Westcott?" Constable Pannu put his coffee down on a table behind him and removed his occurrence book from his jacket.

Jane blinked and tore her eyes away from Jack. When she looked at the cop, he could see a tightening around her mouth as she came forward, past the counter, wiping her hands down the skirt of her apron. "Yes, I am. How can I help you?"

"May I speak with you please?" Pannu asked. His tone became grave when he said, "Privately."

"Sure." Jane walked past him, and Pannu picked up his mug. She led them to the far table, by the west window.

Arlie studied Jack for a moment. "What's going on?"

"Tim Stanhope has or had," Jack lowered his voice, "a letter addressed to Jane in his pocket when I found him." He leaned his hip against the counter.

"Why?" Arlie slowly finished counting change for the ten, leaving coins on the counter for the cop.

"I don't know." Jack ran a weary hand over his face. "At first, I thought he and Jane might be–."

"Not for a moment." Arlie held up one age-spotted hand to cut Jack's words off. "She's been busting her butt here for weeks, working to get this place ready to open. Tim never set foot in the café that whole time."

"How would you know, Dad?"

"Same way I know Stanhope had a thing going on with Lara Finkle. I have eyes." Arlie opened the aforementioned orbs wide at Jack and compressed his lips. "That was a ridiculous thought. I can't believe you'd think that girl would have anything to do with Tim the Tyrant."

"What did you call him?"

"You heard me. It's what everyone called him. He was running the village council like somebody crowned him king. Nothing got done around the village unless it was Tim's idea or if it had his blessing. I bet Bea has a thing or two to say about Tim Stanhope as well. Anita the Hun isn't much better."

"Geeze Dad, keep your voice down." Jack glanced at the cop as he lifted a hand to calm his dad.

"Why? It's the truth. The police can ask any resident in the village and probably get the exact same information." His father said with a sniff.

Jack didn't respond, instead, he stared at his father, not sure what to say.

Arlie stepped to the sink to wash his hands. He came back with a cleaning cloth to wipe up the espresso station. The stainless-steel gleamed.

Jack returned his attention back to Jane. She spoke quietly to officer Pannu, answering his questions. After a couple of minutes, she pulled the envelope out of her apron pocket she'd showed him earlier and handed it to the cop. The constable took out his phone and took pictures of the envelope and the single page letter as Jane held it open for him.

Resolutely, Jack turned his back to the interview going on behind him. He couldn't help Jane at the moment, but something else was puzzling him. "Why did you want a job here, Dad?"

Arlie glanced up and met Jack's eyes briefly, before continuing to put the utensils back in their places. He watched his father's jaw work for a second, and then Arlie sighed. "Because I'm lonely and I need more to do than yard work. I was turning into a busybody, and that's something I don't want to be."

"I see." Jack waited. There had to be more, he merely needed to be patient for it all to come out.

"I need to feel useful. A job gives me that, I should have gone back to work after your mother passed on, but I couldn't." Arlie wiped the cloth up and down on the counter as he spoke.

"Of course not," Jack said. He knew how broken-hearted his father was after his mother's kidney failure took her away from both of them.

He doubted anything remained on the counter to clean, but the action gave his father something to focus on as he allowed the words to tumble out, and Jack was glad. This was the most the two of them had spoken in months about anything which actually mattered.

"I'm only sixty-seven years old. I was younger, back when I applied for some positions in my field on the main island. I never got one answer, not one." He sighed. "I tried for anything and everything. And still, nothing." There was resentment in his dad's tone, but mostly he sounded hurt.

"Retail too?"

"Everything, it didn't matter where I applied. I never received a call back or an interview."

Jack nodded. "They looked at your resume and saw you as over qualified."

"Probably," Arlie agreed as he looked up at Jack. With a shake of his grey head, he said, "Like I expected to be an engineer all my life. I suspect those other businesses thought I would quit and move on to something more lucrative in the engineering field if I got the chance. It didn't matter what I said in my cover letters."

"Short sighted of them and a huge loss." Jack shook his head.

"My thoughts exactly," Arlie nodded and rinsed the cleaning cloth, folded it, and set it in the sink, then dried his hands. "Jane needs help. I saw an opportunity, and I made it easy for her to ask me. And she did."

Jack unzipped his jacket. "I'm glad." He was finally warming up.

"Me too, because the benefits are great."

Jack cut his eyes over to his father. "What do you mean?"

"Leftover cupcakes."

"Ah," said Jack.

"SORRY, WHEN DID YOU say you got this first letter?" Officer Pannu's light-brown eyes watched Jane closely.

"I didn't. Ann, my sister, did in yesterday's mail." She kept her tone even.

"Did she notice if the envelope had been tampered with?" Pannu held his pen poised over his note pad.

Jane nibbled on her lower lip as she thought. "No, she didn't say. I don't think so. Of course, if Tim had mucked around with it, she might not have noticed."

"Why is that?"

"She wouldn't be looking for anything unusual when she opened it. Plus, my sister isn't very patient."

Jane took the letter back from Officer Pannu and slid it into its envelope.

"Why do you have your sister's letter?"

"She left it here last night after dinner. Not on purpose. Ann just...doesn't always remember mundane things. She will no doubt drop in at some point today, and I'll give the letter back to her."

"Aren't you curious to know what the letter means?"

"I think I have it figured out. It's a key. You saw how the word was emphasized. I'm willing to bet the key is for something that will give me and Ann information about our mother, my aunt's sister."

"Why do you think that?"

"Because our mother dumped us off on her sister when I was three and Ann was five. We never saw her again. Later, word came she was dead. Aunt Ethel didn't tell us all the details until I was twelve." Jane lifted one shoulder. "What else could it be? It's not like there is a hidden family fortune or something."

Pannu made another note.

Jane gave up trying to read upside down what the cop wrote. He used some kind of short hand anyway.

"Why do you think Tim Stanhope had your letter in his possession?"

"I have no idea, but he wasn't the most pleasant guy. Bea Merryweather can tell you better than I can. It's tragic for anyone to be murdered, but it's difficult not to feel unsettled about the fact he was found dead with a letter that belonged to me in his pocket. I didn't know the man."

"Why is that?"

"Why didn't I know him?" she asked for clarification, and Pannu nodded. "I'd seen him in the post office twice and only spoke to him once. What I experienced wasn't pleasant, so it colours my opinion of him."

"Thank you, Ms. Westcott." Pannu closed his note pad. "Do you have any questions for me?"

"What's in my letter?"

"I'm afraid I don't know yet. Inspector Zeffler took charge of the evidence."

"Okay, so when can I have my letter back?"

"I'm afraid I don't know that either. You'll have to be patient with the investigation. Once we have everything we need, you will get your property back." Pannu picked up his phone and closed the photo app with a copy of Jane's letter clearly displayed. He'd shown it to her right off the bat. The letter contained her name and address.

Jane nodded. There wasn't much else she could do. This was a murder investigation.

Chapter Thirteen

Jack and Officer Pannu left together after Jane's interview. She suspected they were going to the post office to question Bea.

Jane return to her kitchen and heated up the batch of ham and split pea soup intended for tomorrow's lunch crowd. Staying open this close to the dinner hour required something more than sandwiches. She put Arlie to work on making the sandwiches as he watched the front of the café.

A short time later he popped his head around the doorway. "Your sister's here to see you."

"I'll be right out." Jane turned off the stove. She took the steaming pot off the gas range and poured the contents into a slow cooker. The vessel would keep the creamy soup ready for potential customers. With the lid on top, she carried the appliance out.

As she left the kitchen, she glanced to her right. The oversized kitchen chair she'd left Ruby to sleep on was empty. Where did the little minx go?

"One thing at a time, Jane," she told herself aloud.

As she entered the café, Jane saw her sister accompanied by a young man. His back was to her as he looked up at the wall opposite. His shoulder was level with the top of Ann's head. His jet-black hair was braided into a tight queue down the middle of his back, not a hair escaped. His jeans and jacket were made of the same shade of faded blue denim, and Ann stood close to the man, her hip almost touching his thigh.

"Hi Jane, I'd like you to meet Ben Sinclair." He turned at the mention of his name. His dark eyes sparkled, and he had a ready, friendly smile. The crinkled lines around his eyes made it obvious he wasn't as young as she'd first thought.

"Let me take that." Arlie took the slow cooker. Jane smiled her thanks, as he put it on the counter and plug it in.

"Ben, this is my sister Jane."

Jane offered him her hand. "Hello, nice to meet you, Ben," he had a gentle handshake.

"And you, Jane. I hear you need some mural work done?"

"Yes, have you seen the sketches?"

"I showed him before I asked him to quote on the job," Ann said and glanced up at the tall First Nations man's handsome face.

"I like the sketches, but I wanted to see for myself what I would be painting before I agreed. This," he held up one long fingered hand and gracefully addressed the room, "will be perfect."

"That's good. Can I offer you something hot while we discuss the details?"

"Sure," both Ben and Ann agreed at the same time and glanced at each other briefly before looking away.

Jane's eyebrows rose. Was there something between the two artists?

"What can I get ya?" Arlie asked.

"Hi Arlie, haven't seen you in months." Ben moved forward to shake Arlie's hand.

"I know, how've you been, Ben?" Arlie asked.

Jane took the opportunity to give her sister a meaningful look as the men chatted.

Ann opened her eyes innocently wide. "What?"

"Don't give me 'what,'" Jane said as she tipped her head at Ben.

For the first time in years, Jane witnessed her older sister blush.

ANN AND BEN SLIPPED away a short time later, after the three worked out the logistics for the wall mural.

Jane and Arlie served a few more walk-ins from the village. A woman with three, giggling and soaking wet girls, Sam who left the ferry with part of an old car on the flat bed of his truck, and a pair of older men she didn't know who appeared to be back from a hike, all popped in for soup and hot drinks.

This surprised her, but not as much as the extra ferry run which picked up the coroner's van and the white van which had followed Jack and the RCMP earlier.

Some of the crew members from each vehicle came in for to-go coffees and food. This made staying open longer well worth the effort and the expense, but both she and her new employee were flagging. Five o'clock and the police still hadn't come back, so Jane decided to call it a day.

"How well do you know Ben?" Jane asked Arlie.

"I taught Ben how to weld. I ran a course for teenagers at the drop-in centre, years back, before Sara got sick." They were both in the kitchen dealing with the newly baked muffins. "I taught metal work and a few other things to the kids. Mostly boys, some girls."

"Do you know anything about wrought iron?"

"Yeah, why?"

"Would you consider refurbishing the tables for the patio?"

Arlie raised his bushy eyebrows at her. "Sure, I could, of course. Where's the furniture?"

"In the creepy basement."

Arlie laughed.

"Jane, are you in there?" the voice came from inside the café.

She startled and put a hand over her heart. "I have to get a bell or something on that door," she said to Arlie as she stripped off the disposable gloves.

"Yes, coming." Jane strode through the half door. "Hi Dirk, what can I get for you?"

"I don't need anything. I just wanted to ask if you'd consider seventy-five thousand for the café."

Jane opened her mouth to respond.

"No, please," Dirk held up one hand. "Just think about it first before you answer."

"No," Jane said, overriding his words. "I'm not selling."

Dirk flattened his lips in frustration. After a beat he managed to flash his white smile despite his irritation. "Please think about it anyway."

Jane wanted him out of the café, so she could lock the door. "All right, I will think about it."

Satisfied, Dirk finally left.

Arlie finished the next day's food prep while Jane cleaned. The left-over soup she sent home with Arlie for his and Jack's supper.

Wearily, Jane dug Ruby out from under the armchair in the café. She slowly climbed the stairs to her tiny apartment above, carrying a purring kitten. Earlier, she'd transferred the food dishes from outside to the apartment above. As she rubbed the kitten's ears, tension eased in her shoulders. How could she not smile when the cuddly creature leaned into the attention?

"I'll have to go to the store tomorrow and get everything you need," she told Ruby. "This is the door you can go outside through, and I'd appreciate it if you did. I don't have a litter box for you yet."

It dawned on Jane as she let the cat outside, having Ruby around to talk to would make her slightly less pathetic. Everyone talked to cats, right?

Jane closed the door. If she took a break now, she'd never get supper made. Instead, she went to the fridge in the apartment's tiny kitchen and extracted a couple of chicken breasts. With the meat seasoned, she placed it on a cookie sheet. Then she placed diced potatoes, carrots, onion, and peppers on a square piece of foil. After adding a dollop of butter, she closed the foil, added it to the cookie sheet, and tucked the items into the small oven to cook while she took a shower.

Earlier, her sister had left right after the meeting with Ben. This left Jane no opportunity to explain the events of the day to Ann. Sometime during the evening, she wanted to call her sister. She needed to tell Ann about her letter, and how it was found on Tim's body.

The idea disturbed her more than knowing Tim Stanhope had been murdered. The murder didn't seem real somehow, probably because she didn't want to think about anyone lying dead on one of the hiking trails. Not to mention who could have shot Tim.

She found it hard to get her head around such a serious crime happening in little Musgrave Landing.

Before heading to the bathroom, she opened the door and glanced down the wooden access stairs which clung to the red brick wall. "Here, kitty, kitty?"

Ruby shot up the stairs and past Jane, making her laugh. "I guess you wanted in." A noise in the gathering dark grabbed Jane's attention. It sounded to her like bushes rubbing on nylon as someone passed through the hedge.

Jane frowned as she listened for a moment more. But all went quiet. Still, when she stepped back to close the door, she flipped the deadbolt.

When dinner and dishes were done, Jane picked up the portable phone by the bed and called her sister. It rang several times, before going to voice mail.

"Hey you, call me when you get this, I have tons to tell you." She put the phone down and then looked at Ruby curled up on the single armchair. "I feel like parking my butt too, but I guess I should make up a new soup for tomorrow."

Ruby didn't move a whisker as Jane paused to stroke her soft fur.

"At least the sandwiches are ready, and the muffins are done too. I suppose I should make a new feature treat. I can do that while I wait for Ann to call me back." Ruby still didn't move, although she purred from the attention.

Jane straightened and ignored her runners. Instead, she pushed her feet into comfortably warm red suede slippers. After her shower, she'd dressed in yoga pants and a loose sweater, comfortable clothes she could bake in. She left the apartment door open for Ruby and went down to the big kitchen.

She switched on the overhead lights. The kitchen clock over the stove read just after seven o'clock. Lots of time she noted on her way to the cookbook drawer,

Jane extracted her ring-bound binder from the drawer by the sink and sat at the farm table to leaf through the recipes for ideas.

We've had chocolate and maple, I need something different. She paged through her favourites and paused looking at her aunt's lemon cake recipe. She did have three fresh lemons in the crisper of the commercial refrigerator.

Jane stood and propped the cookbook in the stand on the counter to keep the pages open.

First, she'd get the stock going for tomorrow's soup, and then she could indulge in baking the cake.

Sometime later, chicken broth with a medley of vegetables simmered on the gas stove. Jane closed the oven door on the lemon zest slab cake when the kitchen phone rang.

"Hi Ann," she said with the phone between shoulder and chin. She set the oven timer and moved back to the counter to clean up the cake making mess and prepare for the frosting stage.

"Hey, you, did you hear about Tim Stanhope?"

"Yes, hours ago. The RCMP held their meeting in the café." Jane wiped down the counter.

"Did Jack really find the body?"

"He did, and called in to report it, again from here."

"You are right in the thick of things, aren't you? Why didn't you say anything when I was there with Ben?"

"I don't know, I guess dropping items into the conversation, like 'hey did you hear about the dead guy?' Not really good timing when we were discussing plans for the mural." Jane tucked a stray strand of hair behind her ear as she opened an upper cupboard for her icing sugar and vanilla. "That's only part of it anyway."

"What do you mean?"

"Jack saw a letter in Tim's jacket pocket, addressed to me."

"What? Why would Tim have a piece of your mail?"

"I don't know, but I think the letter was from Aunt Ethel, like yours. The police showed me pictures of it and the letter is the same stationary as Ethel used for yours. I also recognized her handwriting, and Jack agrees with me."

"Jack?" Ann said, surprised. "How is he involved?"

"I told him about your letter and showed it to him. You left it here last night. When he saw yours, he said it matched the one found on Tim, and I think so too."

"What was in that letter?"

"Again, I don't know." The subject was getting old, Jane switched topics. "Did you go to the council meeting?"

"It was cancelled. What with the mayor getting murdered, not surprising really."

"Geeze, no love lost between you and Tim, then."

"I think it's horrible for anyone to be murdered."

"I know, me too," Jane agreed. "I find it hard to believe something like that has happened here."

"Exactly, but you forget I came back to the village a bit before you did. I've had dealings with Tim the Tyrant for a while." Ann didn't sound happy. "Did I tell you he returned a bunch of my mail when I first got back? That is, until I ask Bea what could be going wrong with the change of address notice I paid for on-line."

"This is before you got Aunt Ethel to come to Vancouver for treatment?"

"Yes, clearly he didn't like the way the labels looked or something. My credit cards were put on-hold for lack of payment. I didn't get my bills because of him, and I don't think I was the only person whose mail he was screwing around with."

"You should be banking online and getting your bills through your email," Jane said, knowing she'd mentioned this to her sister many times before.

"Thanks, now you tell me." Ann layer on the sarcasm.

"Heh, I told you right after my cards were compromised."

"By your boyfriend?"

"Arron, yes." She closed her eyes remembering the hurt, humiliation, and anger. "At least, Andrew got the credit card companies to back down after he gave them the report on the incident." However, Jane had to pay the first thousand dollars on each, and she was still out all of her savings. That account was wiped clean.

"You lost all of your investments too, so not fair."

"I agree." Jane rubbed her forehead to ease the beginnings of a headache. "What happens now that the village has no mayor? Is the ECBP on hold?"

"Not as far as I'm concerned. I'll apply for the grants myself and see how far I can go. Dirk is the councillor in charge of funding. I'll see if he can help me."

"You know what bothers me the most?" Jane used a wooden spoon to draw lines in the icing sugar, spreading it around the bowl as she spoke.

"What?"

"Someone in the village is a murderer, and we probably know them."

"More than likely, we do. Tim wasn't at all popular. There could be any number of people who wanted him dead."

"Who would you guess did it?"

Ann sighed, thinking. "I bet it was Lara Finkle. Maybe, Tim wouldn't leave Anita for her."

"A crime of passion?"

"Could be."

"Or, maybe Anita did it, angry at Tim cheating on her, still a crime of passion."

"He was shot on the Eldon Road hiking trail, right?"

"Yeah."

"I don't know if you noticed, but Anita isn't built like someone who likes to hike."

"She could be motivated," Jane suggested.

Ann ignored this. "It might not be murder at all. It may be that a hunter got him, thinking he was a deer or a bear or something. Making it manslaughter instead."

"Enough talk of death. When are you planning to come and start painting?"

"Do you want me to wait until the weekend?"

"No, absolutely not, I think whenever the weather is good, you should start."

"Tomorrow, then?"

"That works for me."

"Okay, what did you think of Ben?" Ann casually circled back to the mural artist.

"He seems nice."

"He's talented too," Ann said that word talented, like it meant more than Ben being an artist. Jane was becoming uncomfortable discussing the man with her sister.

"I should go, I have a cake in the oven." The nagging sound of the oven timer helped Jane to end the call.

Tooth pick in hand, she tested the cake. The dessert was baked to mellow yellow perfection. The scent of lemon filled the oven-warmed kitchen as she slid the long pan on to the cooking rack. She looked down at her handiwork, baking was her passion.

To her, baking wasn't work. To create something out of a handful of ingredients which made people happy was fun. And normally, the quiet kitchen was something Jane embraced. However, tonight the quiet made her uncomfortable. Maybe because of talking about the murder of someone she knew. Whatever it was, she felt unsettled.

As she gave the soup stock one last stir before taking it off the burner, she thought about turning her phone on to play some music over the Bluetooth speakers on the fridge, for company.

Soft, rhythmic thumping made her turn toward the stairs. A sleepy Ruby took the steps one at a time, coming down to the kitchen. Her hesitant movements illustrated how young she still was, and a bit clumsy.

"Hello, Ruby." Jane smiled, watching the newest member of the household wander over and brush against her pant leg before sauntering toward the source of warmth. Jane forgot about the quiet with the steady purring from the kitten as she curled up on the circular rug beside the stove.

Jane picked up the pot full of tomorrow's soup and poured the contents into a ceramic dish she had ready. After placing a lid on it, she set the whole thing in the cooler. Noodles would be added tomorrow.

She returned to the stand mixer and assembled the rest of the ingredients for vanilla icing, measuring and dumping each component into the stainless-steel bowl. When she turned on the mixer, the machine gave a quick, uncharacteristic whirl, and icing hit the red-brick backsplash before Jane got it turned down a notch.

The mixer spun as normal, making even, creamy waves as Jane added the teaspoon of pure vanilla extract, and a favourite baking fragrance wafted in the air.

As the mixer worked, she grabbed the wet dishcloth from the sink and wiped the icing off the smooth red bricks.

She was glad none of the sugar mixture seeped into the grout.

One brick moved under Jane's hand, and she paused with the cleaning. This brick was a different hue than its neighbours, and was loose. When she touched it with her finger tips, the brick moved around in its place in the wall. She squinted and could see a thin sliver of space around the circumference, like it could be easily plucked out.

Jane shut off the mixer and swung the beater up to a forty-five-degree angle to allow the whisk to drip back into the bowl. She looked back at the brick.

On impulse, she reached out and got her fingernails in the gaps to grasp the rectangle and drew the whole brick out of the wall with little effort.

The small opening was exposed. She could see clearly into the space which was lined on five sides with mortar. She could also see the space was empty, even so, she felt around inside it.

Nothing.

"Weird," she said, slightly disappointed at finding nothing in the space. About to put the brick back, her eye caught the glint of something on the back side. She turned the brick over. A strip of grey duct tape was attached to the back. "What is this?" she murmured.

Jane wedged her fingers under the tape and pulled it off. A piece of metal was stuck to the underside.

A key.

She studied it in her hand, approximately three inches long and ended in a fluted tab. The letter Ann received from

Aunt Ethel flashed through her mind as she stared at the club shaped tip.

Had she'd found the key to contentment? Not hardly. Not if she didn't know what it was for.

Jane turned the object over in her hand again. *Why would Aunt Ethel hide a key in a hole in the wall?* She bit her lip when she realized that finding the key was only the first part of the mystery. Now she needed to find the lock the key fit.

Chapter Fourteen

Jane unlocked the front door at just past five-thirty Wednesday morning. This was to allow Arlie to come in when he arrived, but she left the sign off.

She returned to stand by the churning coffee grinder and continued writing a list of things she needed to do today.

Get Arlie setup to be on the payroll software.

Give Arlie his own key, so he could lock up.

Figure out patio table–.

"Ahem." Dirk Ipkiss cleared his throat.

Jane jumped in fright. "Good Lord!" The pen in her left hand flew out of her fingers and straight up, before clattering to the floor.

"We aren't open yet," Jane managed to squeeze out with her heart in her throat as she gripped the counter with both hands. She had to raise her voice over the noise of the grinder.

"Did I startle you?" Dirk grinned wickedly back at her.

She narrowed her eyes at him, he thought it was funny. There was the Dirk she remembered from her childhood, the prankster.

"Dirk–," Jane said between clenched teeth.

The door swung open, and Jack filled the space. He paused for only a second, taking in the scene before moving aside to let his father enter.

"Morning, Jane," Arlie said and gave Dirk a frown.

"Good morning, guys."

Jack gave her a nod and pulled the door closed behind him. He studied Dirk as he strolled forward, giving the other man the once over like he'd never seen him before. Then he spared a glance at Jane but said nothing.

Her lips twisted, who could figure out men and their games? She picked up her pen from the floor.

Dirk ignored the new arrivals as he turned back to Jane. "I just want to see if you thought about my offer."

"For heaven's sake, the answer is no, I'm not selling the café. Please stop asking me," Jane said, impatience flavouring her words. She turned away to check the freshly ground coffee in the hopper. The machine still had yet to brew the three blends the café offered. She dialled the selector for the dark roast first.

"All right, how about I increase my offer to a hundred grand?" the blond man asked insistently with his hands braced on the counter, he leaned forward as he spoke. He sounded like he was humouring her, and his tone further annoyed Jane.

"No," Jane said and put the first container under the spigot. She punched the word with as much finality as she could manage. Maybe then Dirk would finally get the message.

Hot water hit the grounds and the eye-opening aroma of fresh coffee drifted through the room.

"Jane." Jack cleared his throat. "Dad said you want a bell on this door?" His tone made Jane turn her head. He jerked a thumb backward at the entrance.

"I do, actually."

"I told you." Arlie pointed out.

"Yeah, you did Dad, but it's Jane's door. She decides what she wants and where she wants it." Jack gave the older man a meaningful look. "Don't get bossy, I have to put up with it, but Jane doesn't."

Those words fetched Arlie up. His mouth compressed in a flat line, the older man turned to Jane. He held up a small brass bell on a loop of metal. "Will this do, for the door?"

Jane bit her lip to stop the smile threatening to break through at the two men and their good-natured kibitzing. She was happy to come to Arlie's rescue. "Where did you find such a perfect bell?" She walked past a frowning Dirk to get a better look at the brass object.

"Dad is a hoarder." Jack gave her a long-suffering sigh, which earned him a dirty look from Arlie. "It's true," he said, as he grinned at his father. "But his hoarding comes in handy sometimes."

"It should do nicely, thank you." Jane's smile broadened for Arlie and the older man's scowl softened.

"Good, I've been drafted to install it for you." Jack held up a battery powered drill in his hand then crossed back to the door. "Hold these, please." He passed Arlie some screws and a screwdriver bit on the way. They returned to the door, and he drilled two small holes in the frame above to attach the bell.

"You never know when something will come in handy," Arlie defended himself over the whining of the drill.

"I can agree with that." Jane had her back to Dirk. With him behind her, she felt an itch between her shoulder blades. To put distance between them, she moved closer to Arlie and Jack.

He was finished with the second screw and released the bell. It gently tinkled.

Arlie handed Jack a small piece of metal. "Here, put the striker plate on, and you can go to work," he sounded like he was sending Jack off to school.

Jane continued to smile and folded her arms across her chest to enjoy the show. She could see why Jack got the job to install the bell. He was a good seven inches taller than his father and no effort for him to reach the top of the door.

"I thought you needed help with some tables?" Jack used the drill to sink a couple of holes in the door in quick succession, then switched heads on the drill once again, and he attached the striker to the top of the door with screws.

"Right, right," Arlie admitted begrudgingly as he watched Jack open and close the door to test his work, jingling the bell.

The beep on the coffee machine called Jane back behind the counter and once again she had to pass by Dirk. If she ignored him, maybe he'd leave. "Give me a second, and I'll show you where the tables are." She exchanged coffee carafes and handed off the first to Arlie for placement on the self-serve counter.

"They're in the creepy basement," Arlie said.

Jane laughed. "Yes, they are." And she led the way through the patio door. The men followed her around the corner of the building into the side yard.

Dirk trailed after them.

Out of curiosity? Or maybe he actually wanted to help, she thought begrudgingly. And, maybe she wasn't being fair to him.

"This is the basement access." She fished her ring of keys out of her burnt-orange and white-plaid apron pocket. "I'll turn on the light from the inside." She opened the padlock from the hasp, which held the overlapping wooden doors closed, removing it. The angled access was for easy delivery of coal to the basement boiler in days gone by. The coal shoot was replaced by steps, and an oil furnace and tank were installed at some point, probably in the sixties as an upgrade. Some years ago, Ethel converted the building from oil to electric, but the tank remained.

"Grab the other door, Dirk." Jack reached for the right-hand door, and Dirk for the left, the wood swung opened to reveal a black hole. The early morning sun did nothing to light the way, even with the paint-faded wooden doors open. A musty smell, along with damp basement drifted out with the barest hint of heating oil. Concrete steps disappeared down into the gloom.

"I'll get the light." Jane dashed back inside, through the café, and into the kitchen to find the switch. By the time she got back, four of the six wrought-iron tables had been hauled out onto the patio. Dirk and Arlie carried up the fifth, and Jack brought up the sixth.

"Can you fix them?" Jane asked as she wiped spider webs off one, eighteen-inch circular table top. Black paint flaked off and stuck to her hands.

"A couple have leg problems." Arlie teeter-tottered each table back and forth to test their foundations. "Some of this is just surface rust, a bit of paint will fix them up."

"This one needs welding, its joins have come apart," Jack pointed out.

"What are you going to do for chairs?" Dirk asked.

"I don't know yet. I may have to buy some plastic lawn chairs." Jane wiped a second table.

"I don't see anything that can't be fixed." Arlie looked over at Jane.

"How much will you charge me?" Jane hoped the cost would be reasonable. It would be lovely to open the patio, but she had a limited budget which was shrinking fast.

"I estimate twenty dollars apiece, fixed price. No matter what is wrong with them. It could come in cheaper, but not more expensive." Arlie gave her a nod.

"I'll take that deal," Jane agreed. "I have to open now. Do you want me to help you move these to the parking lot?"

"No, no." Arlie waved her away.

"Well thank you, I appreciate this, really."

"We've got this," Jack assured her as he hoisted up one table and carried it around the side of the building. Jane paused to watch him move the heavy metal table.

"Come on, Dirk, grab this side of the table." Arlie directed the third man.

"Hey, it's not like I'm getting paid to be your labourer?" Dirk dusted off the front of his windbreaker.

"Well, you know, you're right. Have a nice day." Jack told the other man as he returned and hoisted another table.

Dirk didn't wait to be asked again. He stalked through the tall grass away from them and in the direction of the marina.

Jane grabbed one side of Arlie's table, and they shuffled it around the front of the building. Jack was already returning and leading Sam, the tow-truck driver, and another man, both from the line of cars. The men headed back around the building, and as they passed Jane and Arlie, greetings were exchanged.

"Looks like we have lots of help now," Arlie said as they deposited the table on the ground by the tailgate of Jack's truck.

One solid bark made Jane start. She glanced through the back window of Jack's truck. A black and tan face with deep black eyes looked back at her, with a doggy grin.

"This is Vimy?" Jane asked Arlie.

"Yep, he's a good dog. You should open, we'll get the rest."

"Okay, thanks. Tell those men and Jack their coffee is on me today." She paused at the passenger's side of the truck and looked in the open window. "Who's a good boy?" Vimy stuck his nose out of the window and sniffed Jane's offered closed fist, then nudged it with his nose. This gave her permission to stroke his soft ears. "You are a handsome boy, aren't you?"

"Jane? Opening up?" Arlie prodded her as he went by.

"I'm going, I'm going." She laughed and gave Vimy one last scratch.

The sun broke through the clouds and brought with it, light, and warmth, promising a fair day.

THE POLICE ARRIVED on the first morning ferry again. Two cars rolled off and parked side by each in the lot.

The villagers gave the officers the 'once over' as the crowd returned to their vehicles after collecting coffee, muffins, and lunch items. A third of the lemon cake went along with them too.

Some of the interest was curiosity, but Jane was sure most of it was the fact that a suspicious death like Tim Stanhope's murder had never happened before in the village.

With the commuters vacating the premises, this left only the authorities with Jane and Arlie. Jack had travelled home to unload the tables before beating it back to the wharf to make the ferry in time for work. Jane half-hoped he'd stop to say good-bye, but that didn't happen.

"Officer Pannu, any word on when I can have my letter?" Jane asked the cop. She figured it was better in the long run to concentrate on her customers and not on thoughts of Jack.

"Not until we have eliminated the letter from our inquiries, sorry," he said and accepted his change for the coffee. He picked up his slice of lemon cake. "And no, I can't disclose what the letter says. But I can tell you, we are taking finger prints off the paper, because the letter was opened."

"I see," said Jane compressing her lips, partly in surprise he shared this detail and partly in frustration at not being able to read her letter. She was also surprised he wanted a slice of cake before seven o'clock in the morning, but if he wanted cake, he could have cake. Who was she to judge?

"I'm sorry, please be patient," he said in a lower tone and put a fork full of cake in his mouth.

Jane nodded. "It's just that I found a key yesterday," she replied in the same low tone.

"Like what was mentioned in your sister's letter?" Pannu asked, intrigued.

Constable Havelange was standing close enough to hear the exchange. "And you're hoping the second letter will tell you something about it?"

"Yes." Jane reached in her apron pocket and extracted the key. "It was weird where I found it too."

"Oh?" As first he, and then Havelange examined the key.

"It was taped to a loose brick in the kitchen wall."

Both sets of eyes snapped up to look at her. "That is weird," said Havelange.

"I know, right? I have to figure out what type of key this is, so I can find the lock it fits." She took the key back and turned it over in her hand.

"It's old, turn of the last century at least, by the patina," the female cop said and shrugged as Pannu looked at her. "What? My mom collects antiques. I learned a couple things from her." She handed Jane a ten-dollar bill. "It looks like an old luggage key."

"Really? Thanks, that's somewhere to start." She slid the key back into her pocket. "What can I get for you?"

"A large Canadiano, double shot, and chocolate chip muffin please."

"Arlie, double shot Canadiano."

"Two minutes," he answered. It quickly became apparent to Jane the shiny new machine was Arlie's favourite toy, and he preferred the hum and hiss of preparing the beverages than waiting on customers. This was fine by her.

"Jack's not here today?" Havelange asked casually.

Pannu rolled his eyes and moved away to sit at a table.

"No, he left for work on the ferry you arrived on, he was the last vehicle," Jane said. She couldn't help the fact she looked for his truck all the time, hoping to get a glimpse of him. As Jane thought about it, she realized she was back in pathetic territory again and needed to stop thinking about the man.

"Ah," was all the cop said as she accepted her muffin.

Did the cop and Jack have history?

"I suppose I shouldn't ask what you guys have planned for today." Jane handed the officer back her change. Havelange dropped a Loonie into the ECBP donation cup. The dollar coin made a satisfying sound as it fell on other change customers had been dropping into the mug all week.

"It's no secret we're meeting with the village council. As soon as Inspector Zeffler gets here that is. He missed the first ferry."

Jane was curious to know why they were speaking with the councillors, but bit back her questions. None of this was her business. If they had the information they could share, no doubt, they would.

Zeffler was on the next ferry, accompanied by a tough looking brunette, who sat next to him in his unmarked car. Her hair was tied back, and she wore a buttoned-down white shirt and black jacket. This was all Jane could see from the café window into the parking lot. The woman's look was familiar. Similar to what Jane used to wear for work in Vancouver, professional and no nonsense, so unlike her current work attire. Jane ran one hand down her aproned front. Maybe, the woman was an interrogator or specialist of some kind.

If she were an interrogator, Jane wondered how she would handle Anita the Hun. Jack told Arlie how it had gone at the village office yesterday, and Arlie had told her.

Including how Anita had thrown everyone out of the office, and how odd he found her behaviour. Even after taking into consideration the violent death of her husband. But again, it was none of her business.

Ann arrived an hour later, wearing serviceable old clothes and driving an aged silver minivan which used to belong to Aunt Ethel. Loaded in the back was the paint, a range of brushes, a ladder, rollers, sawhorses, and a half sheet of plywood, to be set up to serve as a table. All of it came out of the 'Loser Cruiser.' This was the term the girls had tagged the minivan with years ago.

After the authorities had departed, Jane helped Ann unload the paint and supplies from the back of the vehicle.

"Nice to see you got LC running."

"The van just needed a new distributor. Sam took care of it." Her sister slid the sheet of the plywood toward Arlie, and he carried it over to place on the pair of saw horses. "I wouldn't trust the engine enough to take LC out of the village, but it works fine as a truck around here," Ann added.

"I'll go home and grab my weed whacker." Arlie told Jane. "We need to trim the growth around the sides of the building before painting can begin."

"Good, while you cut weeds, I'll wire brush the first wall." Ann told him.

As the sisters watched Arlie cross the street, Ann prodded Jane with her elbow. "He's working out well. Lots of help, am I right?"

"Arlie is amazing. Not only is he a good barista, he's going to fix the patio tables. He gave me a great deal for all six of them." They returned to the van to close the doors. "He and Jack installed a bell over the door this morning. Now I won't jump through the roof every time someone comes in, because I'll hear them."

"Nice!"

"Oh, and I haven't told you the best part." Jane put down the pail of white paint and dug into her apron pocket. "Look what I found last night." She held out the key.

Ann froze and stared at the object. Her eyes tracked up to Jane's face. "Where did you find that?"

"In the kitchen, behind a brick from the wall, if you can imagine," Jane said in an excited rush.

Ann briskly grabbed the can of paint and carried the pail over to the makeshift table. She grabbed a blade type screwdriver and wedged the tool under the lip of the lid. "It looks like a trunk key." Ann pried up the lid from the can of white paint, but she kept her eyes downward.

"That's what I've been told."

Laying the lid aside, Ann took a paint stick, stuck it into the can of white, and gently stirred the contents. "There are trunks in the attic," she said still not looking up at her sister.

Chapter Fifteen

Jane stood by the coffee machine, drumming her fingers on the edge of the stainless-steel frame as she waited for the fresh beans to grind for the noon rush. She listened to the hum and crunch with only half an ear as she thought about her sister's reaction to finding the key.

When Jane showed Ann the key, she hadn't attempted to touch it or even look at it. In Jane's opinion, her sister's reaction was odd to say the least.

Ann's dismissive attitude, especially after her enthusiasm of a couple days earlier, didn't sit right with Jane. Although, she could attribute it to her sister merely being preoccupied with the painting project, but Jane knew better.

Arlie had reacted to the key, the same way as the cops, with curiosity and speculation, when she told him where she'd found it. At least, he confirmed what Jane had been told by the others, it appeared to be a luggage key for a trunk.

Jane dug the piece of metal out of her apron pocket and turned the key over in her hand. She puzzled over it and Ann's reaction, or lack thereof. She didn't have time to investigate at the moment, but once she closed for the day, there would be a trip to the attic.

The bell over the door jangled, and she slipped the key back into its spot in her apron, next to her aunt's letter.

A tall woman with corkscrew platinum curls spilling down her back sauntered in. She wore a form-hugging purple dress with matching jacket. The material, the colour of grape juice, matched her eyeshadow and nail polish, accompanied by a fragrant cloud of perfume.

Jane recognized her as the woman who'd left the village office on Monday, just as she was approaching. The purple lady had warned her not to go into the office.

"Hello, what can I get you?" Jane asked politely.

"Perrier water, perhaps?"

"Sorry, we don't carry that brand. We do have two others to choose from." Jane named the two types she sold, but the woman shook her head.

"Where are the cops?"

"I don't know, at the village office I assume," Jane said.

"I was told to meet them here." She consulted a heavy gold wrist watch. "Ten minutes ago."

"I'm afraid I don't know anything about that. You are welcome to sit and wait."

The blonde heaved a massive sigh and lowered her shape down into the armchair by the windows.

Instantly, Ruby crawled out from under the chair on her belly, gained her feet, and made a beeline for the kitchen. Jane followed with a frown and found the little black cat sitting beside the kitchen door, looking up at her desperately.

"You look like you want out." Jane opened the door and let the poor creature escape. "Yes, that is a lot of perfume."

She murmured an agreement to Ruby as the cat dodged the painting supplies and disappeared around the corner.

Jane returned to the counter, checked on the soup, and made sure all the sandwich trays and muffin baskets were filled. The lemon cake had been a hit, only a third of it left.

The coffee grind was complete, and the machine chugged on to infusing the grounds with hot water.

Both Ann and Arlie were working outside. Ann had begun the base coat of white on the walls.

Arlie was busy clearing away any obstructions that would block painting the exterior. The buzz of the weed whacker ceased abruptly, and Arlie's face popped up, looking inquiringly at her through the patio door.

Jane shook her head and held up ten fingers, and then mouthed the words 'ten minutes.' She could handle the counter until the noon ferry arrived. Arlie nodded, and the buzzing resumed.

"Did you know him?" the blonde asked suddenly.

"I'm sorry, who?" Jane returned her attention back to her lone customer.

"Tim Stanhope, of course," the woman said dryly. "How many people have been murdered around here?" She sounded a touch exasperated.

"Not well, no. Did you know him?"

"All too well." She heaved another sigh.

Jane looked at her as the other woman stared out the window and glared at the parking lot. The village wasn't all that large. "Would you be Lara Finkle?"

"I would, yes." Jane received a sly look around the side of the wingback chair. "You've heard about me, have you?"

Jane walked forward and held out her right hand. "I'm Jane Westcott, pleased to meet you."

Lara looked at Jane's hand in surprise before taking it and gave it a limp shake. "Nice to meet you too, you're the new girl."

From this close distance, Jane could see Lara Finkle was in her late fifties. Probably roughly around Tim's age. She was carefully made up, but few products could hide the neck wrinkles.

"I'm new to you. You didn't live here when I was a kid." She tipped her head to the side. "Sorry for the loss of your friend."

"Thanks." Lara leaned back in the chair and a smile curved her lips. To Jane it looked smug, or maybe resigned. Strange woman.

Jane moved back behind the counter and turned on the radio, the awkward silence was getting on her nerves.

"I think Anita did it," Lara said suddenly.

"Sorry, who did what?"

"Try and keep up, would you? Anita. Anita the Hun, she shot Tim. She killed her husband, and I guess I'm partly to blame."

"Why do you say that?"

"Of course, it may have been Dirk." She ignored Jane's question. "He argued with Tim in the post office Saturday morning. Tim told me Dirk is nothing but a user and a taker. He uses people and takes what he wants from them." She fiddled with one chunky gold ring on her right index finger. "Like Tim was one to talk." She laughed ruefully.

The police cruiser driven by Constable Havelange pulled into the lot. Lara promptly shut up and began fiddling with her purse strap, eyes downcast.

The officer strolled in and stopped in front of the older woman. "Hello, Ms. Finkle, thank you for meeting me here. I'm sorry we couldn't find a private place to speak at the village office."

Lara lifted one shoulder. "What do you want to know?"

Constable Havelange looked at Jane.

"Oh. Would you like to use the old office? It's more of a storage room, but there are a couple of chairs in there and privacy," Jane offered.

"Thank you, that would be fine." The officer smiled at her in relief.

As Lara heaved herself to her feet in a show of being put upon, Jane led the way. She opened the wooden door and flicked on the light.

Arlie had spent a bit of time in the storage room cleaning up the espresso machine debris. It appeared he'd organized and cleaned as well.

She rolled out the two-matching tiger-oak office chairs and push them forward, positioning the chairs opposite each other in the middle of the room.

The cop paused at the doorway to forestall Jane. "I'm waiting on Kenny, our civilian technician. All of our interviews have to be recorded and Kenny is supposed to be bringing the equipment. I gave this location as the meet up point. Thank you, for allowing us usage of some your space."

"You've got it as long as you need it," Jane said. "I'm not using it."

"That's great, now I don't have to see if I can use the community hall." Lea grinned at her.

"No problem, I'm happy to help. I'll knock on the door when Kenny gets here." Jane glanced at Lara as she settled into one of the old wooden office chairs and tucked her crossed ankles under the seat.

In a quiet tone Jane said to Lea, "Lara mentioned she saw Dirk and Tim arguing Saturday morning. It might not mean anything." Jane lifted one shoulder. "I thought I'd mention it, could be important."

The constable held Jane's gaze for a moment. "Good to know, thanks."

"Let me know if you need anything else." She stepped back from the room.

Lea nodded her thanks to Jane, and she closed the door.

Jane chewed her bottom lip as she went through the motions of getting fresh coffee carafes over to the self-serve counter.

When Lara stated she thought Anita murdered Tim, Jane found this a bit shocking. Mostly because when Lara said this, the words held the ring of truth. She was serious about her accusations. Or maybe it was due to the fact Lara was the 'other woman.' Then again, she'd mentioned Dirk argued with Tim. Was Lara merely deflecting any attention from herself? The 'other woman' lived very close to the trail where Tim's body had been found.

But, neither Tim Stanhope's wife nor his alleged mistress, seemed the type to hike into the woods to find Tim and shoot him, but what about Dirk? He could have easily made the trek, he was fit, but then again, what possible reason could Dirk have to want to shoot Tim Stanhope? In Jane's opinion, Anita had the stronger motive, and appearances could always be deceiving.

As the front door opened, the buzzing of the grass trimmer over powered the tinkling of the bell.

Jane glanced right to see a frazzled looking Dirk stalk inside. His usually neat, slicked down blond hair was rumpled, and his sky-blue eyes looked red and raw.

"Jane, is Ann around? I got a phone message from her to meet her here."

"She's outside, painting the west wall." Jane gestured toward the patio door.

Dirk nodded but didn't move. "Did you think about my offer?" he asked instead.

Jane sighed. "Dirk, I told you, I'm not interested in selling the café."

"You were on Monday."

"On Monday, I was curious, that's all. I have no plans to sell. I don't know how I can make it any plainer to you." Without thinking about it, her hand went to cover the pocket that held the trunk key. Dirk's eyes narrowed at her movement, and she dropped her hand.

"One hundred and twenty-five thousand," he said abruptly.

"You're wasting your time."

"Give my offer some serious thought, will you?"

The patio door opened, and Ann—now dressed in disposable white coveralls—walked in. "Dirk, you got my message."

"You said something about applying for grant funding? What type of grants and where are you thinking of applying for them?"

Ann closed the door and came forward, removing her paint-stained latex gloves. "I know things are in an upheaval with the village council, with Tim gone–." She stopped speaking at Dirks derisive snort.

"You could say that. We're officially being audited, the village I mean." Dirk ran his left hand through his hair. "Jane, can I get a bottle of water?"

He turned back to the counter as she extracted one from the fridge.

"Why is Musgrave Landing being audited?" Jane asked as she passed him the bottle.

"Apparently, Tim has a bank account with funds transferred directly from the village account." He broke the seal on the bottle and took a long drink. "I was told the cops poke around in all aspects of a murder victim's life," he said this with a sneer, and he dropped his eyes.

"Funds? How much?" Ann came to stand in front of him, frowning.

"Right around half a million," Dirk said the words like they tasted sour. "The cops aren't saying it openly, but their questions are making me, and the other councillors think Tim must have stolen the money from the village."

"How could he do that?" Ann shook her head.

"Easily. Anita is the administrator, she has access to the bank accounts, she does the taxes and grant deposits, writes cheques and what not, it's part of her job." Dirk ran a careless hand through his hair again and then leaned on the counter like he was suddenly exhausted. "Tim and Anita were both signatories on all the accounts."

"Whose idea was that?" Ann demanded. "Didn't any of the councillors think it might be a conflict of interest if a husband and wife had access to all the village revenue?"

"It was mentioned, in one meeting." Dirk shrugged, he looked slightly sick to Jane. "Nothing was ever done about it."

"You just let it go." Jane nodded in understanding. "It's a small village, no one wanted to create a fuss and upset anyone."

"I guess that was pretty much it, yeah," Dirk agreed, as he picked at the water bottle label.

"Well, that was just stupid." Ann's lips twisted. "Good thing I'm going to apply for grant money without the council involved."

"You are?" Jane looked at her sister.

"I've got an appointment with Mr. Windgate, Aunt Ethel's lawyer in Victoria to set up a foundation for ECBP. We are going to do this properly." Ann brushed hair off her sticky forehead as she answered her sister's look. "I took Andrew's advice."

Jane wanted to ask when her sister had spoken to her ex-husband, but Dirk took over the conversation

"On behalf of Musgrave Landing?" He demanded.

"I got tired of waiting for you to help me." Ann planted her fists on her hips. "We'll lose the summer season if we don't get moving. I have painters, crafts people, sculptors, and gardeners all ready to help. We just need some money for materials and marketing."

Dirk slammed the bottle down on the counter, with enough force to make water shoot out the opening. "Fine! Have fun with that." He turned on his heel and stalked across the café and out the door, leaving the sisters staring after him.

"I think you stepped on his toes." Jane plucked the cloth out of the sink and wiped up the spilled water.

"I'd say so. And he owes you for that water."

Chapter Sixteen

Ann returned to her work outside. Arlie, finished with his grass trimming, came in to wash up and help with the lunch rush.

"Here, I have this for you." Jane handed Arlie a long black apron. "So, you don't ruin your clothes."

"Thanks," Arlie said. He flipped the neck strap over his head and brought the waist ties around him to fasten in a half-hitch in front. He ran a hand over the material. "I remember this one."

"What?"

Arlie met Jane's puzzle expression. "Sara made this apron for Ethel. She sewed all of Ethel's aprons, one of her hobbies after Jack went away to university in Vancouver."

"I didn't know that." Jane touched the bib of her own apron.

"Why would you?" Arlie shrugged.

"Well, she did an amazing job. I love each and every one of the aprons. I look forward to choosing a new one every morning. There have to be at least thirty in the old flour bin."

"Sara had to keep busy. I was gone until six o'clock every night." His eyes shadowed.

With regret for missing time with his wife?

"I only have one black apron. What other colour would you wear? Do you like polka dots?" Jane asked thinking of the stripped, polka dotted, plaid, and paisley prints. "These aren't really geared for guys."

Arlie snorted. "I have others at home Sara made me for barbequing. I'll wear one of those when this one is dirty."

Lara Finkle had been with Constable Havelange for twenty minutes, when a lanky, plain-faced person in their early twenties entered the café, pulling a wheeled, black square case.

Jane wasn't sure of this new person's gender. He or she had light-brown hair pulled back in a half-hearted ponytail and was dressed in a faded plaid shirt over a white T-shirt, jeans, and runners. He-she came to a stop in front of the counter.

"Hi, I'm Kenny. I'm looking for Constable Havelange." Kenny's voice was high and melodious for a male.

"Knock on that door." Jane nodded to the storage room as she juggled two bowls of soup and two sandwiches.

"Thanks," Kenny said and continued to the door.

Jane delivered the food to a table where a teenage girl and a woman who was probably her mother sat. Arlie followed her with a latté for the slender, willowy woman and milk for the girl.

"Can't I have a latte too? Dad lets me have coffee."

"Do I look like your dad?" the woman asked. "Caffeine will stunt your growth, and you'll be short all your life." Her eyes jumped to Jane and widened. "I didn't mean–."

"Don't worry about it." Jane waved her customer's concern away. She looked at the girl. "You, too, can have a body like this if you aren't careful."

The girl's eyes widened.

As Jane turned away, she winked at the mother. The woman hid a smile in her napkin.

"Who's that?" Arlie followed Jane and gestured to the new arrival.

"Kenny, she's some kind of civilian technician from the Duncan Detachment." She frowned, confused. "I mean, he is supposed to set up some kind of recording device for the interviews."

"Looks like we've lost the storage room." Arlie sniffed.

"Only for a while," Jane shrugged, not particularly concerned as she filled more soup bowls for the next order.

"Speak to Inspector Zeffler about renting it." Arlie gave her a level look when she glanced up. But she had no time to consider his words and left to deliver the food.

Later, when she thought about it, Jane's lips parted in surprise. *What a good idea.* If the police needed to use her space, she would be required to stay open longer. Someone would have to pay for it.

Then she experienced a pang of guilt. It felt unsavoury to make money from this awful situation. Even if she did have bills to pay besides the painting, the new expresso machine, and groceries to make product to sell.

"I know what you're thinking." Arlie came back behind the counter. "But this is a business, not a charity. If they want to use the space, they should pay for it."

"We would have to stay open longer, probably until three or four o'clock. Are you prepared for that?" Jane folded her arms.

"We're in this together. If we have to accommodate the RCMP and their use of the storage room as an interrogation room, I'm good with it." Arlie nodded. "Why aren't they using the town office?"

"An auditor is going over the books and has commandeered all the available space in the village office, according to Constable Havelange. That investigation forced the murder investigation to setup camp elsewhere. Money appears to be more important than human life," she said twisting her lips in a cynical line.

"Isn't it always?" Arlie agreed.

BY FIVE-THIRTY, JANE returned to the café from the bank and the post office. She had the place to herself. Everyone was now gone, including Arlie, and the last of the lemon cake.

She also found three loaves of bread on the kitchen table. One white, one brown, and one that looked like it was a whole grain with flax seeds, along with a note written in square, printed letters, and a receipt.

Jane,

Gladys Wyatt stopped by. I bought three loaves for you to try. In trade for the soup and cake you gave me.

Arlie

She picked up one loaf of the sliced bread. It was soft to the touch, with a golden crust. Even through the plastic bag, the aroma of freshly baked bread rose to tease her nose and tempt her. Arlie might just be onto something. He had such good ideas and no doubt, this would not be his last.

Jane moved the loaves to the counter. She had to scrub her work area before she could make up tomorrow's sandwiches. A task best left for later in the evening.

First, she fed Ruby, and then she hauled out the stack of mail from her messenger bag, quickly sorting through it to ensure nothing pressing was in the stack. A task she hated but forced herself to do, much better than being blindsided. There were a few provincial government envelopes, easy to identify their origin by the return address. One envelope contained her goods and services tax number. Another held the tax filing instructions and pin code for logging in online, and the third, the invoice for the espresso machine.

Her hydro-electric bill was next, then an invitation to join the Musgrave Landing chamber of commerce.

The last crisp, white envelope had her post office box number on it, but the address read 'Musgrave Landing Village Council.' She glanced at the top left-hand corner. The windowed envelope was from the BC Government, Economic Diversification Infrastructure Funding Program. Jane knew by the look of it, the envelope held a cheque, but the thick nature of the paper prevented her from reading the amount.

Why did the address contain her box number? She thought back to the mix-up on Monday with ATS

Enterprises, and her post office box. Then there was the fact Tim had one of her letters on him when he died.

She tapped the envelope against the palm of her other hand as she thought. Then stuck the check into her purse to take back to the post office.

Something weird was going on. The funding agency did not pick her box number out of a hat. There was no way this could be random and very likely had everything to do with the half million dollars Dirk mentioned.

The front door key Jane gave Arlie that morning freed both of them up to come and go as needed. While she did errands uptown, he would close up once the cops were done with the storage room, and then see to the cleaning before he left for the day.

Jane did a quick walk-through to ensure the tasks were completed. The place was spotless. *Arlie is quickly becoming indispensable.* She returned to the kitchen.

With a nine by thirteen pan of lasagna slid into the oven, she had thirty minutes to kill before it was ready.

She'd earmarked this gap in her otherwise jam-packed day to take a peek in the attic and was going to take advantage of it. Who knew how grubby the attic might be though, so she ran upstairs to change into old jeans and a T-shirt.

Ruby stood beside the kitchen door when she came back downstairs. Jane paused to let her outside.

She went into the laundry room at the back of the kitchen. The rope, which opened the access to the attic, hung from the ceiling near the back of the room. She stretched up and caught it, tugging firmly a couple of times to lower the wooden ladder.

Dust motes swam in the air as the ladder unfolded and settled on the hardwood floor. Jane waved the cloud away from her face and wrinkled her nose. Her lips twisted as she looked up into the dark yawning space. "I need a light," she said and retraced her route, but diverted to the storage room.

Once there, Jane opened the centre drawer of her aunt's old desk. It contained one sheet of crumpled stationary and a broken pencil. Jane picked up the lone paper and flattened it out on the surface of the desk.

Dear Ann and Jane,
I wanted to tell you

The letter stopped. Possibly, this was the first draft of the separate letters her aunt had sent them. Jane ran her hand over the thick cream-coloured paper. She wished she had her aunt around to ask about the key and the letter. Of course, if Ethel were still living, the questions would be unnecessary. The page went back into the drawer.

She closed it and moved on to the next. This drawer held rolls of tape, a box of staples, no stapler, and loose paperclips scattered about. The last drawer held a small green flashlight.

Jane extracted the light and flipped the switch. The device worked, and a beam of yellow light hit the floor. She returned to the laundry room. As she scaled the wooden stairs, she pulled the string of one lone light bulb which hung from a rafter. The forty-watt thing hardly broke through the dim, forcing her to switch on the flashlight.

The attic was crowded with wooden crates, trunks, and cast-off furniture. Picture frames, broken lampshades, and an old mantel clock sat on a crate. The clock was missing both hands. A small gate-leg table leaned against the wall by the access. All the items wore a thick coat of dust. Close beside the access were two cardboard boxes of toys. Jane recognized these items, the toys used to belong to her and Ann from many years ago.

Did the Crawlys never throw anything away? She scanned the length of the building, above the café and the kitchen. There might be some items of value, but most of it needed donated, recycled, or merely thrown away altogether.

Several trunks lined the south wall. Jane picked her way gingerly over to the collection and shined her light on each one in turn. The four trunks varied in size, obviously a complete set of luggage. Each was a dull brown and flat topped with leather straps unbuckled and hanging loose.

She took a shallow breath to calm the butterflies in her stomach and stepped in front of the first. Beginning with the largest trunk, she tried the lid and it opened. Inside was a cardboard box of oil paintings, each only eight by ten inches. These were her aunt's work, paintings of wild flowers and beach scenes of the Narrows and Stoney Hill. At one time, they had hung in the kitchen below.

With a frown, Jane paused to sort through the canvases. Why had they ever been removed? Did her aunt tire of them?

"Well, you're going back up on the walls," Jane said to the box and set them aside to take back down stairs.

The second trunk too, was unlocked and held old magazines and newspapers. The third was filled with old clothes, musty and moth-eaten. What was the point of saving any of this?

The next trunk held comic books, yellowed and brittle.

Jane shined the flashlight beam on the lock of the last trunk. When she tried to lift the top, it was locked. She'd been stalling, looking through the other trunks and maybe trying to delay disappointment, too.

She wiped the mechanism free of dust and cobwebs. Her hand slid into her pocket and removed the key. It slid into the hasp lock easily, and Jane turned it clockwise. A dull click and the lock opened.

The smell of old paper and turned-to-powder glue drifted upward. She rubbed her nose with the back of her hand. With the flashlight tucked under her chin to shine its light into the trunk, Jane leaned forward.

Stacked neatly inside were several shoeboxes, each wrapped with a rubber band. Jane lifted one lid and found it full of loose black and white photos. It would take some time to sort through the contents.

She moved on to another box. Inside, wrapped in blue tissue paper, was a baby's white baptism gown. A boxed candle and shawl nestled next to the gown. Jane turned the candle box over to find 'Jane Ethel Westcott' written on the back.

Ah, her baptism stuff.

Jane moved the two boxes aside and placed them on the attic floor beside her as she knelt down to dig farther into the trunk.

The next box revealed personal papers. This time she removed the elastic and opened the box properly. A paper copy of her live birth paperwork lay on top, a precursor to her birth certificate. Jane ran her eye down the document. Her mother's name, Stella Ann Westcott appeared on the top line, and her father's name, on the next line, Jonathan Livingston.

Not John Westcott.

Her eyes locked on the line and stared at it. For a second, she was uncomprehending, like the information didn't compute.

Father's name, not the name of the man who'd been the only father Jane could remember, John Westcott, however briefly, who divorced their mother. Not the man who died in a car accident a year later when Jane was three-years-old and Ann five. The same year they'd come to Ethel.

Jane closed her eyes and a vision of a tall man, on the slender side, with black hair and laughing brown eyes came to her mind. With the image, came the warm hugs and giggling laughter as he tickled first Ann, then her. Strong fingers, gently holding her hand as she walked beside him. Her eyes opened, and she looked down again at the paper. Then numbly set it aside.

One more quick rummage through the other shoeboxes revealed some baby clothing, a sample of childhood art work, and a couple old dolls. That was all.

Slowly, Jane closed the trunk. She gathered up the shoebox with the photographs and the other with the personal papers. Using her foot, she pushed the crate of her aunt's paintings toward the access hatch and would come back for those.

She proceeded down the ladder and clicked off the light bulb as she went. Many things whizzed through her thoughts.

Her jaw flexed as she gritted her teeth. Carefully, Jane closed the access and returned to the kitchen to drop the boxes on the wide plank table. She took a breath and let it out slowly to get a grip on her temper.

She needed to talk to Ann.

Chapter Seventeen

Jane's phone rang uselessly in her hand as she waited for her sister to pick up. Again, it went to voice mail.

"You, big chicken," Jane said as she waited for the beep. But all she said after the beep was, "Call me."

She hit the end button and dropped the phone on the kitchen table next to the two shoeboxes.

Slowly, she released her breath in a flustered sigh. It did not take a genius to figure out Ann knew all about the contents of the trunks in the attic. And who had locked that specific trunk and then hidden the key.

The question was why hadn't Ann ever told her?

The aroma of tomato, garlic, and melted mozzarella filled the large kitchen. The warm scent made her stomach growl in anticipation of dinner. A quick glance at the oven timer told her the lasagna would be ready soon. No crisis was too big to force her to miss a meal.

There was a faint meow at the door. Jane crossed the kitchen and let in the damp cat. A fine mist drifted down from the leaden sky and matched Jane's mood perfectly.

Ruby wound herself around Jane's feet, rubbing up against her jean-covered leg. With the door closed, Jane scooped up Ruby and stepped to the right into the laundry room.

"You're a bit wet, let's fix that." Jane placed Ruby on top of the dryer and grabbed a worn towel she used as a duster to wipe the cat down.

Purring from the extra attention, Ruby allowed the drying.

"There you go." Jane tossed the towel into the hamper.

Front paws reached up and touched Jane's shoulder, gently kneading her. Ruby licked the end of Jane's nose and rubbed the top of her head under Jane's chin.

With a chuckle, Jane gathered the cat against her. She scratched Ruby's whiskered cheeks, finding comfort in the little cat's attention.

The oven timer sounded a jarring tone. "My supper's ready, kitty." Jane put the cat down on the floor with one last pat. She stepped back into the kitchen to turn off the timer and the oven, and then moved the lasagna onto the cooling rack, allowing it to rest before slicing.

She was drying wet hands on a towel when a firm knock shook the exterior kitchen door. *Probably Ann, this close to a meal time.*

Jane crossed to the door and swung it open. The cryptic remark she had ready for her sister, died.

"Constable Pannu, Constable Havelange, what can I do for you?"

"Sorry to disturb your supper." Pannu nodded at the bowl of garden salad on the table.

"No, its fine, please come in." Jane stepped back, and the officers strolled in, politely wiping their boots on the mat.

"We have a couple of questions," Havelange said.

"Okay?" Jane lifted one shoulder, ready to share any information.

"Do you own a handgun?"

"No." Jane shook her head.

"Are you sure?"

"I've never owned a gun of any type. I've never even shot one."

"How about one that looks like this?" Pannu held up his smart phone to show Jane.

She leaned in for a closer look. "No, my aunt did though. It belonged to my grandfather, her dad. He was an officer in the army during World War II."

"Did you inherit everything from your aunt?" Havelange had her occurrence notebook out and clicked her pen.

"No, Ann inherited the house and studio. Aunt Ethel left me the café, this building, and the surrounding property." She glanced between the two officers. A disturbing feeling began to grow inside her.

"This Browning is dated before 1946. It's legal for your aunt to own or you even if you or Ethel Crawly never possessed a Restricted Possession or an Acquisition License. You don't hold a gun license, do you?"

"No, Ethel donated the gun to the village museum." Jane pointed out. "I don't have the Browning anymore."

"Where was the pistol stored?" Pannu asked.

"Aunt Ethel used to keep the gun in the strongbox in the store room. Would you care to see?"

"We would, yes."

"How do you know she donated the weapon?" Constable Havelange asked.

"Because she told me she planned on doing just that, along with Grandad's medals. And the pistol isn't in the strongbox now."

Both officers looked a Jane, steadily, but said nothing more. They appeared to be waiting.

"Come with me and I'll show you." Jane grabbed her apron off the hook on the back of the connecting door. She dug out her keys as she led the way through the café and into the storage room.

The floor was clear with the chairs tucked back beside the desk. Jane could walk straight to the back wall, where the metal strongbox sat next to the old roll-top desk. Arlie must have done some more organizing before he went home. The rest of the boxes, odds and ends of furniture, and bags of coffee beans now neatly lined the walls.

The cops followed her into the windowless room and stood to one side as Jane inserted her key into the aging lock, turned it, then swung the paint chipped black door open with a faint creak of hinges.

When she first put her bank deposit bag inside the door, Jane had meant to clean up the box. The recipes cards were tucked in the back and held together by a rubber band. She should shred the old utility bills and sort through the rest of the papers. Her to-do list was never ending it appeared.

Her grandfather's cigar box looked back at her accusingly. She hadn't looked in the box. Would a pistol even fit inside?

"May I?" Pannu asked and gestured to the contents.

"Yes, sure," Jane said as she stepped back.

Pannu leaned down, move aside some of the documents with one hand and reached in with the other. Gently, he removed the old cardboard box and flipped open the top. Pannu tipped it so his partner could see. "The medals," he said simply, and then poked around inside the cabinet, checking behind the recipes before putting the cigar box back. "Nothing else of interest." He straightened.

Jane crossed her arms defensively. "See, no gun."

"We spoke with Marc Whipple. He runs the Musgrave Landing History Museum." Havelange said, and then waited, evident during the long pause, she expected Jane to speak.

But Jane had nothing to add.

The penetrating look was a waste of time as far as Jane was concerned.

"So?" Jane shook her head.

"He said they have a pistol on display already from another villager. The museum board turned down Ethel Crawly's offer to donate her father's sidearm, although they are still interested in Captain Emery Crawly's medals."

"If that's the case, where's the gun?" Jane frowned and glanced at the inside of the strongbox.

"Exactly," Pannu said, and both cops looked back at Jane as she shifted her gaze between the two of them.

Finally, she connected the dots. Jane's jaw dropped in disbelief. "You think my grandfather's pistol was used to kill Tim Stanhope." She ran nervous hands down her thighs.

"Yes, we do." Havelange opened her notes again. "We found what we believe is the murder weapon, a Browning

9mm. The pistol has been sent to Vancouver for ballistics testing. According to the restricted firearms database, there are two Browning pistols in the village. The other pistol is accounted for, yours is missing."

"I don't know what to tell you." Jane dropped her hands as she recovered from the shared information. "There was no pistol in the strongbox when I moved in five weeks ago."

"What about ammunition?" Pannu asked. "Is any ammunition stored on the property? There's none in the box."

"I don't think so. My aunt never learned to use the pistol."

"If there were rounds stored somewhere, where would she keep them?"

"Probably inside the strongbox," Jane said and gestured toward it.

The cops shared another 'look' this habit of theirs was starting to get on Jane's nerves.

"I know it's not legal to store a weapon and ammunition in the same location, but I don't think my aunt knew that."

"She didn't have a trigger lock on the handgun either, did she?"

"Not when I last saw it, but that was years ago." Jane shook her head.

Havelange paged through her notebook. "On February 20th, of this year, a report was made by Arlington Birch that this address had been broken in to, during the previous evening or in the early hours of the morning of the 20th."

"Yes, he told me about it. Arlie also nailed a piece of plywood over the damaged door. No visit was made by the police."

Jane could not help the touch of accusation in her voice.

"He couldn't identify if anything was damaged or missing," the cop continued.

"No, he couldn't. Nor could he, when it happened again the next week." Jane twisted her lips after she spoke.

"There was a second break-in?" Pannu frowned.

"Nothing was reported," Havelange put in.

"I know, Arlie said only the patio door was damaged, so he put up more plywood and didn't bother calling it in. Apparently, because no one from your Detachment came out to investigate the previous incident, so he thought it was a waste of time. You don't have any investigation notes on the previous report either, do you?"

The cops shared another look. "Our resources are stretched thin sometimes. I'm sorry no one came out to speak with Mr. Birch. I'll mention this over site to Inspector Zeffler," Constable Havelange said.

"You can go across the street and speak to Arlie now if you like. He was looking after the place while Ann and I were with our aunt in the hospital." Jane didn't want to get annoyed with the cops, but somehow it appeared they blamed her. "Maybe someone stole the gun during one of the break-ins."

"How would someone get into the strongbox without the key?" Pannu asked.

"My aunt always left the business keys in her apron. Maybe someone besides me knew that. She always hung her apron on the back of the café door. That's where she told me I'd find the keys for everything when I took over the business." Jane opened her palm, facing up. "These keys."

"I see," Havelange said, but did not sound like she believed Jane. "Can you tell us why you left Vancouver, five weeks ago?"

Jane swung the door of the strongbox shut and locked it, playing for time. With a grim set to her mouth, she turned back to the cops. "I had to give up my job and my apartment."

"Why was that?" Pannu grasped the upper straps of his tactical vest and spread his feet as though he was prepared to stand there until he had the full story.

"I had some financial problems."

"What kind of financial problems?" Havelange cocked one hip and tucked her thumbs in her belt.

"Why do you want to know?" Jane frowned.

"The information might be relevant for our inquiries." Pannu returned her frown with a bland look, not judging.

Jane sighed and crossed her arms over her chest, resigned. "My bank cards and credit cards were compromised. You heard about XOplay?"

"XOplay is a credit rating service, it was hacked." Havelange nodded.

"Yes, I use to worked there as an analyst. Mine was one of the customer profiles breached. I lost everything." There was more to it, but none of it was the business of two cops running a murder investigation.

"I'm sorry, that must have been tough," Pannu said.

"It wouldn't have been so bad, if I'd noticed sooner. Ann and I were preoccupied with our aunt. She was dying." Jane shook her head at the memory. "I ended up having to declare bankruptcy." Jane took in a slow breath. Her anger was still raw, and when she got angry, her traitorous eyes teared up.

"When it was all over," she cleared her throat. "We brought our aunt's ashes home for the funeral. I hadn't been home in a while, and I forgot how it was here in the village." She moistened her lips and lifted her chin. "When Aunt Ethel's lawyer read the will, he confirmed I'd inherited the café. By then, I wanted to come home, here."

The cops nodded and filed out of the storage room. They returned to the kitchen, Jane followed, struggling to compose herself as she went.

"Your lasagna smells good," Havelange said as both cops eyed the extra-large pan.

"Tomorrow's special, drop by," Jane told them automatically.

"What kind of lasagna is it?" Pannu studied the dish.

"Chicken and mushroom, with tomato sauce, mozzarella, and parmesan cheese," Jane said as she glanced at her table, set for one. Should she invite the officers to dinner or would that be a conflict of interest, what with the missing pistol?

She spied the stack of mail "Oh, maybe I should give you this." She crossed to the table and snagged her purse from a chair. Dug into it and came up with the envelope addressed to 'Musgrave Landing Village Council.'

"What's this?" Constable Havelange asked taking the envelop.

"That's my post office box number, delivered to me, but I think it may have something to do with Tim Stanhope's murder."

"In what context?" The female officer studied Jane.

"Dirk told me the village books are being audited because someone took a significant amount to money." Both constables looked at Jane in surprise. "Maybe Dirk shouldn't have mentioned the theft or fraud or whatever, but that's water under the bridge now." She lifted one shoulder. "This letter is from a department of the provincial government. Chances are there's a cheque in that envelope. If Tim was alive, I doubt he'd let this piece of mail be delivered to me. He could have been using my box number before I got it, for the cheques he was possibly stealing."

"According to Councillor Weldon Ingram, almost all the village's requests for grant money were refused," Pannu said as he flipped through his notes.

"But were they refused? Grants could be the source of the money in Tim Stanhope's bank account." Constable Havelange tapped the envelope against her opposite hand as she spoke, much as Jane had.

"We can trace a cheque back quicker than getting the bank records." Pannu nodded. "Then we'll know. Come on, we want to catch the six o'clock ferry."

The constables took their leave, and Jane firmly closed the kitchen door behind them.

Chapter Eighteen

Thursday morning before the café opened, Jack arrived with Arlie again. A pleasant routine, Arlie enjoyed having his son back home.

"Pecan Coconut muffins," Jane said after Jack asked what she recommended this morning.

"They smell good. I'd like one." Jack smiled at her, but Jane merely looked back at him.

Arlie sighed. His son attempted to smooth over the awkwardness with Jane since he'd asked if she was seeing Tim Stanhope.

Yeah, good luck with that, buddy.

The two of them had always gotten along okay, most of the time. And, having someone else around for the evening meal, gave Arlie a reason to cook a proper dinner, instead of merely making do. But Arlie wasn't fooled at all. He knew who the main attraction was, and it wasn't dear old dad.

"You should take a sandwich too. Gladys Wyatt baked the bread." Arlie placed an oversized mug of coffee on the counter for his son. "If you're on the road today, I doubt you have anywhere you could reheat a slice of lasagna."

"No, I wouldn't. I'm driving out to Lake Cowichan today. I'll take a roast beef then, please." Jack tried to hand Jane money while his father loaded a paper bag.

"No, it's on me," she said.

"Jane, you can't–."

But she cut off his words with a shake of her head. "You help me out every time you come in here." She waved her hand at the front door.

Just this morning Jack had installed a motion arm on the back of the door, so it closed slowly and automatically, instead of threatening to smack into the wall if the wind caught it.

"I didn't want to see your wall damaged." Jack put his money away.

"I know, and I thank you for your thoughtfulness. You saved me from needing to hire someone to do exactly that or having the door repaired later on."

"Just do as the lady says," Arlie put in. Maybe Jane had forgiven Jack.

"Thank you." Jack gave her a nod. His discomfort created an awkward pause. "Is Gladys supplying the café with bread now?"

"Maybe, if we can come to an agreement on price," Jane said and smiled, showing she was grateful Jack let the matter drop. "We both have to make a bit on the transaction and the margin on food is pretty tight." Their eyes met briefly, and then they both looked away.

No, Arlie wasn't fooled at all about why his son had moved back to Musgrave Landing, but the boy still had some work to do on that end.

"Stop making googly eyes at Jane if you're not going to do anything about it." Arlie handed his son lunch. "Of course, there is the Community Spring Dance coming up, you could take her to that." He gestured to the poster he'd placed in the window the day before.

Both Jane and Jack looked at each other again, then away. Probably uncomfortable at the mention of the social event, or maybe his 'googly eyes' crack.

Arlie shook his head in disgust. What was wrong with these two kids? Couldn't they see they were made for each other? Just as he and Sara had been.

He sighed and went back to his favourite machine to give it a wipe down before putting together the first shot of espresso of the day.

Jack picked up his items and moved off to a table.

Arlie knew he had to do something about these two. They needed more interaction between them. "Did you tell Jane the cops were over at our house last night?" He poured himself a small drip coffee and added the shot of espresso to it, then joined Jack at the table.

"No." Jack pulled his mug toward him.

The microwaved toned. Jane took out Jack's breakfast wrap and brought it over with her coffee to sit with them.

Arlie smiled at Jane. This was progress.

"Did they ask you about the break-ins?" Jane wrapped her hands around her cup.

"Yep." Arlie nodded. "I told them the same thing I told you and about putting up the plywood. They asked if I went into the café, and what I saw."

"What did you tell them?" Jane looked at him over the rim of her mug as she sipped.

"I didn't see anything damaged or missing as far as I could tell." Arlie lifted one shoulder.

"Which is strange, why break-in and not take anything?" Jack wiped his mouth with a napkin. "I got the feeling there was more to it than they were saying."

"There was," Jane nodded. "You found the murder weapon, the Browning pistol." She looked at Jack. "It's probably the same one that belonged to my grandfather. Aunt Ethel had the gun stored in the strongbox in the back room, but now it's gone."

"That explains it." Arlie leaned back in his chair. "Whoever broke in wanted a gun, and they knew they could find one here. With Ethel in the hospital on the mainland, they had plenty of opportunity to take it."

"They also knew where she kept her keys." Jane gave Arlie a meaningful look, like it was a clear indicator of who the burglar could be.

"That fact won't narrow it down much. Lots of people knew Ethel kept her keys in her apron pocket. I knew," Arlie said with a shrug. "Anyone who saw her unlock the storage room would know."

"How many people would know there was a gun in the strongbox?" Jack asked.

"Now there, that might be a shorter list." Arlie rubbed his chin thoughtfully.

"Constable Havelange said Marc Whipple knew. Aunt Ethel offered him the pistol and my grandfather's medals for the museum."

"I can't see Marc wanting to kill Tim. Plus, there's no way his medi-scooter could travel down that hiking trail. It's strictly for paved streets, no off-road capabilities." Arlie waved the thought of Marc Whipple away.

Jack and Jane shared a look, both amused, but Arlie ignored them.

"Who else knew Ethel offered her father's effects to the museum?" Jack asked, sobering.

"Anyone on the museum board, I'd imagine. Dirk and Anita for sure, and possibly Earl Moffatt," Arlie said. "When the cops get here today, I'll be sure and mention it."

"I WANT TO THANK YOU for the use of your storage room," Inspector Zeffler said to Jane as she handed him a pecan coconut muffin to go with his coffee.

"It's no trouble." Jane watched Kenny roll the black box back into her storage room.

Before Jack left for work, she'd asked him and Arlie to bring down the table she'd seen in the attic yesterday. It would give their recording equipment a place rest, and allow the officers a sort of desk to write down their notes.

Arlie delivered an espresso to Constable Pannu, and no doubt told the cop the low down on the museum board. The constable put down his cup and dug out his notepad, then waved the other constable over.

She thought about Arlie's suggestion regarding the storage room space. Money was tight, and she had to make good business decisions. "I won't ask for any rental fee for the space, if you and your people use the café for lunch and what not."

Zeffler lifted his heavy black eyebrows. "Good point. Yes, I'm sure we can do that. Would you be able to supply lunch to us in the village office? Denise McKenzie and I will be working there again today."

"That will be no problem we are featuring chicken lasagna along with the soup or salad of the day, tomato noodle, and the regular assortment of sandwiches. The featured treat is strawberry cheesecake."

"Can I put my order in now?" Zeffler asked eagerly.

"Certainly." Jane smiled back and grabbed her note pad.

Shortly after that, the police filed out, taking the auditor with them. Kenny was left at a back table playing on a smartphone he pulled from a backpack.

"Do you have Wi-Fi?" Kenny asked, wandering over to the counter. The tech wore the same uniform as the day before, shirt over a T-shirt and jeans. Jane studied the young person's face.

"Not for the public, no, I'm sorry," Jane said. "Would you like something? Coffee, juice, or water, maybe?" She held back on the offer of milk. She didn't want to imply anything about Kenny's age. Although right now he-she looked about twelve-years-old.

"No, I don't drink coffee. Fruit sugar is fattening, and no one should use water bottles. They're bad for the environment."

From the corner of her eye, Jane could see Arlie's lips moving. He was thinking about refuting the kid's statements and if he did, it would not end well.

"How about a glass of tap water?" Jane asked.

Kenny paused, and then nodded.

Jane filled a glass and handed it over.

With a smile, Kenny wandered away, glass in hand, oblivious to Arlie's narrowed-eye look as the tech went by him.

"Have you figured Kenny out? Is he a guy or is she a girl?" Arlie asked in a low tone as he added more muffins to the baskets.

"No, and you know what, it really doesn't matter." Jane picked up a cleaning cloth and wiped down the back counter.

"I suppose you're right, as long as Kenny does his job."

The bell jingled as the door opened, and a senior citizen entered. He held the door wide for a man on a mobility scooter. As Jane watched the silver-haired senior maneuver his scooter into the café, she was glad they had installed the wide French doors instead of reducing the size of the portal for a regular sized one.

"Hello gentlemen, what can I get for you?"

"We'd like to welcome you back to Musgrave Landing, Jane. Ethel was so excited when she thought you were coming back. I'm Marc Whipple." The man sitting on the scooter reached out and Jane moved around the counter, so they could shake hands.

"Lovely to meet you," she said smiling at the man with his warm brown eyes and weather-beaten flushed face.

"What he said. I'm Earl Moffatt." Jane shook his long boney hand. She remembered Earl from the first day she opened, but if he wanted to pretend it never happened that was okay with her.

"Nice to meet you too," Jane said and gave the other man a warm smile as well. She could not remember either of the men from her youth.

"Fellas," Arlie said with a nod.

"Hi Arlie, you workin' here now?" Earl asked.

"Yep, started this week."

Jane watched the three men chat for a moment before they turned back to her.

"We'll each take a drip coffee to-go," Earl said.

"When you get your feet under Jane, give either of us a call. Ethel offered to put your grandfather's medals into the museum, and we would love to have them as part of our World War II exhibit."

"Thank you."

Arlie handled the sale. "The cups and such are on the self-serve counter behind you."

"I'll get it," Earl told Marc and crossed to the windows.

"I wish you'd have taken the medals and the Browning pistol when Aunt Ethel offered them to you. Maybe then the gun wouldn't have been stolen," Jane said as she stood by Marc.

"I heard about that. The police mentioned it when they came to see me." He lifted one shoulder. "It seemed the best thing to do at the time. Emery Crawly's weapon was still operational, and we thought since we had Anita's uncles Browning in the display, that would be enough."

"Anita Stanhope's pistol doesn't fire?" Arlie asked.

"No, the firing pin is damaged. We feel safer having a broken pistol in the display than a working one." Marc accepted his coffee from Earl. "No one would know the difference anyway."

Jane glanced at Arlie, and he raised one eyebrow at her as Earl and Marc moved over to a table. Earl slid out a chair to accommodate his friend's scooter.

The bell jingled again, and Bea Merryweather strolled in. She called a greeting over at the other villagers as she paused to remove a dripping wet pink scarf from her head. Her blond curls sprang back into her signature hairstyle. No doubt due to some industrial strength hairspray the woman must use, Jane figured. How else could she keep her helmet of curls in place?

The postmaster shrugged out of her coat and gave her matching pink rain jacket a snap to remove the built-up water.

"Good thing she's standing on the mat," Arlie muttered sarcastically as he went to the kitchen for the mop.

Oblivious to the wet trail she left behind her, Bea crossed the wooden floor to the counter. She gave her coat one more shake and spattered water droplets in a dozen directions. "Sorry," she said offhandedly. "It's windy again and raining hard, spring is not being very cooperative, I'm afraid." She pushed up the sleeves of her pink yoga shirt. The top matched her stretchy pink pants and shoes.

"No problem, Bea, what can I get for you?" Jane asked as Arlie noisily dropped the mop to the floor and cleaned up water with exaggerated swings of the mop, muttering words under his breath.

"I'm supposed to meet Constable Havelange here. Apparently, she has some questions for me." Bea frowned at Arlie as he mopped the floor around her in a circle.

"This way, please, ma'am." Kenny appeared at Bea's elbow before Jane could say anything. The tech gestured toward the setup in the back room.

By the sound of the car pulling into the lot, Constable Havelange had arrived as well.

"Can I get you anything, Bea?" Jane offered again.

"No, thanks." She followed Kenny to the back room.

Arlie waited by the door with the mop as the constable came into the café. He nodded in approval as she wiped her feet on the mat before striding over to the temporary interrogation room.

The café telephone rang.

"Arlie, I bet it's Josh for you," Jane called over to him.

LATER, AS JANE POURED the contents of her soup pot into the slow cooker, Ann strolled into the café.

Her sister still hadn't returned Jane's call from the night before, which annoyed Jane to a large degree. And when Jane looked up from her task, a flash of guilt entered Ann's eyes but vanished quickly, even before she shed her navy-blue wrap. Jane compressed her lips and shook her head.

Ben Sinclair was behind Ann. He entered, carrying a pair of wooden cases. The rain must have stopped, neither was wet.

Jane wasn't getting any answers from her sister with other people around. Family business had always been a sensitive issue with Ann about what was and what wasn't discussed in public. No doubt a hold-back from when they were kids and had to explain to the other children at school why they didn't have a mother or a father.

She wasn't angry at Ann exactly. Merely puzzled with why her sister avoided telling her the truth, and yes, that hurt.

Today, both artists dressed for work in old jeans and sweat shirts, and they carried in an assortment of painting gear.

Jane placed the lid on the pot and selected the heat setting, taking her time acknowledging Ann and Ben. It gave her a moment to center herself and figure out what to say.

"Looks like some work is going to get done on the inside today," Arlie remarked as he picked up the stainless-steel pot. He had on a red apron, in contrast to Jane's yellow and white one. Arlie had taken on washing up the café dishes, which could not go into the dishwasher, like Jane's chef quality cookware. With the vessel in hand, he headed into the kitchen.

Ann moved toward Jane with a weak smile. "I hope it's okay if we start to draw out the design." Ann's tone was a touch hesitant. "Ben wants to do most of the painting during the weekend when the café is closed, if that's all right."

"Sure, no problem, as long as you know the customers will probably watch and possibly critique today."

"That's fine, it can't be any worse than when my family comes to a gallery showing." Ben grinned to display white teeth against dusky skin. He was either ignoring the tension between the two women or he was focused on the job at hand. And knowing how artistic types functioned, Jane figured it was the latter.

"Okay, then." Jane nodded.

Ann met her sister's eyes briefly, and Jane saw pain in their depths. She immediately let go of her own hurt.

It appeared the information bothered Ann as well as it did Jane, and it wasn't as if the facts were going to fade away. Ann would speak to her about the trunk contents when she was ready. Jane could afford to give her sister some time.

Instead, she helped the pair of artists rearrange a couple of tables giving them space to work and access to the north wall. With supplies spread out across a canvas drop cloth on the floor, they set to work.

The phone rang again. It was Zeffler with the rest of the lunch orders. She added the items to the initial order and applied the cost to the credit card number he supplied. They also agreed to a pick-up time.

During the call, the storage room door opened, and Bea left, looking white around the mouth. She didn't even bother to put on her coat. Minutes later, the constable followed her out and left in her cruiser.

"I bet the cops told Bea stuff about Tim she didn't know." Arlie took the note from Jane concerning the lunch order.

"Could be," Jane agreed. "Someone will be by to pick up the RCMP's lunch around noon. They are all having the lasagna, garden salad, and cheesecake," Jane told him. "I think I have a cardboard box we can use."

"Bea wasn't in with the cop very long. I wonder who they're rounding up next," Arlie said as he looked over the lunch order.

Ann and Ben continued to sketch out the image of sea life on the opposite wall.

"Maybe Dirk or Anita? I'll bet Pannu is still looking into the gun Jack found."

"Could be," Arlie said with a nod, repeating her words.

Shortly after the mid-morning ferry departed, Anita Stanhope was escorted into the café by both the constables.

Jane noted the woman's red-rimmed eyes. Her blonde, curly permed hair was flat on one side, and Anita's clothes were creased and rumpled as if she'd been sleeping in them. When she looked Jane's way, Anita lifted her top lip at Jane in a surly manner.

The village administrator's attitude surprised Jane. She'd only ever spoken to the woman one time. Maybe the older woman had a problem with people in general at the moment. It can't have been easy to live in the same town as 'the other woman,' let alone told your husband was murdered.

Jane felt sorry for Anita. She knew what it was like to be hauled in front of the authorities, repeatedly, to explain your actions, and it wasn't pleasant. Let alone, treated like a pariah and then lose all your friends.

All the customers' eyes were drawn to the village administrator. Even Ann and Ben paused in drawing a killer whale on the wall to watch Anita dodge the handful of villagers as she speed-walked across the café and disappeared into the interrogation room.

As soon as the door closed, comments ensued.

Constable Havelange ignored everyone's questioning glances as she closed the door.

Pannu stopped at the counter. "May I have three bottles of water please?"

"Sure." Jane grabbed the water out of the refrigerator. Money changed hands. "Do you want your receipt?"

"Oh, yes, thanks. I have to expense these." Pannu took the slip from Jane, and he followed his partner.

"I'd love to be a fly on the wall during this interrogation," Arlie said. He dragged out the case of water and added more bottles to the fridge.

"Why? I don't care for the woman, but it's still tragic her husband was murdered."

"That may be." Arlie snorted. "But I think she's the one that pulled the trigger."

"Really? You think Anita has the where-with-all to break into the café, steal the pistol, and track Tim down on a hiking trail to shoot him?"

"I think so, she hates Lara Finkle." Arlie stored the extra water bottles under the counter, and then stood. "She was motivated."

"How long had the affair been going on?"

"At least a couple of years," Arlie said with a shrug. "Tim wasn't exactly subtle about it."

"So why shoot Tim now?" Jane tipped her head to one side as she thought out loud. "Something had to trigger a change in behaviour."

"I don't know," Arlie said with a shrug. "Maybe she finally got tired of Tim's shenanigans." He moved past the counter. "I should go check the washrooms."

Jane frowned as Arlie entered the men's room. The washrooms shared a common wall with the storage room. She shook her head and hoped he wasn't eavesdropping.

The bell jangled again, forcing Jane to forget about Arlie and wait on her next customer. An older woman entered, dressed in a periwinkle-blue dress and shoes, and carrying a black umbrella. She collapsed her umbrella and left it by the door.

Her silver hair marked her age around seventy as she pattered up to the counter. She looked vaguely familiar to Jane. "Hello dear, I'm Mindy Sowinsky," the small, fragile looking woman said.

"Nice to meet you, I'm Jane Westcott." Jane extended her hand and a thin boned one grasped it limply.

"I know," Mindy smiled and exposed tiny teeth. "You're Ethel's niece. I used to work in the grocery store when you and your sister came in for penny candy. I'm retired now, you know."

"I remember you, Mrs. Sowinsky. How have you been?" Mindy had been head-cashier, incredibly fast and efficient. She also never left her post at the front of the store. Mindy was always on duty to ring through a customer at B&H Country Grocers.

"Very busy, I make custom patio stones out of concrete. Thought I'd bring you a few samples, so you could see my work. The patio out back needs a few stones replaced and mine would fit right in." She looked over her shoulder at

Ann and Ben. "I see you're sprucing up the place already. The mural on the outside walls is very interesting. It might be nice when it's done."

Jane looked down at Mrs. Sowinsky, not more than four and a half feet tall which tempted Jane to ask how the woman could bring samples. It seemed impossible for the senior citizen to lift even one patio stone. If she managed the feat, the stone might squash the poor woman flat.

"Yes, it's a work in progress," was all Jane said.

Mrs. Sowinsky reached into her large, black handbag and extracted a half-sized photo album. She laid it on the counter in front of her.

An album, this of course, made perfect sense. Jane felt a bit silly at her assumption. Dutifully, she leafed through the photos of the six-sided concrete blocks in various styles, colours, and designs.

"These are lovely, how much for one?" Jane asked. She particularly like the dragonfly and lady bug designs.

"Sixty dollars each. But, if you buy two or more, I'll give you a deal."

"I do need to replace a few of the patio stones, but I'm afraid my budget for renovations is currently tapped out." Jane glanced over at Ben and Ann as they drew dolphins on the north wall.

Mrs. Sowinsky studied the two artists then turned slowly back to Jane. "How about this?" She tapped an index finger against her pale lips. "Could I display some of my stones here in the café? You could sell them for me, at say a five percent commission."

Jane pursed her lips and tipped her head toward the patio door. "How about this instead, I'll pick out your best six stones, and I'll buy them at twenty dollars apiece. In return, the stones will be on permanent display. You can leave six different samples under the eve against the wall, and I'll sell them at your price for a ten percent commission?"

Mindy opened her mouth to argue, and Jane held up one finger to stall her.

"I won't take the commission right away. The money will go against the six I received until they are paid off. You get a venue to show off your work, and I get my patio repaired. If you have business cards, you can display them here at the cash register and the album too. And," Jane tapped the donation mug. "You could be one of the Ethel Crawly Beautification Project members. Ann is working on grant money to pay the artist for the beautification of the village."

At the mention of grant money, Mrs. Sowinsky's silver eyebrows climbed upward. "I'll think about it," she said, closing and stowing her album, and then went to collect her umbrella.

Jane was sure the deal died, but Mrs. Sowinsky left the café through the patio door. She tottered all over the patio looking at the stones. And Jane grew hopeful the retired cashier might take the deal. It would be nice to get the patio fixed.

She glanced at the clock and compressed her lips. "I wonder what Arlie found to clean in the washrooms that would take this long," she muttered and headed to the washroom and knocked on the door.

The noon ferry was drawing into its berth. The café was going to get busy again.

Chapter Nineteen

"I can't believe you!" Jane hissed at Arlie as he quickly washed his hands. Customers were coming through the parking lot door.

"What? Aren't you curious to know what Anita is saying?"

"No. Okay, yes, but you shouldn't be pressing your ear against the ladies' room wall to hear what's going on. Doing so has to be a breach of privacy of some kind. Not to mention, probably against the law."

"I couldn't hear anything in the men's room."

"Arlie, you're killing me here. What if a female customer needed to use the facilities?"

"Pah," Arlie scoffed and tossed the paper towel he used to dry his hands into the garbage. "If the police wanted privacy, they should have dragged all their suspects back to Duncan for questioning."

"They're trying to disrupt people's lives as little as possible and also solve the murder as fast as possible," Jane pointed out dryly.

Arlie merely opened his hands in a 'whatever' motion.

They were both too busy after that to discuss it any further. Several customers drifted in from the newly arrived ferry as did two more which were from the cars preparing to depart.

Finally, when a break came in the food and beverage requests, Jane couldn't stand it any longer.

"So? What is Anita saying?" Jane asked as the customers in the room clustered around the artists to watch the landscape of Samsum Narrows appear on the wall, out of earshot.

Arlie chuckled smugly. "I knew you were curious."

"Did she confess?" Jane pressed.

"No, she's denying everything." Arlie ticked the items off on his fingers. "Anita says she didn't break into the café. She also doesn't know how to fire a gun. She said she loved her husband and no, she didn't know about his affair with Lara Finkle. What horse pucky." The last was Arlie's own comment.

"She claims she had nothing to do with any money transfers from the village to her husband's account either. Anita suggested Tim must have copied her banking access ID and passwords to transfer the money himself."

"What about the grant money, she had to have deposited the cheques?" Jane asked.

"Anita said she didn't know anything about any grant money. Only the village council, or rather Dirk, had applied for several endowments and as far as she knew, all the submissions were denied." He placed a cardboard box on the counter next to the cash register.

Jane had brought it in from the kitchen to pack the RCMP's lunch order into.

The microwave beeped, and Jane transferred slices of lasagna into cardboard meal containers and closed the lids to keep the food hot. She handed each to Arlie, and he packed them in the bottom of the box.

"Do you think the constables were buying it?" Jane handed him the four containers of garden salad, each with a raspberry vinaigrette dressing.

"I don't know, I couldn't tell. They didn't give much away, just asked lots of questions."

"Innocent, until proven guilty, I assume," she said collecting the dessert for the order. Jane knew the actuality of the saying all too well. The paper bag with the smaller containers of strawberry cheesecake went into the box too.

"Yep, and don't worry. I won't say anything to anyone else. It's no one else's business."

"I know you won't, because if the RCMP gets wind of you listening in you'll lose your source of information." Jane extracted two bottles of water and two soft drinks from the fridge.

"That too," Arlie agreed and gave her a mischievous grin as he added the drinks to the box of food.

A few minutes after twelve-thirty came and went, the storage room door abruptly opened, and Anita stomped out. Her heels struck the floor loudly as she tramped across the café. She elbowed a young man out of the way to get to the door. Her bad mood was as evident as her flushed red face, and the anger burning in her eyes.

"Her exit would have been more dramatic if she could have slammed the door," Arlie commented as he tucked napkins and plastic cutlery into the police lunch.

"I expect you're right. Good thing Jack installed the arm restraint this morning."

"Good thing I found one in my parts pile in the metal shop." They both waited by the counter for the cops to leave the back room.

"Speaking of which, how are the patio tables coming?"

"Fine, Jack's been welding up the breaks, and I've been painting the tables. We should have them ready to deliver this weekend, probably Sunday." He paused, keeping his eyes on Ben Sinclair as the artist added a thin layer of black paint to the dorsal fin of a killer whale. "It's good to have Jack home."

Jane glanced at Arlie and realized his words conveyed much more than their surface meaning. She patted his arm, but all she said was, "That's great, thank you. Now all I need to do is find some chairs to go along with the tables."

The constables exited the storage room. Jane watched as they paused to speak to Kenny and he nodded and went into the old office.

Constable Havelange stepped over to the counter. "Is this our lunch?" She gestured at the cardboard box all packed up.

"Yes, it is. Inspector Zeffler didn't say anything about your technician," Jane said.

"Kenny's going to pack up the tapes and take them back to the Detachment. Is it all right to leave the equipment in the room while she's gone?"

Jane blinked, she'd gotten it wrong, Kenny was female. But what did it matter?

"Yes, absolutely, use it as long as you need the space." Jane slid the box toward the constable.

"Great, thanks. The food is paid for?"

"It is, the receipt is in the box."

The constable gave them a nod and picked up the box. "Thanks again, see you later."

Pannu held the door open for her and they left.

"Ann?" Jane called over to her sister. After no response, "Ann, are you and Ben stopping for lunch?" Jane called a second time to get her sister's attention.

At the mention of lunch, both artists finally turned to look her, their gazes slightly unfocused, like they were only now coming back down to earth.

"What's wrong with them?" Arlie asked.

"They were, 'in the zone.' When Aunt Ethel or Ann worked on a painting, they both had the ability to ignore distractions, like blocking out the whole world. I guess Ben does the same thing."

"Artistic types are strange."

"You have no idea," Jane agreed.

THE RAIN STAYED AWAY in the afternoon, but the sky held onto its leaden cast, giving the day a sullen feel.

The RCMP did not return, and neither did Kenny.

Ruby curled up under her usual chair by the windows, and no new customers stopped in with the last ferry.

The café needed some food items, and Jane didn't feel like trekking down to B&H Country Grocers. She gave the list to Arlie, and he drove down to do the shopping.

Saturday, Jane planned a trip to the wholesalers Ethel frequented on the big island. As much as possible she bought locally, but some things the village didn't offer, like the imported coffee beans the café had used for the last twenty-five years.

Ann and Ben had made good progress on the inside murals, they even got as far as outlining all the pencil drawings with black paint. The sea life appeared to leap off the walls and made the space feel bigger already.

"This is all we can do today." Ben cleaned his thin paint brush with a soft rag as he spoke to Jane. "Is it all right to come back tomorrow to continue?" he asked politely.

"Sure, it's fascinating watching you guys work." Jane leaned on the front counter. She divided her time watching the art on the wall take shape and looking through her recipe binder. She'd been looking for an idea for tomorrow's treat. Peanut butter cookies rated high on her list.

"Great, see you tomorrow morning then." Ben gave Jane a grin. He spoke quietly to Ann, as they packed up their brushes and supplies. She shook her head at him as she glanced at Jane. Ben picked up his cases and left with a quick wave.

As the sound of the bell's tinkle died, Jane studied her sister. She leaned a hip against the counter, arms folded.

Ann delayed acknowledging Jane's regard as her sister cleaned brushes and replaced them in the case.

Finally, Jane could wait no more. "Would you like some tea?"

Ann's dark eyes shifted to look at Jane. There was sorrow and regret in their depths. "Yes, please."

As Jane heated the pot and spooned tea leaves into the strainer, Ann washed her hands. After she dried them, she went to sit at the closest table to the counter.

Jane carried the brown striped teapot and two cups to the table. Still, her sister said nothing about the elephant in the room. "Do you want to tell me about the trunk in the attic, or do you want me to ask you questions?" Jane slid her sister's jade-green cup over to her.

Ann wrapped her long, slender digits around it as though she hoped the heat would thaw her fingers. "No, I'll tell you straight out." She met Jane's steady gaze before taking a sip of the brew and swallowing. "The summer before I went to the University of British Columbia I made extra money working for Aunt Ethel, by cleaning in my evenings. The attic was the last room I reorganized for her."

"I remember."

"I got rid of a lot of junk, by sorting through each trunk and crate. Books and old clothes were donated to different organizations." She lifted a shoulder. "But there was lots of stuff she didn't want to let go."

Jane was not going to prod her sister to get to the point, Ann would explain in her own time. Instead, Jane took a swallow of the rich chamomile and rose hip tea. The combination of flavours and the teas properties helped to keep her words behind her teeth.

Ann's gaze dropped to stare into her cup. "I found the trunk full of mother's things last, shoved in the back corner. The trunk was under a pile of broken furniture. I didn't know if Aunt Ethel forgot it was there, or if she wanted me to find it. But that doesn't matter now."

"No," Jane said simply.

"At first, I was excited. I was going to go straight away and tell you about it. Then I found your birth certificate and live birth papers. I was shocked to see some man named Jonathan Livingston documented as your father and not our dad, my dad. It confused me, and I went to ask Ethel, how this could be, and why we didn't know."

"What did she say?" Strangely, Jane felt detached from the conversation. Ann had kept the information from her for years, decades. *Unreal.*

"She said you weren't old enough or mature enough to know about your father yet, but I could tell Ethel didn't want to tell you. I didn't either, because I knew you'd be hurt."

"Not as hurt as my sister, my best friend, keeping this from me."

Ann nodded as she looked up at Jane. "First, let me say I didn't want to hurt you. I didn't want you to find out by accident either, so I locked the trunk and hid the key." She sighed and rubbed her forehead, pushing her wispy hair away from her face. "I had some idea that I'd tell you when you were older. When you could handle it, at least that's what I told myself." She moistened her lips. "I found the loose brick in the kitchen the week before when I was cleaning. Aunt Ethel knew it was there, she said when she and mom were kids they would hide messages behind the brick. Leave notes for each other. Anyway, I hid the key there." Ann raised her head and attentively looked back at Jane. "I knew you would find out someday, but someday got pushed farther and farther away, until I forgot about the trunk." She leaned forward and put her hand on Jane's. "I'm sorry I didn't tell you sooner, I really am."

"Okay, I accept that." Jane compressed her lips, but she was not actually angry with Ann. "What did Ethel say about my birth father?"

Ann rolled her bottom lip over her teeth. "You're not going to like it."

"I don't like it now. How bad could it be?"

Ann met her sister's gaze squarely for the first time that day. "Dad found out Mom had an affair with her art teacher. You are the result." She swallowed and continued, "Apparently, the affair went on for years, even after you were born."

"This was after I turned two, when Dad found out, and he divorced our mother," Jane concluded, she wanted it all out on the table, no more stalling. She still thought of John Westcott as Dad, because that was who he'd been to her.

"There was a little more to it than that. Mom was in the process of leaving Dad to go live with Jonathan Livingston before the divorce. She was going to take us with her," Ann said dryly, like she didn't believe it. "But our dad wanted custody of both of us according to Aunt Ethel. He felt you were just as much his daughter as I was. That's when things got nasty, and it was during the custody fight when he had the car accident."

"Dad was hit by a drunk driver," Jane nodded. Now it was her turn to stare into her teacup as the feelings of loss crept over her. "He died instantly."

"Yes," Ann said simply. "We weren't allowed at the funeral. Our mother thought it would be too traumatizing for us. Aunt Ethel disagreed, they argued, but Mom wouldn't give in."

"I remember thinking Daddy would come home soon. I didn't understand." Jane shook her head.

"You were only three by then, how could you understand?" Ann scooted her chair over and slipped an arm around her sister to draw her close.

"What about you? You didn't get to say good-bye either." Jane hugged her sister back.

"I know." She nodded against Jane's shoulder. "But what's done is done. We could visit his grave in Victoria, and we did."

"Only because Aunt Ethel took us, Mom never did." Jane let go of her sister and got up to make a trip into the kitchen. "Here." She handed Ann tissues and deposited a paper napkin with chocolate chip cookies on the table between them as she retook her chair.

"Thanks," first the tissues were used, then they bit into their cookies. "Tell me what happened to the art teacher, Jonathan." Jane swept up her crumbs and bundled them into her napkin.

"Mom was wrong. He didn't want us. Jonathan only wanted our mother."

Jane stared at Ann. "And that's why she dumped us on Aunt Ethel. I thought she was going to work overseas for some charity."

"Where did you get that idea?" Ann frowned at her.

"I don't know, maybe something she said, it was a long time ago."

"Well, no, as far as Aunt Ethel knew, our mother went chasing after the guy, Jonathan. They met up again in Costa Rica. There was a postcard in the box of pictures. Did you find the pictures?"

Jane made a second trip into the kitchen and came back with the shoebox. She removed the rubber band and dumped the contents on the table. Ann sorted quickly through the old photos and plucked out the card. She glanced at the back, and then handed it to Jane.

Dear Ethel,

I have found my sole-mate again. My kindred spirit! He is working for a school here, teaching children art. I'm helping him for the next month or so. Then we plan to go to Columbia. I'll let you know when we get there.

Hi to the girls.

Much love,

Stella

Jane checked the address, post marked from some place she had never heard of in Costa Rica. With a sigh, she tossed it on the table.

"And they disappeared." The same hollow sensation crept into Jane's chest she always experienced when thinking about her mother.

"Reported dead, six months later," Anne said with a nod.

"Did Ethel ever find out what happened?"

"Nope. Does it matter? Mom's body was sent back, buried in the cemetery here next to St. Michael's church. End of story."

"You're still angry with Mom." Jane blinked at this realization.

"A little, yes, I admit it. I want to blame her for everything. For all the bad decisions. The ones she made, the ones I've made," Ann said, but held up her hand. "Before you say anything, no, I know I've made my own messes. I can't lay my divorce at Mom's feet. We are who we are made to be, by our family, our experiences, and our own choices." She shrugged and dropped her hand. "It doesn't mean I can't still harbour some bad feelings about her choosing that man over her own children."

"I feel a bit the same way," Jane agreed. Then she inhaled a long breath, and they began sorting through the pictures. "It's up to us to learn from the situation and get over it. To forgive, so these bad feelings don't own us." She didn't know if Ann agreed completely with this sentiment.

All Ann did was give a small nod.

Could the baggage from their parents be part of the reason Ann's marriage ended? Jane looked at her sister curiously. Ann never talked about it, but whenever Jane brought up her sister's failed marriage, she ducked the issue.

Ann picked up a photo and smiled. She turned it, so Jane could see, sparking a laugh from her sister. The two girls were roughly eight and ten-years-old, grinning for the camera in matching blue and white pyjamas, their short hair rolled up into curlers. "Remember this?"

Chapter Twenty

Arlie brought the groceries into the kitchen. "I met Gladys at the store. She told me she'd drop by Monday to discuss supplying bread for the café. She also told me the village is going to have an election," Arlie said in a rush. "Bea was acclaimed acting mayor at the meeting this afternoon, but she doesn't want the headache of the position." Arlie handed over Jane's change and the receipt.

"That doesn't surprise me. I wouldn't want to sort out the money issues and deal with the results of the audit either." Jane unpacked the items from the grocery bags onto the table. "Thanks for picking this stuff up, I appreciate it."

"No problem." Arlie put the cold items into the stainless-steel refrigerator. "I think Ann should run for mayor." He glanced over his shoulder at Jane to gauge her reaction as he stacked bricks of butter on the shelf.

Jane paused with a bag of crushed walnuts in her hand. "Ann would be good as mayor, but it would eat into her ECBP project," she said as she considered the idea.

"She could champion the project easier if she were mayor. Especially now some money has been found."

"I wonder where all that money came from." Jane lined up her ingredients for tomorrow's featured treat on the kitchen counter.

"Half a million isn't all that much, not for a village of this size, but it is a lot to embezzle." Arlie folded the cloth grocery bags and laid them over the back of a chair.

Jane reached behind her for her cup of tea and found the brew had gone cold. "Any amount that is stolen is unacceptable." She dumped the tea out and rinsed the cup. "The thief needs to be held accountable." She gripped the handle of the mug too tight, and her knuckles showed white. She forced herself to relax the grip. All thieves should be held accountable.

"Gladys heard there's even more money. The auditor found another account with seven hundred and fifty thousand on deposit. The question is; what was Tim planning to do with the funds?"

"Maybe Tim had a trip to Vegas planned." Jane placed the cup inside the dishwasher. "I wonder if Lara Finkle knew."

"She just might have known." His tone was odd to Jane's ear.

Jane narrowed her eyes at Arlie. "How many times did you eavesdrop on the interviews?"

Arlie had the grace to look a bit sheepish. "Maybe a couple of times," he admitted.

"I bet. When Lara Finkle was waiting for the constable, she told me she thought Anita killed Tim."

"She would say that, she was the other woman," Arlie put in. "She told the cops the same thing."

The bell in the café jangled. "I'll get it." Arlie shrugged out of his jacket as he returned to the café, and Jane turned back to her baking.

"Jane," Arlie called back to her, not even a minute later. "You need to come out here, please."

She put down the container of peanut butter and joined Arlie in the café. A stern looking woman in a navy, polyester pantsuit stood primly in front of the counter. Her short, jet-black hair matched her plastic-rimmed glasses, and her eyes held a bored expression. World weary, Jane thought, noting the woman also clutched a clipboard and pen.

"Jane, this is Anna-Bell Pinquest–," Arlie began, but she cut him off.

"Ms. Westcott, I represent the food inspection department of the provincial Health Ministry." She placed her business card down on the counter with a crisp snap. "We've had some calls, with regard to this establishment's hygiene."

Jane opened her mouth to offer every bit of cooperation she could.

Ruby chose that precise moment to claw her way out from under her usual hiding spot and scoot between three people's feet. The cat made a beeline straight into the kitchen and up the stairs to the apartment above.

Jane noticed the floral scent the inspector wore, and it made Jane's eyes itch.

Anna-Bell lifted her steely gaze from staring after Ruby's exit to meet Jane's wide-eyed expression. "How many pets do you keep in this restaurant, Ms. Westcott?" Anna-Bell opened her clipboard and gave her pen an aggressive click.

JACK TIED VIMY'S LEASH to the hitching post under the window, outside the café. He was curious as to why the place was open this late in the day. Through the window, he saw Jane working behind the counter as he leaned down to scratch behind the dog's ears.

The German shepherd dropped his head to the dish and began lapping water.

"I won't be too long, boy." Vimy glanced at him briefly. Then the dog stilled, his nose pointed toward the flowering shrubs which bordered the parking lot.

Jack removed his sunglasses and hung them from his shirt pocket, as he tried to see what had caught Vimy's attention. He did not have to wait long. A small black cat slunk out from between the shrubs and paced the short distance to the other side of the water dish. Vimy stared steadily at the kitten.

Thankfully, the German shepherd didn't growl at the cat with one orange ear.

"Make a friend, Vimy," Jack instructed and received a look from his canine friend that spoke 'what have I ever done to you, to deserve this?'

"Go on," he prodded, and the dog heaved a sigh.

Vimy leaned forward with his nose and the cat did likewise. Their noses touched briefly, and then he went back to lapping up the water, ignoring the feline.

With a soft chuckle, Jack opened the door. His eyes found Jane, still working behind the counter. The same warm sensation consumed his chest each time he saw her.

"I'm surprised the café is still open." Jack crossed the room to where she was head and shoulders deep inside the display case. At Jane's elbow sat a steel bowl of soapy water, also inside the case. She gave him an odd look through the glass and dropped the cleaning cloth into the water.

"I thought I'd get ahead of the weekly clean. We had a visit from the health inspector today." Jane pulled her head out of the case to stand up as she spoke.

"Oh? How did that go?" Jack asked cautiously.

"Ruby chose that moment to climb out from under her chair to run into the kitchen." She compressed her lips. "Inspector Anna-Bell is not a cat person, and Ruby is not an inspector friendly cat."

"Not good."

"Not so much, no, but your dad saved the day." A half-smile drifted over her lips.

Jack raised his eyebrows in question as he leaned a hip against the counter and folded his arms to listen.

"He looked the inspector right in the eye and said Ruby was his service cat. He suffers from depression and Ruby helps him deal with it."

"Seriously?" Jack asked with a chuckle.

"No kidding." She smiled along with him. "He's home right now on the internet, registering Ruby as his service animal with the provincial health authority, or wherever you do that."

Jack laughed harder, and he was gratified to see her smile widen. "He's a devious old guy." He shook his head at his father's antics.

"I am just now, finding this out." Jane nodded in agreement.

"Let me know if he starts getting out of hand. My mom was the only one who could rein him in, but sometimes I can too."

"He's fine, just spirited. I'll say one thing, though. It's never dull around here."

Jack searched for something innocuous to say. He didn't want to go too fast in his pursuit of Jane. He was determined but didn't want to spook her. They were only now getting to know each other again.

Instead, he picked the most obvious subject. "The exterior painting is going well. I like what you've done so far."

"That's all Ann, she's the creative one."

"You have other talents." He gazed into her deep brown eyes and wished he had kept this thought to himself when she blinked in surprise at his words. He saw caution creep into her expression. "I meant your cooking."

"Oh." Her uncertainty died, and the smile was back.

Go slow Jack, don't scare her.

"Thanks." Jane gestured behind him. "What do you think about the mural?"

Jack turned away to take in the opposite wall. "Impressive, the art inside and outside will attract customers for sure. Once it's completed, you should give the Cowichan Valley paper a call. I know the editor. I'm sure he'd do a feature on the café and the paintings."

"Ann would love that, and no doubt Ben would too. Thanks for the suggestion."

Jack was happy he made Jane smile again. "Ben Sinclair?" Jack said, impressed. "How did you get him to paint for you?" Ben ran his own gallery on Vancouver Island, just outside of Sooke. People flocked there to buy his work.

"He's a friend of Ann's. They're coming back tomorrow to work on the interior mural. He'll do most of his painting over the weekend when we're closed." Jane adjusted a purple lily in the flower arrangement beside the cash register. The flowers he'd given her, turning the lily to show off the darker interior of the flower. He watched her gently stroke the petal of a pink rose.

"The work should go faster with the café closed and no one around," Jack agreed. He hoped his conversation didn't sound too lame. He found it difficult not to say what he truly wanted. To stay on safer ground, he said, "Dad and I have the wrought-iron tables more than half-finished. We should be able to drop them off on Sunday afternoon."

"Great, thanks." Jane looked at Jack, he looked right back at her. Neither spoke for a moment.

Stop stalling and go for it, Jack.

"Jane, would you be interested–," he broke off as the door swung open and the bell tinkled.

"Hi Jane, why are you still open?" Ann breezed in.

He scowled at the bell and made himself straighten away from the counter.

"Hello, Jack." Ann batted her eyelashes at him playfully. "Is that your dog tied up out there?"

"That's Vimy, isn't he beautiful?" Jane addressed her sister.

"He looks fierce," Ann said.

"He's a pussy cat, unless you're a criminal," Jack said and turned back to Jane. "I should go. I'll see you tomorrow morning." He gave Jane a nod.

"See you in the morning."

"Bye Jack," Ann sang at him and gave him a little wave.

Ann always put his teeth on edge, but for Jane's benefit, he gave her sister a brief nod. "Bye, Ann."

JANE WATCHED HIM LEAVE. She was unhappy they couldn't finish their conversation, she had the feeling Jack was working up to asking her something. Regretfully, she looked over at the source of the interruption. "I didn't bother locking the door. I was working in here anyway, so it didn't matter."

"Never mind, I was just at the village emergency council meeting. I thought I'd come by and let you know what's happening," Ann said, eagerly. She had completely dismissed Jack and already moved on to a new subject.

"There's going to be an election," Jane said as she extracted the bowl of soapy water from the display case and dumped it into the sink.

"Yes, how did you know?" Ann frowned.

"Arlie heard it from Gladys. Both he and I think you should run for mayor," Jane said as she crossed the room and turned off the 'Open' sign.

"You do?"

"Yes," Jane said and locked the door.

Jack and Vimy were long gone. Only Ruby was left stalking some poor bug in the parking lot. She'd call the cat in later through the kitchen door.

"Coincidently, I was thinking the same thing too. I could do a lot of good for ECBP and the village, but it will be tough."

"Why? Bea doesn't want the mayor's chair." Jane turned off the lights. Ann picked up her things and followed Jane through to the kitchen.

"Weldon and Dirk each want the position. They both put their names forward." Ann dropped her bag and wrap on a kitchen chair.

"Like they would be competition for you," Jane said in a 'perish the thought' tone, she closed the connecting door and untied her damp apron.

"You're right. I could take the election if I put my mind to it." Ann took a seat. "The audit is turning up strange details, more money in oddball accounts."

Jane hung her apron on the door hook and picked up her oven mitts, time to check dinner. She opened the oven door to release the aroma of bay leaves, spices, roast beef, with a hint of garlic and onion. "Something like seven hundred and fifty thousand?" She removed the roaster lid and placed the previously peeled carrot and potato chunks into the roaster, ensuring the broth lapped over the top of the vegetables.

"Arlie, again," Ann said, sounding a touch frustrated.

"Yep." Jane found it funny Arlie had stolen Ann's thunder, but bit her lip to control it.

"Okay, did he know all sorts of grants were applied for and awarded for village civic improvements? I think the auditor and the cops think the Stanhopes embezzled the money."

"Can they prove it was both of them? Maybe it was only Tim who's guilty of theft." Jane thought about the things Arlie had overheard.

"Right, like Anita would ever be taken advantage of, or used. You've met the woman."

"Okay, maybe not where her job was concerned," Jane said as she closed the oven door and turned to her sister. "But, certainly in her personal life. Tim was cheating on her."

"True. Plus, that fact makes Anita the most likely suspect in Tim's murder. She has all the motives."

"Wait a minute, didn't you tell me Dirk is in charge of securing grants for the village?" Jane dropped the oven mitts onto the table.

"Well, yes...," Ann allowed.

"He could be involved with the grant money scam too."

The sisters looked at each other. "Nah," they said in unison.

"He's not smart enough, but the Stanhopes could have used Dirk's name on the applications. How would he know?" Ann suggested.

"Maybe, but do you see Anita tramping through the bush, down a hiking trail to shoot Tim? Or for that matter break into the strongbox in the storage room to steal Grandad's handgun?" Jane shook her head.

"What?" Ann said in shock.

"Oh, I forgot to tell you about that. The cops figure the murder weapon is Grandad's old service revolver. They've sent it out to be tested." Jane sat down in her usual spot. "You remember the two break-ins Arlie told us about? That may have been when the gun was stolen."

"Holy crap," Ann breathed.

"Yes, I found it a bit freaky too."

A brisk rap sounded at the kitchen door.

Jane got up and opened the door. Ruby dashed in and slid to a halt in front of her food dishes.

Her new employee stood on the back step.

"Come in, Arlie." Jane stepped back. She ignored Ann, who narrowed her eyes at the older man, no doubt because he'd one-upped her with the village gossip.

"No, I just thought I'd let you know I've registered Ruby as a service animal. You shouldn't get any more flak from the health inspector."

"Lovely, thank you for that," Jane said.

"I also wanted to give you this." He handed a book to Jane, and she curiously looked down at it then saw the cover picture and read the title. "I also have a small favour to ask," Arlie added.

"You'd like Nanaimo bars for Jack's birthday." Jane nodded as she looked into Arlie's watery blue eyes, and his seamed face folded into a smile.

"Yeah, you remembered."

"How could I forget? Mrs. Birch made the best Nanaimo bars I've ever tasted. I remember they're Jack's favourite." Jane opened the photographic cookbook. "Your sister had this book made up for Mrs. Birch. I remember she showed it to me when she first received it."

"Shelley didn't want Sara's recipe to get lost," Arlie said as Jane turned the pages to show a laughing and happy Sara

Birch measuring, stirring, and preparing the chocolate treat. "My sister also wanted to make sure the process was documented. She said it was an important part of the recipe." Arlie nodded.

"I'll copy it and get the book back to you tomorrow."

"No, you keep it. Sara would want you to have it. We never had a daughter to give it to, and even though Jack loves them, he'll never make Nanaimo bars."

Jane hugged the book to her chest and gave Arlie a gentle smile. "Thank you. Of course, I'll make them for him."

Chapter Twenty-One

From hooded eyes, Jack watched Dirk enter the café. He assessed the other man with the usual mild distaste. Slicked back hair, the two-hundred-dollar cashmere sweater over a dress shirt and suit pants. He wore leather deck shoes and probably had a manicure too.

Hard to believe they had ever been friends. When Jack thought about it, they hadn't been. Dirk just took to showing up at Jack's house with the other kids. His mother never excluded anyone from their backyard, unless he or she did something that warranted a temporary expulsion.

His mother was a good person, easy to forgive and live and let live. Her son, not so much, at least, when it came to Dirk and the attention he paid to Jane.

The other man was around Jane far too much in Jack's opinion. It didn't matter they all used to hang around together as kids.

As the years progress, they'd never formed any kind of friendship. They moved in different circles. And now, Dirk was sniffing around Jane, and Jack didn't like it.

"Have you thought about my offer?" Dirk placed his hands on the counter and leaned forward, like he wanted to give Jane a kiss.

"Please, stop asking me that. I have absolutely no plans to sell the café, so give it up." Jane took a half-step back.

Even from across the room, Jack could tell Dirk had an agenda concerning Jane. And he didn't think it was all about finding the right price to buy the café.

Jack climbed to his feet and dusted toast crumbs off his jeans and green cotton work shirt. He picked up his oversized, red coffee mug and plate. Time to let Jane know why he decided to move back to Musgrave Landing.

His boots didn't make much noise as he crossed the painted wooden floor. He stopped short of Dirk at the counter and loomed over the shorter man.

"So, would you?" Dirk was asking Jane something else. But by her expression Jack knew she wasn't comfortable with the question.

Dirk was oblivious to the fact his nemesis stood behind him.

Jane's dark-brown eyes flickered over his shoulder and up, to meet Jack's eyes. He gave her a half-smile.

Relief flooded her expression.

"I'm sorry, no, Jack asked me first," she said with such a firm nod that her chestnut braid bounced down her back.

What had he already asked Jane? He reviewed their conversation from before and found nothing.

Dirk turned, and glanced over his shoulder, his eyes opened wide for a second, but he covered his surprise quickly.

Amusement lit Jack's face at the shorter man's startled expression.

Then the other man narrowed his eyes at Jack. "How did you know about the Community Centre Spring Dance?" an accusation said through clenched teeth.

Jack raised one eyebrow at Dirk. His reaction seemed over the top.

"I told him about the dance." Arlie popped his grey head around the storage room door. "I put up the poster in the window, day before yesterday." The older man disappeared again.

"It's true," Jack nodded and set his coffee mug on the counter. "Thanks for breakfast, Jane. The egg and bacon wrap was delicious as usual."

"Glad you liked it." Jane gave him a quick smile and snagged his dirty dishes for the dishwasher.

"You're out of luck, Dirk." Jack pulled out his wallet and removed a ten to pay Jane.

"No problem." Dirk shrugged, acting like Jane dating someone else didn't bother him. "I'll ask someone else. I'm going to get a large coffee to-go." His tone petulant, was this high school? Dirk stalked over to the self-serve counter.

Jane met his eyes briefly as she handed Jack his change. He dumped it all into the ECBP mug. "Thank you for going along with my story," she said in a low tone.

"Anytime." Jack winked at her and was pleased to see he triggered a blush.

"The ferry will be here in about five minutes, have a good day at work," she said this louder.

"Thanks." Jack glanced over his shoulder briefly at Dirk, and then turned back to Jane. "Can I get a kiss good-bye?" He lifted his eyebrows in mock innocence.

"I..." Jane's soft pink lips parted in astonishment. Her eyes darted over to Dirk, so she knew he was watching them. "Yes, of course." She stepped around the counter and aimed a quick kiss for his cheek.

But Jack grasped her shoulders as he turned his head, and their lips met. Her kiss tasted sweet, her lips carried a faint touch of cherry, and he couldn't get enough. He slipped his arms around her, and she melted willingly against him.

"Oh, for God's sake," Dirk snapped in disgust. Neither one of them heard his curse, or when Dirk threw money on the floor and exited the café.

Gently, Jack broke the kiss, and her eyes fluttered open.

"Why did you do that?" she whispered.

"Because I've wanted to kiss you for too long, and because I never grabbed the opportunity before, but I knew I had to. It's time I let you know how I feel about you."

"What about Ann?"

"What about her?" he frowned.

"I thought." Jane swallowed as she leaned away from Jack, but the counter pinned her in place. "I thought you and Ann had something between you."

He shook his head. "No. When we were teenagers, it was Ann who wanted something between her and me. I was never interested."

"Who were you interested in?"

"You."

"Me?" Jane blinked in surprise.

"Yeah, but you were far too young. You were thirteen, and I was eighteen. I had to go to university on the mainland. I doubted you'd wait for me, and of course, you didn't." Jack lifted his broad shoulders in a shrug. "Life got in the way."

"By the time you got back, I was gone." Jane covered her mouth with her fingers as she stared at him.

"Exactly. And you found someone else, Eggbert something?" Jack moved back, allowing Jane some space, but still held her hand.

"Aaron Herbert. He was the biggest mistake of my life." Jane shoved herself away from the counter and slipped her hand out of his grasp. She crossed the room to the self-serve counter. "One of my mistakes, anyway," she amended as she straightened up the station.

Jack studied her, frowning slightly. "I thought so too." He walked slowly to her, as she gave him a solemn look over her shoulder.

He paused and picked up the money Dirk tossed on the floor.

What a jerk.

He wiped the two dollar-coin off with a sweep of his thumb and handed it to her. She took the money and looked up at Jack, a hesitant smile flirting with her lips. "Are you really taking me to the spring dance?"

"Yes, I am. When is it?"

"Next Saturday night."

"Do you think I could learn to dance between now and next Saturday?" he asked with a grin.

"No, probably not, but I don't care. We can shuffle around on the floor together."

Jack took her hands in his. "That works for me, would you care to go out to dinner with me tonight?"

"I–," she started to say.

"Be sensible, Jack. The girl will be exhausted. Invite her to our house, cook something for her." Arlie walked out of the backroom with a sack of coffee beans in his hands. "Thank God, you finally told her you like her. I couldn't stay in the storage room forever, you know." He went around to the back of the counter to load the beans into the roaster.

She bit her lip to stop from laughing, but nothing could diminish the sparkle in her deep-brown eyes

Jack inhaled deeply through his nose and released it, striving for patience. "Would you care to join me for dinner? It's my birthday."

"I would love to. I'll bring dessert, and happy birthday."

Chapter Twenty-Two

Jane didn't know if Anna-Bell, the health inspector, was on the same email list as Mr. Conroy, the fire inspector. Even so, it seemed more than a coincidence when Mr. Conroy strolled into the café after the nine o'clock ferry arrived.

How did all these separate agencies know to come to the village of Musgrave Landing and inspect Jane's Eats & Treats? She only mailed the paperwork to the various government agencies on Wednesday.

"Our department was notified the café reopened." This was Mr. Conroy's explanation. "I'm here to examine the premises for fire code adherence. What electrical changes did you make with your renovations?" the wiry young man asked.

"Who informed you, Mr. Conroy, we were re-opened?" Jane asked with a slight frown, something felt off to her.

"I'm afraid I don't know. That information is not on my paperwork." Mr. Conroy gave her a brief shrug. "I get my schedule for the week and make my rounds. That's all I know." He handed her his card. It looked right.

"I've got this, Jane," Arlie assured her.

"Thanks, Arlie." Jane stepped back and let the older man handle the young man's questions. Once again, she was glad she'd hired the experienced man and not just because she wouldn't have to go down into the creepy basement.

Hiring Arlie was one of the better decisions she'd made concerning the café. Maybe her judgement was improving.

After a twenty-minute tour–wherein Kenny showed up and Jane let her in the back room to retrieve the recording equipment–Arlie and Mr. Conroy were back in the main part of the café.

"You're building meets all the fire codes, with the exception of requiring a new smoke alarm in the kitchen. The current one is over twenty-years-old, and it may fail. There's no point in taking chances."

"I'll have a new one installed within the hour," Arlie promised Jane and Conroy. "I'll run down to the hardware store right away."

The inspector consulted his metal clipboard one more time. "You should also arrange to have the furnace fuel tank in the basement removed. You heat with electricity now, anyway. By leaving the tank inside the building, you are putting your business and yourself at risk. The tank needs to be emptied and removed. It's not mandatory, but I'd recommend it."

"The tank is empty. I remember my aunt ran it dry before she had the furnace disconnected." Jane told him.

"The company she contracted should have recommended removal."

"They did, but it's not a cheap thing to have done. As soon as I can afford it, I will," Jane said.

Conroy nodded. "Those tanks are never completely dry. The fuel is a low-grade diesel and leaves residue behind in the tank. It's not as flammable as gasoline but still, if you don't plan to use it, it should be removed from the premises for safety and environmental reasons." He made a note on his clip board.

"THE COST TO HAVE AN oil tank removed can range from eight hundred to twenty-five hundred dollars, depending on the size and condition of the tank, and the location of the installation." Jane explained to Arlie as they ate their lunch. The pumpkin and butternut squash soup turn out well, but she had no appetite and absently stirred her soup around in her bowl.

"Who did you call for the estimate?" Arlie asked, as he used his napkin to wipe his mouth.

"I did an internet search for companies on Salt Spring Island and on the main Island. The general estimates are all similar." She rubbed the side of her face, feeling tired. Her poor little bank account was taking a kicking, just with the regular expenses for operating the café. The cost of arranging for the fuel tank removal would empty her account completely. It would just have to wait, even if she was feeling pressure from Mr. Conroy.

"The tank has been in the basement for decades. It's not hurting anything." Arlie stood and collected their dishes.

"That's true, but now I know it should come out, it's bothering me. Guess I'll just have to put aside a few dollars every month until I can afford to have the work done." Jane stood and retrieved the cleaning spray and a dry cloth to do all the tabletops and counter now that lunch was over.

"That sounds like the best idea." Arlie agreed. "I'll go put up that new smoke detector in the kitchen."

"Thanks, Arlie."

After being in operation for five days, the café had brought in some money, but the additional expenses were sucking up all the profits. Jane glanced at the half-finished mural on the north wall. Ben called earlier to say he couldn't paint today. His mother needed to be taken in to see her doctor, so he promised to be back first thing in the morning.

Why had she rushed into having everything done at once? She should have concentrated on the infrastructure and regular operations. The actual cost, per week, to run the café was not a known actual expense yet. All she had were mocked-up estimates.

"And here I thought I was making better decisions," she muttered as she wiped the last table down.

Dirk's offer to buy the café popped up in her mind. Tempting as it was to sell, Dirk's offer was ridiculously low, but she could put the whole thing on the market with a commercial realtor.

Jane immediately discarded the idea. *I'm not going to cut and run at the first sign of adversity.* Besides, where would she go? She loved her sister, but there was no way she would live with Ann. The very thought made he groan.

"What was that?" Arlie called from the kitchen.

"Nothing," Jane answered. She shook her head and checked the coffee carafes, then wiped down the self-serve area too.

The door opened with the bell sounding, and Ann strolled in. "Hey there, little sister."

"Hi Ann." Jane gathered up her cleaning supplies and returned to the counter.

"No cops today?" Ann rested her oversized bag on the counter top.

"Nope, I haven't seen them, or the auditor."

"I believe the auditor is finished. She'll write up her report and send it to the village council, which is why I'm here." Ann extracted a set of papers from her purse and laid them on the counter. "Can I get you to sign as a witness, on my nomination papers?"

"Absolutely." Jane smiled at her sister. "I'm so glad you're running for mayor."

"Thanks." Ann actually blushed as she handed her sister a pen and pointed to the appropriate locations for Jane's signature. She looked around the empty café. "Where's Ben?"

"He couldn't make it today; he'll be here tomorrow."

"I will too. I'll get the rest of the flowers on the west side finished tomorrow and hopefully start on the north side."

"That would be great, thanks. I have to head over to Nanaimo and do my shopping." Jane handed her sister the papers back.

"So, what's for sup–," Ann began, both women jumped at the sudden noise. The blaring of the smoke detector blotted out her words.

"Arlie!" Jane covered her ears.

The blaring died. "Sorry, I was just testing it."

"Good lord," Ann said. "That noise would wake the dead."

"Probably not a bad thing," Jane allowed.

"Anyway, what are you doing about supper?"

"Why, are you inviting me over to your place?" Ann had eaten most lunches and evening meals at Jane's over the past five weeks.

"Um, no," Ann said awkwardly.

Jane tipped her head and folded her arms, as she looked at her sister. "Actually, I've been invited out this evening."

"Really, where? And with who?"

"To Jack and Arlie's for dinner. Its Jack's birthday."

"Oh." Her sister appeared to be at a loss for words.

"Yes." Jane lifted her eyebrows as she gave her sister a steady look. While it was true Ann did help Jane out a little in the evening with the café prep for the next day, she left all the dishes and clean up for Jane. Ann also let her sister know she expected payment for the painting jobs, inside and out.

If she hoped to save up enough money to have the fuel tank removed, she needed to get the free meal thing under control. Occasionally feeding her sister was not out of the question, but every day was becoming a bit much. Or, she could cancel the painting projects, but that would hurt Ann more than having to cook her own meals.

"I'm going to the nomination meeting this afternoon. Would you come with me?"

"For moral support? Sure, just let me talk to Arlie."

ARLIE WOULD RUN THE café until three o'clock, and then lock up. This let the sisters leave and walk side-by-side to the nomination meeting in the Musgrave Landing Community Centre.

"Does attending this meeting feel a bit weird to you?" Jane asked her sister.

"How so?"

"Tim Stanhope was found dead, Tuesday. Someone in the village is guilty of murder, the council is preoccupied with replacing the mayor, and there hasn't even been a funeral announcement yet. This is all moving fairly fast."

"I don't know how they do things for funerals when the deceased was murdered, but I think the burial has to wait until the body is released from the coroner," Ann said. "And as for the nomination meeting, well somebody has to run the show, and Bea stated categorically she won't do it because she doesn't have the time." She glanced sideways at her sister. "No doubt because Tim was the assistant postmaster, and his body was found with your letter in his pocket. Now an investigation is being conducted by Canada Post to see if he stole other people's mail."

"I didn't know. When did this happen?"

"Like Wednesday morning, as soon as the cops told Bea. She had to report it to her bosses, and now the post office has its own audit going on. See that?" Ann paused on the sidewalk outside the post office and pointed to the sign in the window. "It says that if anyone has any information about missing mail or parcels to go see Bea. That went up two days ago."

"I never noticed the sign."

"I'm surprised Arlie didn't tell you," Ann said dryly.

Jane ignored the remark. "Bea is up to her eyeballs in alligators."

"You could say that. Anita's house and property were searched too."

"Did the police find anything?" Jane resettled her purse strap on her shoulder as they began to walk again.

"I don't know." Ann shook her head.

When the women arrived at the community centre, a couple dozen people were milling around. Another handful had already taken their seats. Some had young children with them, but most were retired seniors or villagers who worked in the community. One older woman, extremely well-dressed in an expense cream suit, and matching hat was helped to sit in an aisle seat near the front. Her lanky attendant looked around him as he settled a cashmere blanket over her lap, like he dared anyone to come close. She patted his hand and folded her own around a gold headed cane.

"Who's that?" Jane whispered to her sister.

Ann glanced in the direction her sister gestured. "Mrs. Frost-Highmere, she owns the estate across from the ferry wharf. She led Jane to the front row, centre, and they took their seats.

Jane glanced at her sister, a small smile playing on her lips. Ann appeared keyed up with excitement, no doubt looking forward to tossing her name in the ring.

Dirk was walking around the assembled villagers, shaking hands and chatting. When he approached Mrs. Frost-Highmere, her elderly attendant glared. Dirk immediately turned in the opposite direction.

"It looks like your competition has already started his campaign for mayor."

"I think the three-piece suit is a bit much."

"Maybe, but the dark suit contrasts well with his features and makes his blond hair and white teeth stand out." Jane gave her an innocent look.

Ann snickered.

A table was set up on the stage for theatrical performances. In days gone by, when she and Ann were school kids, they'd participated in a few events. The scent of the floor wax brought back a host of memories as Jane looked around.

Spoken poetry contests, Christmas concerts, and Sunday afternoon movies. Where the kids would use the floor as a place to sit, and some old family film was projected on the back wall while they ate burnt popcorn.

"This place still smells the same." Jack sat down next to Jane.

"Stale popcorn and floor wax." Jane smiled broadly at him. "Are you going to put your name forward for mayor too?"

"No way. I wouldn't have the patience for the job," Jack said. He tipped his head in a nod. "Ann," he said in that careful tone he used for her sister.

"Nice to see you, Jack." Ann leaned over and smiled at him. "I hope I can count on your support," she said, ignoring Jane as she rolled her eyes.

"I'll have to hear about the platform you're running on first," he said in a serious tone.

"Well, I want–," Ann began, and Jane poked her sister with her elbow.

"He's kidding."

"Oh." She blinked. Before she could comment more, Bea walked onto the stage and sat down at the middle of the table in front of the microphone. Weldon Ingram, Dirk Ipkiss, and Celine Nickels filed out as well and took seats along the table. Last, Anita Stanhope plodded to the far end of the table and dropped into one of the folding metal chairs.

"How is Anita still part of the council?" Jane whispered to her sister.

Ann shrugged; her eyes glued to the small group of people as Bea opened the meeting.

"No charges have been laid against her. Nothing's been proven yet as far as embezzlement goes, at least not yet," Jack said in a low tone to Jane, and she nodded.

"If my husband were murdered, I don't think I could handle being in public only a couple days later," Ann remarked to her sister.

"Me neither," Jane whispered.

"Nominations are now open for the position of mayor on this council," Bea said. "But before that, I'd like to give you an update on the situation as it is today."

She cleared her throat, and Weldon slid a glass of water over to her. Bea nodded her thanks and took a sip.

"Okay, the total amount in the revenue account is $2014.06 as of yesterday." Bea shuffled her papers. "Total amount in the contingency account is $3115.00. And the amount the Village of Musgrave Landing expects to have returned, post the forensic audit performed by the RCMP, is 2.4 million." A gasp rippled through the room, and murmured comments flowed.

"That's even more than we expected." Jack shook his head.

"A lot more," Jane agreed.

Ann grinned from ear to ear. "I can work with that."

She was hushed by the people behind her.

"The plan for this grant money needs to be filed by the end of May or the village loses out on the benefits." Bea continued to speak and overrode the noise of the audience's feedback. "Filing an overall plan will be the most pressing responsibility of the new mayor and council. That being said, I am not running for the mayor's seat." She leaned back in her chair, and Celine leaned forward to speak into the microphone.

"We were all saddened to hear about the death of our mayor, Tim Stanhope." Celine began and continued to say a few nice things about Tim.

Anita brushed away a few tears, Bea's lips twisted as she folded her arms. Weldon and Dirk gave little reaction. The villagers in the audience were strangely silent.

Jane remembered Ann's remark about Tim the Tyrant. The man had not been well liked, and it didn't appear many would miss him.

"I now move that we open the floor to nominations," Celine announced. The motion was seconded by Weldon and the vote unanimous.

Anita kept her head down and wrote in a book. Jane suspected Anita was recording the minutes.

Lara Finkle stood up and called out in a clear, loud voice, "I nominate Dirk Ipkiss." Then she sat down.

"I accept." Dirk leaned toward the mic with a wide grin at the smattering of polite applause.

Roberta Ingram stood. "I nominate Weldon Ingram." She and her husband owned the liquor outlet, dry cleaners, and florist, all contained in one store.

Her husband stared at her for a moment as he cleared his throat. "I accept," Weldon said gravely as he stood to more polite applause.

Ann poked Jane sharply with her elbow.

She rose to her feet. "I nominate Ann Westcott."

Jane had barely gotten the words out when Ann shot to her feet. "I accept." There was applause for Ann too and a touch of laughter. Especially as Ann waved and beamed at the crowd, and Jane retook her seat, slightly embarrassed.

She shared a look with Jack, who waggled his eyebrows. "I doubt the election will be boring."

"Oh, lord." Jane just got an image of what was to come.

"Are there any further nominations from the public?" Celine asked the crowd after a few moments of quiet, and it appeared not. "Councillors are there any further nominations among you?" Head shakes from the councillors accompanied a bit of mumbling from the audience. "The election will be held in seven days. Bea Merryweather has been appointed as returning officer. Please return to the community centre between the hours of eight o'clock in the morning and four o'clock in the afternoon for the vote, in one week." Celine leaned away from the mic.

"Please file your nomination papers by noon tomorrow, with the village office." Bea put in. "Thank you all for coming out today. This meeting is adjourned."

"When you are elected mayor, a full reckoning should be done on the village books. Going back to before the Stanhopes got involved in the village council." Jane suggested to her sister as she stood.

"That's not a bad idea." Ann nodded.

"Celine is an accountant. She should be more involved with the running of the village finances," Jack said as he stood next to Jane.

"Really?" Ann looked back at the professionally dressed black woman. A new determination entered her eyes.

"I'm headed back to the café, are you staying, Ann?" Jane called after her sister.

"Yes, I'd like to speak to a few people." Her eyes were locked on Celine.

"Good luck."

"Thanks for nominating me." Ann waved at her sister, and then proceeded toward the stage.

"Can I give you a lift home?" Jack asked as they paused on the sidewalk.

"Yes, please. I have a dessert to make for dinner tonight." She gave Jack a mischievous grin.

"Can I get a hint at what you're making?"

"Sorry, but no, just be patient."

Jack opened the passenger door. "Vimy, hop in the back please," Jack said.

"No, he's fine." Jane offered her knuckles to the German shepherd.

The dog looked at Jack.

"Make a friend," he said with a smile twitching his lips. Vimy licked Jane's fingers and pushed his head under her hand, so she could scratch his ears.

"Your ears are so soft," Jane told the canine as she climbed into the truck, and Jack closed the door. "Who's a good boy?" He leaned against Jane's leg in the cramped space, only cramped because Vimy was a larger than average dog. He rested his chin on her knee and looked up at her with soft, black eyes.

"Did you train him?" Jane asked as she continued to give the dog attention he craved.

"No." Jack started the truck. "A buddy of mine is a K–9 officer. Vimy is retired, but Soto isn't and has a new baby. It's a bit much to keep two large dogs." Jack placed a fond hand on the dog's head and then was required to perform the same ear-scratching maneuver. "He's my buddy too."

As he drove them back to the café, Jane relaxed back in her seat, comfortable sitting there beside Jack. Her thoughts shifted back to that morning and the kiss they'd shared. Was this all really happening?

"What time should I come over for dinner?" Jane asked, suddenly feeling shy.

Jack gave her a slow smile, and then looked back at the road to steer around a pothole. "Come for a drink around five-thirty, we'll eat around six o'clock."

"I'm looking forward to it." She returned his smile as they pulled into the café parking lot.

"Me too," Jack said warmly.

She gave Vimy a last pat and would have slipped out of the truck, but Jack grasped her wrist. She was drawn to look up at him.

Without a word he leaned forward and pressed his lips to hers briefly.

"See you later," he whispered, and his warm breath brushed against her lips.

Chapter Twenty-Three

After Jane got out of the truck, it took a moment to get her feet back under her again. She walked into the building in a bit of a daze, wondering about the second kiss, brief but heated. It promised things and made her think about things. Things, she needed to put away for now. She had a lot to get done if she was going to get ready for dinner and still make dessert.

Jane blew through her chores, which left her plenty of time to assemble a large batch of Nanaimo bars. She followed Sara Birch's recipe closely and popped the nine by thirteen glass pan into the refrigerator for the chocolate and custard bars to setup while she showered and changed.

Dressed in a comfortable, cream-coloured cable knit sweater and jeans, Jane carefully added a touch of makeup. She pulled her hair away her face and piled it up in a loose whirl as she slid a wooden clip into the tresses to hold them in place.

Back in the kitchen, she put wet cat food in Ruby's dish, but the cat went to sit by the door, so she let the feline out. No doubt Ruby would be back when she got hungry.

The dessert had setup nicely, and Jane cut it up into squares and loaded a bakery box. As she closed the lid, she spied the bag of walnuts on the counter. She hadn't included the nuts in the recipe, even though she knew the ingredient was on the list. How had she missed the step to add the walnuts?

Hopefully, the bars tasted okay, but the white box needed something. This was Jack's birthday after all.

She dug a navy-blue ribbon out of a drawer to tie around the box. She didn't have a birthday card; the Nanaimo bars would have to do on their own.

At five-thirty, Jane locked the kitchen door and strolled the short way down the street to the Birch residence. She didn't bother with a jacket, the air was still warm, and sunset wouldn't happen for another couple of hours. In minutes, she passed the towering cedar hedge and walked up the path beside the driveway.

Jane loved the look of the Birch house. The scoop of the Tudor roofline, the wide veranda with square columns holding up the roof, the black and white two-story clapboard always felt welcoming. As kids, on hot afternoons, they would hang out there in the summer, play music, and talk about what the future held for them.

She walked up the steps and reached for the doorbell beside the forest-green front door. It opened before she could press the bell. Vimy bounded out and ran a circle around Jane, before he into the yard and leapt the gate to the backyard.

"Hi." Jack grinned at her as he swung the wide door open. He was fresh from a shower. His damp auburn hair appeared darker, virtually black and combed neatly off his forehead. A subtle hint of aftershave drifted her way, a fresh tantalizing aroma.

He wore a grey long-sleeve shirt with the cuffs rolled up to expose tanned forearms and well-worn jeans which clung nicely to his trim waist and long muscular legs.

"Happy Birthday," Jane wished him as she offered him the bow wrapped box.

"Thank you," he said. "Come in." Jack took the box and closed the door. "I'm working in the kitchen, come with me, and I'll pour you a glass of wine."

"Sounds good," Jane said as she walked beside Jack. She felt awkward as they reached the heart of the house, somehow it didn't feel real.

The aroma of sautéed mushrooms and onions wafted through the kitchen as they entered, making Jane's tummy rumble. The large kitchen with its black and white checkered floor and white lace curtains had not changed. Although, it looked as if the built-in shelves—which framed the back door—had a fresh coat of white paint. So too, did the shaker-style cupboards and cabinets with their black hardware.

"Have a seat," Jack invited.

The appliances were newer than she remembered from her last visit. She'd dropped in once on Christmas holiday to visit Mrs. Birch. And with the hope she would see Jack too, but he wasn't home at the time.

Soft music drifted in from the living room. She didn't know what to do with her hands, so she tucked them into the pockets of her jeans. "Where's your dad?" She climbed onto one of the kitchen stools that surrounded the granite peninsula.

"He's gone to his community theatre practice. He's playing Nicely-Nicely Johnson in 'Guys and Dolls.' Gladys Wyatt is in the play too." Jack waggled his eyebrows at her, and Jane connected the dots.

"Oh, so that's why he wanted me to buy her bread. Much becomes clear."

"When you say it like that, it sounds naughty." Jack put the box down on the counter and pulled on the bow. "As far as I know the two of them are just friends."

"I'll have to discuss the meaning of full disclosure and conflict of interest with your dad. However, Gladys does make great bread, so maybe not."

Jack opened the box and stared at the treat inside. He lifted his eyes to look at Jane. "I haven't had Nanaimo bars since before Mom passed away," he said solemnly.

"I hope they taste okay; I used your mother's recipe. I've never made them before." Jane rolled her bottom lip over her teeth and nibbled it nervously. "Try one and let me know what you think."

He plucked one out of the box and bit into it tentatively. Then he closed his eyes and chewed. "Perfect," he said after swallowing. "You nailed it."

"I'm glad." Jane allowed a smile. "Your dad gave me your mother's recipe. The book his sister made up for her," Jane clarified. "Arlie said she'd want me to have it, but you cook, you should take the book back."

Jack shook his head. "I used to help Mom make these when I was a kid." He finished off the treat and licked his fingers for good measure. "Mostly, I got in the way. I'm not much of a baker, so if you promise to make me a batch, now and then, you can keep the book."

"I will, any time you want," Jane promised, and he gave her a pleased grin.

He opened the fridge door and slid the box onto a shelf, and then looked at Jane. "Red or white wine? I'm going to barbeque a steak for you."

"Then red, please." she tipped her head. "This is a new experience, having a man cook for me."

"It won't be the last time I like to cook for you. I enjoy making food taste as I expect it to, and for more than just myself." He closed the fridge and stepped around the corner. Jack walked under an archway which led to the dining room. When he returned, he held a bottle of red wine. "I have to get some shelves built in the basement and move the wine down there." He opened it and poured the whole bottle through an aerator and into a glass pitcher. "We'll let it breathe for a minute and you can pour us each a glass, if you don't mind." Jack placed the pitcher and red wineglasses on the counter, near to Jane's hand.

"Sure, no problem." She watched Jack pick up a chef's knife and deftly cut up a red pepper for their salad. "I have one question about your mom's recipe."

"Shoot."

"Where do the walnuts go, into the base? I forgot to put them in."

Jack chuckled as he dumped the diced peppers into the bowl of lush butter lettuce. "You didn't forget." His eyes danced as he glanced at her. "I'm not a fan of nuts, so Mom never used them, even though crushed walnuts are mentioned in the recipe."

"Well, that's a relief." Jane poured their wine and passed Jack a glass.

"Here's to Jane coming home to Musgrave Landing." Jack toasted her.

"Thank you, and happy birthday to you." They sipped at the same time, and Jane felt the smooth bodied wine glide over her tongue.

"Why did you decide to come home?" Jack asked carefully as he went to work on an English cucumber.

Jane paused, why was she hiding it anymore? "You know about Aaron Herbert." At Jack's nod, she continued, "He and I dated a long time, years. I thought we were in a serious relationship." Jane swallowed, she wasn't proud of this part. "Aaron and I both worked at XOplay, and while I was on the business analytical side, Arron was on the information technology side." She watched Jack extract the New York strip steaks out of the fridge and drizzle oil on them.

"Go on," Jack said as he added spices and rubbed them into the rich, red meat, and then set the platter aside to wash his hands.

She was grateful he didn't look at her directly as she told the story, somehow it made explaining easier.

"Aaron complained about not being respected. No one valued his opinion when it came to security." She lifted one shoulder. "Anyway, he would rant and rave about how our company was going to get hacked, and the customer data would be compromised. It would be management's fault because no one listened to him." Jane dropped her gaze to stare at her glass as she slowly turned it in a circle and spoke, "To prove his point, and without any company approval, he secretly arranged for a white hat ethical breach of XOplay's data stores. No one knew, not even me." She took a sip of wine.

Jack said nothing.

"I think he thought he would be hailed as some kind of genius or hero it he found a chink in the company's protection. After the hack was discovered, it took a week to track the transactions. The hackers were good. They broke into the Virtual Private Network and hopped through multiple servers and used various IP addresses. The group masked their penetration very well." Jane sighed as the dark feelings that made her stomach hurt surfaced, but she pushed on. "After that, it took another week of security interviewing staff to figure out who was involved. They knew the hackers couldn't get in past the firewalls without help. Security tracked all the relevant IDs, and of course, mine came up because security was right, they did have help."

"What?" Jack's tone was cautious.

Jane could feel his eyes on her now, but she couldn't look at him, not yet.

"I was a senior analyst." Jane continued to stare at the deep burgundy wine as she spoke, "I had all the access the hackers could want."

"You didn't give the hackers your ID as a favour to Aaron?" A question but it came out sounding rhetorical.

Jane gave him a half-smile for his faith in her. "No, Aaron compromised my access. I should have guarded my credentials better, but I thought we were in a relationship and could trust him. It never occurred to me that Aaron would betray my trust and our employer. He took my laptop and loaded a software algorithm on it to capture my keystrokes, to get my passwords, and encryption key pin number."

"He stole your ID and passwords."

Jane lifted her eyes and met Jack's frown. "True, but I did give him the password to the laptop, itself, when he asked for it, which was the first stepping stone. If I hadn't, he would've been dead in the water, and so would the hackers. My fault too, I should've never shared my company laptop access." She shook her head at the pivotal mistake she'd made. "When you hire on, you go through a course, you sign an agreement, and there are several levels of education about what not to do. I broke the rules as soon as some guy asked me to."

"Did he get fired?"

"Yes, and he went to prison. Aaron was sentenced to eighteen months."

"For disregarding–no." Jack broke off as he watched Jane.

She could tell when he figured it all out, and she nodded.

"Oh yes, the white hats were black hats in disguise, and they stole a crap load of XOplay's data before the breach was found. Aaron's and my data included." She took a fortifying sip of her wine. "They took everything I had, cracked my bank accounts, credit cards, everything. They also sold my information. It cost me my identity, my job, and my whole life in Vancouver, because my bosses could not believe I wasn't somehow involved. They couldn't prove anything, but..."

"Guilt by association," Jack finished for her.

"Yes, and I do feel responsible."

"You could fight it as wrongful dismissal."

"I don't want my job back. I don't want Aaron or my old life back either. He showed his true colours when he was arrested. He was trying to figure out how to get hired by the black hats and go work for them when his involvement was discovered."

"Wow, nice guy. What happened to your identity and your money?"

"I have a guy working on it. Hopefully, Andrew can get my investment funds back and my savings. There is some negligence on the part of the bank, and the pension company my old employer used." Jane sipped from her glass. "Andrew is a lawyer and Ann's ex-husband. He's negotiating with XOplay and my bank, but in the meantime, I have the café." Jane looked up at Jack to gauge his opinion, but his expression showed only understanding and a touch of sympathy. No accusations and no recriminations.

"I'm sorry that happened to you," Jack said as he came around the island and pulled her into a hug.

Jane slipped her arms around him too, burying her face against his shoulder. She breathed him in. Now, she knew for sure why she was back in Musgrave Landing, because of how it felt when he held her. She was home.

"It was humiliating. I feel guilty for the other people caught up in this mess. I was also an idiot to allow myself to be manipulated like that," she said against the material of his shirt, and then rested her cheek against his shoulder.

"You're being too hard on yourself. People make mistakes. You didn't do anything criminal, not like Aaron did."

"Two hundred thousand people were affected. I still feel so bad about it all."

"Because you are a good person at heart and only want the best for everyone." He held her close.

Jane's stomach rumbled in answer.

"I suppose I should start the barbeque," he murmured against the top of her head.

"In a minute."

Chapter Twenty-Four

Jane carried their refilled wineglasses outside to the deck off the living room. The sun had slipped behind Stoney Hill, but the evening remained warm even as dusk settled in.

"You can supervise from here." Jack tossed a couple of cushions on to two Adirondack chairs, and then went to light the grill.

"This is an amazing view." Jane placed their glasses on the wooden table between the chairs and went to lean on the railing. The cedar deck overlooked the backyard, where Vimy was currently dashing around. From the elevated position, she had a good view of the water. The ferry was making its last run of the day across The Narrows and heading back to the opposite wharf where it would tie-up for the night.

She also saw the parking lot side of the café, the giant yellow daffodils, and glowing deep-purple pansies looked incredible on her building's exterior from that distance.

"It took some doing to get Dad to agree to put the deck on. Once it was in place, of course it became all his idea." Jack's eyes crinkled at her as he put the black, cast-iron lid down to allow the grill to heat up.

"Of course." Jane grinned back. After telling Jack about her debacle on the mainland, she felt lighter, light hearted even. Confession was good for the soul. "When did you guys build it?"

"A month after Mom passed away. I needed to get Dad busy doing something. He was wasting away by inches." Jack lowered his large frame into one of the chairs, and she joined him in the other.

"I'm sorry I brought Aaron to the funeral. I should have been a better friend to you instead of wrangling him. I don't know why he thought he should come with me, when I look back on it now." The light breeze grabbed a strand of her hair, and Jane pulled the errant lock away from her eyes. "I have a lot to apologize for," she said as she tucked the strand behind her ear.

"Don't worry about it. Most of my old friends didn't come at all."

"Some people don't know what to say or do when they are faced with someone else's loss," Jane said, trying to be charitable.

"It doesn't matter now." Jack reached out and clasped Jane's hand. "I should have told you a long time ago I liked you. I could have cleared up this misunderstanding with Ann."

Jane threaded her fingers through his. "You must have met someone between university and now?"

He gave her a careful look, and Jane hoped he could see she merely wanted honesty between them. "I did, Cassy, but it didn't last."

"Why not?"

"She wasn't you," Jack said simply, and kissed her fingers. "You are the biggest part of the reason I moved back to Musgrave Landing." His eyes watched her reaction as he spoke. "Sure, Dad needs some looking after, but it was you, who drew me back."

Jane moistened her lips as she took in his honest words. "I'm glad, I did hope–." She was forestalled from saying anything further as Vimy chose that moment to bound onto the deck, chased by Ruby.

"Grab your glass," he cautioned and held his aloft as the animals thundered around the furniture and then back down the deck stairs to the lawn.

"So, this is where she goes." Jane laughed, holding her wineglass. "I wondered where Ruby disappeared to when she went outside."

"Yep," Jack said as he climbed to his feet. "The first time she showed up to check out my dog, I thought there was going to be blood. But I told Vimy to make a friend with her." He got to his feet and sauntered over to the warming barbeque. "I guess they did."

"I think it's cute."

"Those two are the reason I set the table in the dining room. I can't eat with animals charging around me. Plus, you may not know this, but your cat begs."

"No, I didn't, and I see your point," Jane said as she crossed to the railing again to watch the pair of animals chase each other around the backyard. "Have they ever hurt anything doing that? Broken anything?"

"You mean one of Mom's hideous gnomes? No, they're good."

When Jack told her the meat was about cooked, she went to finish setting the table inside. She added the salad Jack made, the sautéed mushrooms and onions, and the casserole dish of scalloped potatoes he had in the oven, impressed with Jack's skill.

"This is amazing, thank you for inviting me." Jane opened her napkin and laid it on her lap, eager to dig in.

"I'm glad you're sharing my birthday with me." Jack refilled their glasses, draining the pitcher. "Should I open another?"

"Let's see how it goes," Jane said giving him an impish smile. "I'm good for the moment."

"That sounds promising." Jack grinned as he took his seat. Anticipation was thick in the air between them as they looked at each other across the table.

Don't rush this, Jane. She blinked and looked down at her plate. "This all smells amazing. I have to say, you surprised me."

"Why?" He picked up his knife and fork to cut the steak on his plate. "Every guy can barbeque, it's one of the two things men know how to cook."

"The other item being?" she asked, digging her fork into the fluffy casserole.

"Spaghetti, every guy can make spaghetti." He popped a piece of meat into his mouth and chewed experimentally. "How's your steak?"

"Perfectly tender, just pink enough, it's delicious," Jane assured him.

As she cut another piece of meat to sample with her potatoes, the doorbell pealed.

They looked at each other.

"I'm not expecting anyone." Jack frowned and left the table to answer the door.

Jane ate with relish. The meal was beautifully prepared, and it was a treat to eat someone else's cooking. She was unconcerned about Jack's visitor, until she caught the familiar voice.

"After the meeting broke up, I stopped by the café to talk to Jane about the news that Weldon has stepped down. The contest is now between Dirk and me," Ann spoke quickly and non-stop in her excitement.

Jane's shoulders slumped in resignation, and then she quickly sat up as Jack led her sister into the dining room.

Jack gave Jane such a dramatic eye roll it almost made her spit wine. Instead, she covered her mouth with her napkin to contain the laugh.

Ann was oblivious to the byplay.

"I thought since it's your birthday, I'd drop by and wish you a happy one." Ann offered Jack the bottle of wine in a festive gift bag.

"Thank you, Ann. This was thoughtful of you."

"Not at all, oh, are you just eating dinner?"

"Like you didn't know," Jane muttered.

"What?" her sister asked.

"Nice of you to drop by," Jane said instead and forced a smile for her sister, too late to salvage the date since a third wheel had arrived.

"Would you like some dinner?" Jack asked politely.

"Oh no, I'm sorry, I should have called ahead." Ann waved a dismissive hand.

Jane compressed her lips into a flat line at her sister's insincere attitude.

Jack lifted his eyebrows at Jane in question, and she lifted one shoulder in return.

"There's plenty to go around. No problem." Jack turned to snag a wineglass out of the rack.

Jane got up and collected a place setting for her sister.

"Well, if it isn't too much trouble...," Ann dropped her wrap and bag by the door and grabbed a chair and dragged it to the table.

Chapter Twenty-Five

His father had returned an hour ago from play practice, in time for dessert. The four of them shared the Nanaimo bars and one more glass of wine. Then, much to Jack's relief, Ann went her separate way home.

Jack offered to walk Jane home. Partly, because it was after eleven o'clock, and partly because he didn't want his evening with her to end yet.

The moon had begun its climb into the night sky and lit the way as they strolled down the sidewalk

"This has been a great birthday, thanks," Jack said as he took her hand and turned her to look at him. All they had was the moon, but it was all they needed.

"Next time we do this, I won't tell Ann where I'm going," Jane promised as she curled her fingers around his as they approached her kitchen door.

The warmth of her touch sent a surge of anticipation through him. "I like the sound of that," he said with a pleased smile. "Your sister's okay, but you are the one I'm interested in."

She rewarded his words with a pleased smile. "I could have cooked for you," she said as he studied her lips.

Good things were coming. "You've been doing the cooking all week, and you made my birthday present."

"I like to cook, and I love to bake. I think that's my superpower."

"Maybe one of your superpowers," he said and gave her a small nod. "But maybe next time you can make dinner and I'll bring dessert."

"Deal," she breathed as he leaned in.

When Jack's mouth touched hers, Jane parted her lips to deepen the contact. Without thinking, and he pulled her against him and was rewarded with a pleased sound.

He wrapped his arms around her and she slid her hands up his chest to encircle his neck. The increased contact heated up the kiss and it was some time before Jack could bring himself to break the contact. This was where Jane belonged, in his arms.

When he finally drew back, a bright sparkle lit Jane's dark eyes and her parted soft lips enticed him to return. This time, he gathered Jane closer when he kissed her again. His thumb brushed the velvet skin of her cheek as he explored her sweet mouth. Jack liked the feel of her hands as they ran up his back and held him close.

When they parted, Jack was fascinated by the way Jane rolled her bottom lip in over her teeth. She ran her tongue over it, as if she still needed to taste his kiss.

"I think I know what your superpower is," she said huskily.

"You do?"

"Yes, you make me feel thing. Things that are going to make taking this thing between us slow, hard to do."

"Good," Jack chuckled and pulled her in for a last hug. He liked the feel of her resting against him. It felt completely right. "I should let you go."

"I'll see you tomorrow?"

"And every day after that," he promised.

RUBY JUMPED DOWN FROM the bed with a thump. This was the third time in the past ten minutes by Jane's reckoning, and she sighed. All week the cat appeared quite happy to sleep on the end of the bed by Jane's feet, but tonight or actually it felt like morning, something was not right with the feline.

Jane groaned as she read the glowing numbers on her alarm clock, it was just after four in the morning. She listened to Ruby nose the door open and run lightly down the stairs to the kitchen.

Maybe she was hungry, the kitten was still growing. She had plenty of dry food in the dish in the kitchen. Jane rolled over and closed her eyes to go back to sleep before the alarm went off.

Even though it was Saturday, and the café was closed, Jane still had a long list of tasks to complete, items to buy, and prep for the coming week, not to mention some housework and laundry. An early morning was required to get all of it accomplished, so no sleeping-in allowed. What did they say? No rest for the wicked?

Ruby ran up the stairs again, but the cat didn't return to the small bedroom.

Jane opened one eye. A sliver of ambient light from the kitchen appliances shone through the doorway. She could see the little cat standing at the top of the stairs, looking downward. Jane let her eye fall shut and then frowned as Ruby emitted a growl.

Something was definitely not right downstairs. A mouse maybe?

As the sound of the cat's distress continued, something triggered inside Jane, and she tossed back the covers and sat up. Something was wrong.

She grabbed her robe off the end of the bed at the same time as she stuck her feet into her slippers. She'd barely stood up when the fire alarm in the kitchen sounded.

"For heaven's sake," Jane muttered as she scrambled to get the belt on the robe tied. Her left foot refused to be wedged into the stubborn moccasin and made her stumble as she hurried to the door. The noise would surely wake the dead and the neighbours.

Jane pushed the door fully open. The heavy odour of fuel oil and smoke drifted up the stairs as the alarm blared its battery heart out.

"Oh, my God!"

No longer sleep-muddled, Jane moved.

She snatched Ruby up and then slammed the apartment door shut to cut off the smoke. Jane was glad for the thick terry-cloth robe. The material absorbed Ruby's claws as the wee cat clung onto her shoulder. Hugging Ruby, Jane ran back into the tiny living room and grabbed her mobile phone off the desk.

The cat might not like the jostling, but she held on as Jane ran to the back door and hurriedly unlocked it. She flung the door opened and pounded down the outside steps, at the same time dialling her phone.

"911, what's your emergency?"

"My business is on fire," Jane said breathlessly as she ran down the dark path that led to the street. When she made it to the parking lot out front, false dawn lightened the eastern sky as she turned to look back at her home. There were no flames to see, but Jane was sure she could make out inky black smoke filling the café. The smell of fuel hung in the air.

"This is a mobile phone number–please give me your address."

Jane did so, and the dispatcher told her to hold on the line. It didn't matter she was outside, the smoke alarm's ear-splitting shriek sounded. Even over the dogs barking.

As she waited for the operator to come back, she stared at the building with trepidation. Her home, her livelihood, it could all be gone if the fire was not put out in time. This realization made her chest tighten with fear. She took a shaky breath as she crossed the deserted street.

"Your local fire department has been notified." The operator came back on the line. "Is there anyone still in the building?" the operator asked.

"No, we are outside."

"Thank you. Please stay on the line."

"I will," Jane said blinking to stop tears from gathering. Everything she owned was in that building. The café was home. She'd never forgive herself if the place was destroyed.

Smoke billowed out and up from the backside of the residence, darker than the indigo sky. The black cloud moved sluggishly upward.

"I should have closed the back door," Jane said to Ruby. "I should have grabbed my purse."

Ruby squirmed and Jane let the cat down. The animal streaked across the street and headed straight for Jack's house.

"Smart kitty." Jane quickened her steps as she jogged briskly toward the house, the phone bumping against her ear as she moved.

Jack came sprinting down the driveway. He was dressed in jeans and beat-up runners. He was struggling to pull a twisted T-shirt over his head and shoulders and down his chest when he caught sight of her.

The spectacle of Jack, partially dressed, distracted her for a moment.

"Jane, are you all right?" He ran up to her, his hands grasped her shoulders as he searched her face.

"Yes, I'm fine, but my café is on fire," she said weakly, clutching her phone tight. "And I left my purse in there." She flung a hand behind her at the building across the street.

"What happened?" Jack slipped his arm around her and turned her toward his house.

"I don't know." She relaxed against his shoulder. "The smoke detector went off. I smelled something, like diesel or kerosene so I didn't hang around. I grabbed Ruby and called 911." Jack walked her up the driveway. She welcomed the feeling of security his touch brought.

"I'm glad you left right away." A siren wailed in the distance, it cut over the fire alarm and increased in volume as it got closer. "That'll be the fire department. Are you cold? Do you want to go inside?"

Jane shook her head as she turned to stare at her home and business, and then wrapped one arm around herself. The other hand still held the mobile phone to her ear.

"Okay, please stay here," Jack raised his voice so she could hear him over the din. "I'm going to help them," he said as he drew her to the sidewalk beside the driveway.

She kept the cell phone to her ear. Vaguely, she knew Jack left her to stride to his truck and open the storage compartment, but she could not tear her eyes away from the smoke rising up into the air.

Two trucks roared down the hill toward the bottom of High Street. One, the fire engine and the other, was the emergency medical services truck, both had sirens and red flashing lights. The emergency service vehicles were closely followed by a line of cars and trucks. Members of the Musgrave Landing Volunteer Fire Fighters. The long pumper truck parked and the sirens cut off, leaving only the red flashing lights.

The firefighters, both male and female, parked haphazardly along the street, but well away from the café. They spilled out of their cars, pop trunks or hauled out tough totes and suited up.

"You can tell the dispatcher the fire department is on scene," Jack called over to her.

Her eyes followed Jack. He had donned firefighting gear and was fastening his canvas coat as he strode over to a young man who climbed out of the larger truck. He too, was dressed in typical firefighting gear, helmet, heavy coat, pants, and large black boots. He issued orders to the assembled people.

"Hello?" Jane said into her phone.

"Is the Fire Department on scene?" the female dispatcher asked.

"Yes, thank you for your help."

"Good luck," she said and ended the call.

A tall man with 'fire chief' on the back of his coat paused to listen to Jack. Then he and several others disappeared behind the café, carrying axes, fire extinguishers, and dragging a long hose.

"What's going on?"

Jane glanced behind her at Arlie. "The café is on fire." She surprised herself at how calm she sounded.

"I smell smoke and hear a lot of noise, but I don't see any flames. That might be a good thing." He came to a halt beside her. Arlie too was dressed in pyjamas, slippers and a robe.

"I hope the fire isn't too far along. Ruby woke me even before the smoke alarm went off."

"Well, that was handy." Arlie nodded as they watched the hubbub. "Where do you think it started?"

"I think maybe the basement. The smoke smelled like fuel. The fire inspector was right. I have to get rid of that tank," Jane said and rubbed a shaky hand across her brow, feeling a headache coming on.

Arlie patted her shoulder. "It'll be okay."

When the smoke alarm abruptly stopped screaming, she hoped so too.

"WE OPENED ALL THE WINDOWS and put a couple of fans in the doorways. That will help air it out." Fire chief Fred Quamichan explained to Jane.

"Thank you, I appreciate this."

"It's what we do." He grinned at her.

"I find it interesting that the fire inspector was here only yesterday and did a full walk through. Then today, we have a fire," Arlie said rubbing his hand over his whisker-stubbled chin.

"Who came to inspect?" Jack asked with a slight frown.

The four of them were standing in the café parking lot sometime after the fire department arrived. The sun was climbing a clear blue sky, and the day promised to be fair and clear, maybe even warmer than expected.

"Conroy," Arlie said.

Fred nodded. "I'll be giving him a call to report this. I expect he'll want to come back out and have a look-see."

"Thank you for saving my home, Fred," Jane said as she put a hand on his arm. "Can I get you and the firefighters some coffee or something?"

"No, but thank you for the offer. We are selling tickets to the Community Centre Spring Dance, it's a fundraiser for new Scott air packs," he said, hopefully.

"We will be there. Jack's going to sell me a couple of tickets, and he's taking Jane," Arlie said with a nod at his son. His tone said, 'I told you so.'

"That's great, thanks, we'll see you there," Fred said shifting his eyes from Jack to Jane and back again. He gave Jack a knowing grin, and then headed back to his truck.

"What a week this has been. Murder, fire, what else can happen?" Arlie threw his hands up in disgust. "Pancakes and sausages will be ready in twenty minutes, Jane. You get changed and come over." He stalked across the street and up his driveway.

"Why is your dad angry?" Jane watched Arlie disappear behind the hedge.

"He gets cranky when things like this happen, and he feels powerless to fix them, the same as when Mom got sick."

"Can we go inside my building?" The ferry had arrived while they were talking. "I really don't want to be the centre of attention for the locals." She was still in her bathrobe.

"Of course, but you just can't go downstairs into the basement until Conroy comes out and has a look," Jack said. "There's hazard tape across both entrances."

"Fine by me, I don't need to go into the basement." Jane led the way through the café front door.

A sticky odour of smoke greeted her. "It's not too bad in here," she commented then frowned at the counter and ran a finger over the surface. It felt greasy.

"Yeah, that's going to be an issue." Jack saw her reaction.

"Everything will need to be washed down." She couldn't think about the huge cleaning job she had ahead of her just now. Instead, she continued through into the kitchen. This room was where the smell of smoke and diesel was the strongest. Jane could taste it in the back of her throat. "It's a good thing it's Saturday, and I don't have any food out in the café or in here."

"You were pretty lucky." Jack adjusted the fan in the back door to a better angle to bring in fresh air from the beach. "This could have been much worse."

"I know. I could have lost everything." Tears chose that moment to spring into her eyes. Jack walked over and pulled her into a hug. She buried her face in the curve of his neck, not caring about the rough material of his coat. She only wanted to feel his arms around her and breathe in his male scent mixed with smoke and sweat.

"I'm just glad you didn't get hurt," he said with his lips against her hair.

"Me too." Jane used her sleeve to wipe her eyes. "I don't know why I'm crying, I should be happy it isn't worse."

"It's probably stress." Jack leaned back to look at her and brushed more tears away with his thumb. "Come on, you need breakfast. You haven't lived until you've had Dad's pancakes. We'll eat then come back here and start cleaning up."

"Thank you," she sniffed. "I should call Ann, too."

"How about we eat first?" Jack asked.

His pained expression made Jane laugh.

She made a detour upstairs. When she opened the door, Jane was relieved to find her tiny apartment, while not completely unscathed, held only the barest hint of smoke. She changed quickly into jeans and a sweatshirt and exchanged her slippers for socks and shoes.

After she rejoined Jack, they crossed the street to his house.

"Is it normal for a fire inspector to come and look at a building after a fire?" Jane asked as they stopped by the garage. Jack shucked his fire fighter equipment and laid the gear over a couple of sawhorses for cleaning later.

"Sometimes, particularly if there is the suspicion of arson." Jack opened the screen door for her, and he had them pause in the foyer.

"Do you think it was arson?" Jane asked. She knew her voice was shaky but didn't care.

"I'm sorry to say, yes."

Jane closed her eyes for a second to get a grip.

"Jane?"

"I'm fine, let's go eat."

Jack placed his hands on her arms to look seriously down at her. "You need to know some things. The access to the basement was broken open. There was a pile of rags under the connection between the old furnace and the fuel oil tank. The flange was loosened to allow the residual fuel to drip onto the rags."

"The rags were set on fire?"

"Yeah, they were," Jack said with a nod.

"I never left any rags in the basement," Jane said as she looked up at Jack.

"I know."

At his tone, Jane bit her lip.

"You'll be staying here, tonight. I don't want you over there by yourself, until we know what's going on and catch whoever did this," Jack said firmly. "Are you willing to do that?"

"I could stay with Ann," Jane offered.

They made their way to the kitchen and the welcoming aroma of maple sausages and fresh pancakes.

"I want you here." The protective tone in his voice sent a shiver through her from head to toe.

"I'll make sure he behaves himself," Arlie called over to them from the kitchen.

Jack chuckled and shook his head as Jane smiled too.

"Arlie is a master at eavesdropping," she commented as they continued to the kitchen.

"I heard that." Arlie pointed a pair of tongs at Jane.

"Good," she said as Jack pulled out a stool for her and then crossed to the cupboard to grab the coffee pot.

"Conroy took pictures yesterday. They will show there was nothing wrong with the furnace connection to the tank," Arlie said. He exchanged the tongs for a spatula and flipped a golden yellow pancake onto the top of the stack. "Nor were there rags piled up anywhere," Arlie put in. He and Jack exchanged another serious look.

Fresh fear wrapped around Jane's heart as she clutched her coffee mug between her cold hands.

"I locked the padlock on the door after we took out the patio tables." Jane took the placemats and silverware Jack offered her. "I know I did."

"The hasp was pried off. The fact that the door to the basement was jimmied, points to arson too," Jack said. "Fred is going to call the Duncan RCMP Detachment and report it. Conroy should be out here later today too. So, don't touch anything in the basement."

"But why would someone burn down my café, and my home?" Jane swallowed hard and gave Jack a desperate look.

"I don't know." He put a glass of orange juice down in front of her.

Jack looked worried to her.

"I bet it has something to do with Tim Stanhope's murder." Arlie dropped a ladle of batter into the skillet. It hissed in the silence.

Chapter Twenty-Six

"You could have been killed," Ann said, horrified at Jane's brush with death.

"I know, but I'm fine. The question is, why would someone do this?"

"I don't know, but I'll be over shortly to help you clean up." Ann ended the call.

Jane looked around her kitchen. A fine layer of greasy smoke residue coated every surface. She opened a cupboard and was relieved to find the dishes still clean, so that was something. Probably due to the tight fit of the doors in the old shaker style cabinets. However, all the items on exposed shelves needed to be taken down and washed along with the shelves, walls, ceilings, and floors.

She pushed up her sleeves and walked to the sink. Jane placed her wash bucket under the tap. Time to get started. Jack, Arlie, and Ann would help when they got here.

The former were rounding up more buckets and some industrial soap Arlie swore by. Fine by Jane, she was ready to take all the help she could get.

Just as she dumped in some floor washing soap into the bucket of hot water, a knock sounded at the back door. Jane shut off the water and walked over.

Dirk stood outside the kitchen door and looked in at her through the small window.

Jane looked back at him, and he gave her an innocent little wave. She hesitated about allowing him in, she did not feel comfortable with the idea of Dirk in her kitchen, but what else could she do?

She unlocked the deadbolt and opened the door part-way. "I'm kind of busy Dirk, you probably heard about the fire?"

"I did, and thought I'd let you know how sorry I am about that. I feel so bad about what happened." His eyes opened wide, and he nodded as he spoke, like he was trying to look and sound sincere.

Jane narrowed her eyes at the man. "Uh huh," she said, waiting for him to add more.

"I'll up my offer to one hundred and fifty thousand if you want to dump the property." He twisted his pinky ring as he spoke. "This fire must be a lot to take after everything that's gone on." He gave her a soft, understanding smile.

"For the absolute last time Dirk, no, the café is not for sale. Besides, the property is worth much more than what you are offering. Now I have tons of work to do so if you would excuse me," she said as she swung the door to close it.

"Jane, you aren't being sensible," Dirk said and pushed the door to widen the gap. He braced his foot in the opening.

A bad feeling fluttered in Jane's stomach, and she wished one of her helpers would show up soon. It should be fine to be in here alone during the day, but Dirk was changing her mind.

"What are you doing? Get out of my house." Jane pushed back against the door. Unfortunately, Dirk was the stronger of the two. He shoved her back farther into the kitchen. The idea she'd be pinned between the wall and the door decided it for Jane. She let go of the door, and Dirk walked in.

"Look, I've been very patient with you. I thought maybe you and I could be partners, or even something more, but you still only have eyes for Jack." He shook his head at her, and Jane backed up another couple of steps. "I'm the one who wants things to improve in the village. The same as you do. I got Tim to apply for the grants, how could I know he'd pretend the village was denied the money, and he pocketed it all instead?"

Jane frowned. Dirk's words did not have the ring of truth to them.

"Tim discovered you and your sister had money coming to you, he told me he saw Ethel writing letters to you. Letters with ridiculous clues to find some stupid key. I looked around here, but I didn't find anything, and I don't have time for wild goose chases anyway."

"It was you who broke in." Jane's chest tighten. She couldn't wait to be rescued, she had to do something. She backed up farther, putting distance between her and Dirk.

Jane thought quickly as she moved out of his path and dashed to the counter by the stove. If Dirk was going to make himself a problem, he would live to regret it.

"We need to sit down like civilized people and discuss my offer." Dirk raised his hands like he presented no threat as she turned to glare at him.

Jane pulled the chef's knife out of the butcher's block.

He advanced toward her as Jane lifted the long, sharp, knife level with his chest. "You need to leave," Jane said firmly with a white-knuckle grip on the knife handle and pointed the tip at Dirk.

"What are you doing?" he asked incredulously.

"Defending myself. Now get out!"

Dirk shook his head at her as he advanced.

"Stay back," Jane warned.

A shot exploded in the kitchen.

The sound was deafening and closely followed by ceramic shattering above Jane's head. On the other side of the wall, in the café, hung the shelves where she stored the teapots. What was left of the brown striped teapot was in pieces on the floor in the doorway.

Jane froze and stupidly stared down at the mess.

Shock made Dirk's mouth hang open as he turned to look behind him, when a second shot rang out.

This time, Jane saw Dirk lurch to the left and stumble as he grabbed his midsection.

"You shot me. I can't believe you shot me." Dirk fell to his knees. Almost in slow motion, he sank all the way to the floor.

Anita advanced out of the laundry room with the muzzle of a gun pointed at him.

Jane didn't move as the older woman came forward, not sure if she was relieved Dirk couldn't hurt her now, or if she was more scared Anita would shoot her too.

He gasped as he stared incredulously at Anita. "Why did you do that? Why did you shoot me?" Dirk asked over the barking dog next door.

Anita stared at the hole in Dirk's stomach.

He looked downward and sucked in a breath as his white shirt became marred by a slow-spreading red stain.

She paled visibly at the result of her actions, but blinked, and curled her lip into an ugly snarl. "You killed Tim. You ruined everything." Anita gestured with the barrel of the black handgun she held.

"Oh, my God." Jane blinked, was that squeaky voice hers? Dirk was the killer. She tightened her grip on the knife as she realized Anita wasn't much better.

The enraged woman turned her eyes on Jane. "Put the knife down," she ordered. "If anyone's going to kill Dirk, it's me." The words were said with such calm, they belied her fever-bright eyes.

"I didn't kill Tim. I didn't do anything to him," Dirk denied in a whining voice, but Jane ignored him. He was no longer the biggest threat in the room.

Anita was, and from what Jane could see the woman was unhinged and eager to use the gun again.

Jane swallowed and raised her hands. "I'll put the knife down." Slowly, so she wouldn't alarm the other woman, Jane slid the knife back into its slot in the block on the counter.

She never took her eyes away from Anita as she returned the knife. As though breaking eye contact would give Anita permission to shoot.

"I'm going to die! Please, somebody, call an ambulance. I need help."

Jane glanced at the table, hoping she'd left the phone there. No, it was across the kitchen on the counter by the door, close to Anita.

She didn't like Dirk, but she still didn't want to see him dead. As he writhed on the floor, Jane wondered at herself for pulling the knife and if she could have ever used it on him.

"Don't be any more of an idiot than you are," Anita said to him. "Everybody dies sometime. There's no way I'll ever work for you if you are elected mayor. I'm taking you out of the running." She gave him a weird wavering smile. Jane watched in horror as Anita pointed the pistol at him again.

"That's my gun," Dirk said. "You stole it."

"You should store your firearms in a more secure location. Your night table isn't very safe, and it's also against the law, if I'm not mistaken." Her pudgy finger was on the trigger again.

As the two exchanged words, Jane edged away from Anita and toward the door connecting to the café. Her ears still rung from the shots fired so close in the confines of the kitchen. She had to take charge of the situation, or Anita could quite possibly continue shooting.

With a slow reach, she grabbed a tea towel off the stove door handle and held it behind her back. "You stay put," Anita said to Dirk, and glanced at Jane. "Somebody should shut that damn dog up. That barking is driving me crazy." She moved to the right and reached for the kitchen door, no doubt to close it. The frenzied barking was getting louder.

"Here, use this to stop the bleeding," Jane said and tossed Dirk the towel.

"Get away from him," Anita snarled. She pushed at the kitchen door to close it.

Dirk grimaced and whimpered as he used the towel to compress his wound. The gunshot only bled sluggishly. This had to be a good sign, right?

Vimy punched through the screen as he launched himself into the kitchen. A jarring impact smacked the wooden door and sent Anita flying backward. He wasted no time after hitting the floor and lunged. The dog grabbed Anita's wrist between his jaws. He hung on as the woman's gun hand as she flailed around, stumbling and finally fell screaming to the floor. "Get it off, get it off!"

Without waiting for the outcome, Jane turned and ran through the connecting door, and through to the café. She desperately hoped Vimy could hang on to Anita until she returned with help, with Jack.

Valuable seconds were wasted opening the front door. She flung it wide and ran for Jack's house across the road.

"Jane!"

Her head snapped to the left as she recognized Jack's voice.

Chapter Twenty-Seven

"Oh," she said breathlessly as she collided with him and hung on to his shirt. "Call the police. Anita has a gun. She shot Dirk. Your dog knocked her down, but she might hurt Vimy," Jane said in a rush.

"It's okay, Jane, I've got you." Jack wrapped an arm around her and escorted her up onto his driveway. "Dad," he called out.

"I'm here. I called the shots into the RCMP. The dispatcher said they are on their way, but you know, it will take some time." Arlie came up beside them and patted Jane's arm. "I never thought I'd wish for that road to go through to Fulfort Harbour, but I do now." He shook his head and looked at Jack. "What's the plan?" he asked his son.

"I'm going to make a citizen's arrest," Jack said, and he gripped her shoulders. "You stay here, Jane."

"I will not." Jane stepped forward and broke his hold. "You'll need help."

"Dad will back me up."

"Fine, then I'll back up Arlie."

His father opened his mouth to argue, but shut it at the look they both saw in Jane's eyes.

"We don't have time for this," Jack said, and recognized the stubborn set to Jane's chin. He turned and jogged across the road. "Stay behind Dad, Jane."

"Yes, fine." Jane and Arlie were hot on his heels as the three of them ran across the road. "But be careful Jack, she shot Dirk and my favourite teapot."

"Not the brown striped one?" Arlie made a tsk sound at Jane's nod. Jack shook his head, what a pair.

They made it to the open kitchen door and found Vimy with a death grip on Anita's arm. Blood stained her coat sleeve, but the former K-9 was not being overly rough. He was growling, but merely held the woman in place, albeit by the point of his teeth.

"Let go, make it let go of me!" Anita shrieked in panic as tears and snot ran down her face.

"Give me the Glock, and I'll tell him to release you." Jack put one hand on her right wrist, above Vimy's muzzle. The hand which held the automatic pistol gripped the handle tightly.

Jack had to be careful to make sure the business end pointed away from him and Vimy. By the mad light in Anita's eyes, he wasn't sure she would comply. Jack had to keep Jane, his father, and Vimy safe. "Anita, look at me," Jack commanded. "It's over," he said firmly.

There was a moment's hesitation, then, with a final whimper, she opened her hand, and Jack took the gun away, careful not to touch the trigger. He flicked on the safety and ejected the clip.

Vimy rolled dark eyes to look at Jack. "Release, Vimy," Jack told his dog, and he opened his jaws.

Anita rolled on to her side, in the fetal position, quietly sobbing as she clutched her arm.

Arlie got past Jack and went to kneel by Dirk. The injured man lay on his back, panting in pain, and pressing a towel against his stomach.

Jane dashed by Jack and into the laundry room as Vimy went to Ruby's water dish and sucked up the contents then moved on to the cat food.

Jack placed the Glock and its clip on the counter. "Good boy," he gave the dog a pat. Only then did Jack notice the cooler air coming out of the open basement door.

The yellow 'do not cross' caution tape was torn aside. Jane was well back from the door but stared down into the dark maw. He moved forward into the laundry room and only touching the top of the door, closed it with his fingertips.

"I hate that basement," she said and gathered up clean towels and turned to Jack. "Here, wrap Anita's arm in this," she said as she handed him a hand towel.

"I love a woman who doesn't panic in the face of danger," Jack touched her cheek gently.

Jane's stricken-look faded, and she blinked and huffed a laugh. "I don't have time right now to panic." She touched his arm and gave the muscle a grateful squeeze before returning to the kitchen.

Briskly she walked over to Dirk and knelt down beside the dark red pool of blood on her floor. "Roll him toward you, Arlie." As he did as she asked, Jane slipped a folded towel under Dirk's back and rolled him back. "That should help stop the bleeding."

"I'll call the clinic emergency number. We need Bea." Arlie climbed to his feet as Jane put a towel under Dirks head and covered him with a bath sheet.

"Thanks, Dad." Jack lifted Anita's arm and pushed up her sleeve to look at the injury. "This isn't too bad as bites go." The punctured and bruised limb bled a bit. "It's nothing life threatening, not like the round you put into Dirk."

Her tearful eyes met his, and her lower lip trembled, but something in her reaction didn't feel genuine.

"This is what happens when thieves fall out. You'll live." He told the woman as he wrapped her arm in the towel. The clean scent of soap and fabric softener wafted to his nose.

"Why call Bea?" Jane asked.

"She's a trained EMT," Jack replied.

"He started the fire," Anita said. She jerked her chin at Dirk and then looked up at Jack wide-eyed. "Jane could have been killed."

Jack cut his eyes to Dirk. The coward turned his head away and closed his eyes in resignation.

"Then it's a good thing Arlie put a new smoke alarm here in the kitchen," Jane said. "Thanks for calling the fire inspector's office, Anita. We wouldn't have installed it if Mr. Conroy hadn't visited the café."

"How did you know...," Anita trailed off, realizing she just admitted her guilt.

"I didn't, not for sure, but I do now." There was no anger in Jane's voice, she merely sounded tired. "Dirk helped you to kill Tim too, didn't he?" Jane looked down at Dirk as she put a new towel over his front wound. "Didn't you?"

"No, I did not. But Tim thought he could blackmail me." Dirk's voice sounded strained, but he kept talking. "He wanted all the money for himself, and Lara. He took the biggest share from the grants, even though I came up with the idea, and I had to do all the paperwork. Then he wanted my share too." He swallowed hard. "But I didn't kill him. If I die, please tell my parents I didn't kill Tim."

"You're not going to die," Jane said firmly.

"Can I get some water please?" Dirk asked weakly.

Arlie came in and stood at Jane's shoulder. "You've been gut shot, so no," Arlie said, and not with much sympathy. "Water's a bad idea."

"Dirk was going after the café and the land. It's worth a pretty penny, at least half a million." Anita sneered from her location on the floor by the door.

Her shooting victim laughed contemptuously. "Don't be stupid, the housing development I planned would make each lot worth twice that. There is enough land in the parcel for ten lots." He panted and swallowed. "It still doesn't change the fact he was blackmailing me or that you helped him, Anita. Tim must have told you he was getting ready to leave, and you weren't going with him. You must have been pissed. You killed him for leaving you for Lara, I know you did."

"I didn't shoot Tim," Anita said weakly in reply. "He was my husband, and I loved him."

"You are complicit. You moved the money around." Dirk looked up at Jane. "There's more money, the cops didn't find all of it. She's got money stashed in a safety deposit box in their bank in Duncan."

"Shut up, you idiot," Anita snarled. "He wouldn't have left me. Tim loved me." This was said with misery. Jack doubted she believed her own words.

"Why did you come here tonight, Dirk?" Jane asked quietly. "How did you think you'd convince me to sell to you?" Jane shook her head at him. "You tried to make my life difficult, getting Anita to call in the inspectors to give me grief and cost me money to fix things they found wrong, except there wasn't much. Your next plan was to try with the fire."

"I hoped you'd get scared and sell out. Worried someone was after you too." He closed his eyes as he spoke.

Now anger flared in Jane's eyes, and Jack wondered if he should intercede, if only so he would be the one to punish Dirk.

Jane tipped her head to look directly down at the wounded man. "Were you planning on killing me too? That would've been a stupid move, Ann would inherit the property," she said bitterly.

"Not after the hand written will he had Tim counterfeit surfaced." Anita rolled to a sitting position. "Check his jacket pocket." Jane leaned forward and pushed Dirk's jacket open. He tried to roll to his side, winced, and lay still. She reached in and pulled the cream-coloured envelope from his pocket.

"That's Ethel's stationary," Arlie said. The envelope held a single sheet of paper and Jane removed it

"I couldn't find the stationary anywhere. I was forced to steal it from Ethel's office here in the café. It took Tim a long time to master her cursive writing style, but it was easy to get examples from the letters she sent."

"Tim stole my aunt's letters. He was in the perfect position to take them, like he was when he stole my mail." Jane didn't sound shocked, Jack realized as he watched her, just resigned.

"What does the will say, Jane? Is Dirk, Ethel's long-lost son, or something?" Arlie asked.

"No," Jane said as she read the signed and dated document. "Apparently, Aunt Ethel felt she didn't want to burden me or Ann with the business, so she left it to Dirk for the sum of one hundred thousand, to be paid to me."

"The will was why Tim was blackmailing Dirk," Jack nodded. As convoluted as the situation was, it was starting to make more sense.

"Tim was excellent at forgery," Anita said, proudly. "Too bad he took up with Lara Finkle. If he'd kept her under control, I wouldn't have had to do anything." She pulled her lips back off her teeth. "She kept coming into my office, my work, and tried to make a fool out of me, taunting me." Jack wondered if Lara Finkle was next on Anita's list. He was certain she had to be the killer. It was obvious Dirk didn't have it in him.

"It's easy to refute this last will and testament. It won't have any of Ethel's finger prints on it." Arlie interjected.

"Good point," Jane said as she returned the handwritten will to the envelope.

"You gave Tim the idea to blackmail me!" Dirk accused his former partner.

Anita merely shrugged, and Vimy glanced up from the cat food dish to watch her. Anita froze as she returned the dog's stare. Then moving slowly, she cradled her arm against her chest. "Tim used to be easy to manipulate, but he stopped listening to me. He only listened to that woman." She gathered her feet under her as if she was preparing to stand. "You would have been a good partner Dirk, but you are obsessed with this dump of a village."

"Vimy, here," Jack said as he stood. The shepherd trotted over to Jack's side. "Watch her." Jack pointed to Anita. The dog turned steady eyes on his charge and dropped his head in an aggressive stance.

Anita let her feet slide away from her, and she shrank up against the wall.

"Why did you kill Tim?" Jack asked her. If they could get all the information out in the open, the cops could arrest Dirk and Anita. Then Jane would be safe.

"I didn't kill him, I told you. Even though, I was tempted when he got greedy and I found the other accounts he had setup. He was going to leave me and take off with that woman." Anita's anger died, and the weird, manic glint reappeared. "All together there is over three million, with Tim's cut, my money, and Dirk's. I could have lived well in Victoria or like a queen in Central America." She looked away from Jack, her gaze unfocused, as though she was looking off into her potential future.

"Tim only thought about himself. If he'd given Dirk his full share, like I told him to, he could have bought this place from you." She looked over at Jane. "You would have gone back to Vancouver, and Tim wouldn't be dead now," she said the last bit wistfully. And then shook her head. "He brought it on himself. I guess he deserved it when you shot him, Dirk."

"I didn't kill him. Even though he used me, both of you did," Dirk accused her.

"You can't cheat an honest man," Arlie put in.

"Did you know about the letter Tim had in his coat when he was killed?" Jane asked.

"What letter?" Dirk rolled his head to look at her.

"A letter addressed to me, using this same stationary, it was found on the body."

"I don't know anything about a letter." Dirk closed his eyes.

Jane stared at him a minute then glanced over at Anita.

"What about you, Anita?" Jack asked.

"I don't know anything about a letter either." Unfortunately, to Jack's ear they both sounded sincere, which would almost be funny considering all the lies the two had spewed over the past week.

"Hello," a new voice called.

"That'll be Bea," Arlie walked back into the café and led her back into the kitchen.

Flashing lights glanced off the windows as the sound of a powerful outboard engine split the air.

"That should be the RCMP." Jack looked at Jane. "I don't want to leave these two. Can you signal them?"

"Absolutely," Jane stood.

"What the hell is going on now?"

They all heard the shrill voice from the café as Bea entered the kitchen

"Ann's here."

WITH HER ARM BANDAGED, Anita sat miserably in a kitchen chair while Arlie went to help Bea with Dirk.

She was not deemed much of a threat after Constable Pannu took possession of the Glock and ammunition. Her good arm was handcuffed to her belt loop, and she was going to be charged with assault with a deadly weapon and possibly attempted murder. Zeffler told them he would let the Crown Attorney decide that one.

Bea helped the EMS technician finish bandaging Dirk's wound and rose to her feet. "You'll need surgery to ensure none of the slug still needs to be extracted," the female EMS tech said. "We called it in, so you will probably go straight into the OR."

The postmaster stepped back to allow the EMS attendants to load him onto the gurney. She pulled her gloves off tiredly. "I'm so sorry this happened to you," she said as she patted his shoulder. "So much violence, it's wrong."

"I'll ride in with him." Constable Havelange stepped forward to help the ambulance crew with the doors.

"Dirk Ipkiss, you are under arrest for embezzlement, attempted arson, and a few other charges yet to be resolved," Zeffler informed him. "However," he caught the constable's eye. "You are as yet, not charged with murder."

He turned to look at the Bea.

Jane frowned when she realized the inspector was watching the woman steadily with a slight tip to his head. The look in his eyes was penetrating.

"But sir–," Havelange began.

"Dirk didn't kill Tim, I did." Bea said with a large sigh. She squared her shoulders and looked directly at the inspector.

"What?" Anita stared at her friend, for the first time, nonplussed.

Jane's eyes widened as Jack inhale between his teeth. Everyone was shocked into silence as they looked on.

"I had to do something about him," she said and lifted her chin. "I discovered Tim was using my post office to embezzle grant funds from the village. He was also guilty of forgery, deceit, theft, and it was unacceptable." She jutted out her jaw in anger a she spoke. "It wasn't until the audit was begun that I realized how big a thief he really was and figured out who was involved with him." She gave the patient on the gurney a sour look as he was being strapped in.

"But worst of all," Bea said defiantly. "Tim was stealing mail," she said this as though that crime was worse than murder.

"This is incredible." Jane shook her head in amazement at the postmaster. As though feeling her disquiet, Vimy leaned against her leg, and Jane rubbed his neck. Jack squeezed her hand.

"I had no proof of any of this, just what I'd observed. I told our regional office I suspected Tim was stealing mail, but they didn't take me seriously. I know he must have taken the cheques and replaced them with rejection letters, and then stuck the rejections into the Council's mail box." Again, she shook her head as she turned to Anita.

"Bea, how could you?" Anita found her voice.

"You disappointed me, Anita." Bea made no protest as Zeffler signalled Havelange to cuff the postmaster. "You coolly sat in the meetings and said nothing."

"I didn't do anything!" Anita exclaimed.

"You transferred money from the council's accounts to Tim's. Both you and Tim had signing authority. With the two signatures, the cheques could be cashed." Bea put her hands behind her back, folded like she was praying. "Tim ruined his marriage, he destroyed the village finances, and he compromised our postal reputation. Too much, so I acted."

"You were the one who broke into the café." Jane looked at Bea in a whole new way.

"The second time," Arlie interjected.

"I needed a gun. Ethel had one." Bea shrugged. "I knew she kept her keys in her apron behind the door. I thought I could use the first break-in to cover the theft of the gun, but that stupid door gave me problems and I lost my temper."

"You broke the door handle right off and damaged the hinges," Arlie said. "What did you use?"

"A crowbar."

"Beatrice Merryweather, I am arresting you for murder in the first degree." Inspector Zeffler stepped forward. "Constable Pannu, read Mrs. Merryweather her rights."

Chapter Twenty-Eight

"I'm a little disappointed," Ann called to her sister as she collapsed into the kitchen chair.

Jane frowned and turned back to her task. She dumped the bucket of dirty water into the laundry sink. "Why are you disappointed?" she called from the laundry room. With a grimace at her filthy apron, she stripped it off and tossed it into the hamper. She knew she had to get to the laundry soon. The thing was near over-flowing.

"I thought we'd find at least one key by now," Ann said with a long-suffering sigh.

"Maybe I was wrong on the key thing." Jane crossed to the sink and washed her hands. "Maybe Aunt Ethel was using the word key as a metaphor."

"Now you tell me. I've been searching the house and studio all week for a real key."

"It serves you right for hiding the stuff inside the trunk in the attic in the first place." Jane grinned at her sister, drying her hands on a towel.

"I guess," Ann muttered. She rested her cheeks on closed fists, elbows on the table. "I'd kill for a cup of tea."

"I'll make you one, it's the least I can do for all your help with the cleanup." She opened the linen drawer to extract a clean apron, the last one left.

"Helping you clean up from the fire is the least I can do for mooching so many meals off you," Ann said ruefully.

Jane smiled as she unfolded the red and white pinstriped creation. "Do you remember this one?" She dropped the neck strap over her head and flipped the polka dotted ties around her waist, tying them into a bow.

Ann expression lightened too. "That was Aunt Ethel's favourite."

"It was," Jane agreed as she smoothed the skirt down her thighs. "Right, some tea," she said as she automatically slipped her hand into the right pocket and froze. "Ann." Jane slowly turned back to her sister.

"Hm?" Ann looked tiredly up at her.

"Look." Jane withdrew her hand from the apron pocket. She held up two keys.

Ann's jaw dropped as she sat up straight and blinked. "Are you kidding me?"

"There's a note too." Jane quickly unfolded it.

Dear Ann and Jane,

These are the safety deposit box keys to your inheritance from your father's insurance policy. I bought securities for both of you after his death. I used part of your inheritance to pay for your education, and I left the rest to mature so you would each have a nest egg after I'm gone.

I wanted you to be certain of what you wanted and to avoid any impulsive actions after my death.

The plan is to wait sixty days before you get the money.

See my lawyer, Mr. Wingate in Victoria, if he hasn't contacted you yet. He is a signatory on the box at the bank, but you both have the keys.

Love you always,

Aunt Ethel

"Everyone knew Aunt Ethel kept her keys in her apron pocket." Jane laughed.

The End

Don't miss out!

Visit the website below and you can sign up to receive emails whenever Yvonne Rediger publishes a new book. There's no charge and no obligation.

https://books2read.com/r/B-A-SFCV-JFSDF

BOOKS 2 READ

Connecting independent readers to independent writers.

Did you love *Death and Cupcakes*? Then you should read *The Common Touch*[1] by Yvonne Rediger!

[2]

Major Zara Dare, air force brat from CFB Moose Jaw, home of 15 Wing. Zara followed in her father's footsteps by joining the air force. Unfortunately she did not attain his pilot status. Her talents lie elsewhere. She always felt the need to make her dad proud, but knew she fell short. Now she has a tough new assignment. While His Royal Highness is attending the international Connaught Ranges annual shooting event in Ottawa, Zara is tasked to be part of his security detail. She must ensure the safety of the outspoken

---

1. https://books2read.com/u/3GVzDL

2. https://books2read.com/u/3GVzDL

and unpredictable Royal. It would all be fine if she could keep their relationship on a professional footing, but minutes after they meet at the Governor General's gala, the prince begins changing things to suit him.

His Royal Highness, Prince James Argyle Sandhurst Fleming is third in line to the Riocht Oilean throne. James would be happier if there were several dozen more people between him and that particular mantle. Maybe why he continually shakes off his security to lose himself in the crowd. He too, had a successful military career, until the media's fascination made life impossible to continue without placing others at risk. While he takes his royal duties seriously, he is bitter about giving up his chosen career. He's not sure the life of a prince is what he wants. Then he meets Zara.

Read more at blackyvy50.wix.com/yvonnerediger.

About the Author

Yvonne Rediger was born in southern Saskatchewan. She lived and worked in northern Manitoba, New Brunswick, Alberta, and Vancouver Island. She now resides in central Saskatchewan with her husband. She has two grown children.

Read more at blackyvy50.wix.com/yvonnerediger.